Safe HAVEN

OTHER TITLES BY KRISTEN PROBY

Triple Creek Ranch

Safe Keeping

The Blackwells of Montana

When We Burn

When We Break

Where We Bloom

When You Blush

Where You Belong

The Wilds of Montana

Wild for You

Chasing Wild

Wildest Dreams

On the Wild Side

She's a Wild One

With Me in Seattle

Come Away With Me

Under The Mistletoe With Me

Fight With Me

Play With Me

Rock With Me

Safe With Me

Tied With Me

Breathe With Me

Forever With Me

Stay With Me

Indulge With Me

Love With Me

Dance With Me

Dream With Me

You Belong With Me

Imagine With Me

Escape With Me

Flirt With Me

Take a Chance With Me

Single in Seattle

The Secret

The Surprise

The Scandal

The Score

The Setup

The Stand-In

Love Under the Big Sky

Loving Cara

Seducing Lauren

Falling for Jillian

Saving Grace

Big Sky

Charming Hannah

Kissing Jenna

Waiting for Willa

Soaring with Fallon

Big Sky Royals

Enchanting Sebastian

Enticing Liam

Taunting Callum

Heroes of Big Sky

Honor

Courage

Shelter

Curse of the Blood Moon

Hallows End

Cauldrons Call

Salems Song

Bayou Magic

Shadows

Spells

Serendipity

Romancing Manhattan

All the Way

All It Takes

After All

Boudreaux

Easy Love

Easy Charm

Easy Melody

Easy Kisses

Easy Magic

Easy Fortune

Easy Nights

Fusion

Listen to Me

Close to You

Blush for Me

The Beauty of Us

Savor You

KRISTEN PROBY

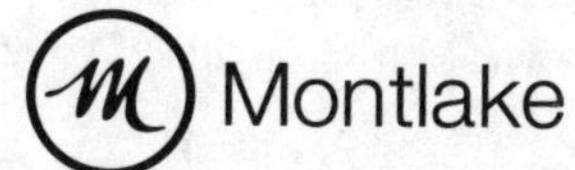

This is a work of fiction. Names, characters, organizations, places, events, and incidents are either products of the author's imagination or are used fictitiously. Otherwise, any resemblance to actual persons, living or dead, is purely coincidental.

Published by Montlake, Seattle

www.apub.com

EU product safety contact:
Amazon Media EU S. à r.l.
38, avenue John F. Kennedy, L-1855 Luxembourg
amazonpublishing-gpsr@amazon.com

ISBN-13: 9781662532962 (paperback)
ISBN-13: 9781662532955 (digital)

Cover design by Hang Le
Cover image: © Wander Aguiar Photography; © Ashley Hadzopoulos, © district4.studio, © Jiwsurreal, © Elvira Savchuk, © svekloid / Shutterstock

Printed in the United States of America

This book is dedicated to G.
We've come a long way, baby.

Prologue

Ryker

Fifteen Years Old

Gideon hauls off and punches me in the thigh. *Freaking hard.* Giving me an instant muscle cramp.

With a glare, I sock him in the shoulder.

"You might want to cut that out." Reggie glowers at us both in the rearview mirror and then shakes his head, as if he's disappointed in us.

I don't really care what Reggie thinks of me. He may be in charge at the boys' home—a.k.a. hell house—I've been living in for the past six months, but as far as I'm concerned, he can kiss my ass.

"Loser," Gideon whispers at me, and I want to punch him again. He's still sporting the black eye from the last time I knocked his ass out.

"Fuck off," I snarl at him.

"Okay, enough," Reggie snaps. "I get it, you hate each other. That's fair. You don't have to like everyone in this life, but you don't get to mouth off and put hands on every single person that ticks you off."

"Why do we have to go to this stupid ranch?" I ask him.

Not that I really mind the thought of leaving the hell house and moving to a ranch in the middle of nowhere. I like animals, and I like being outside.

It would be great if I didn't have to go with the dickface next to me.

"You need to learn what it is to work hard," Reggie says, dragging his hand down his face.

"Basically, we're screwups and you want to get rid of us," Gideon adds, but Reggie shakes his head.

"No, Gideon, I don't think you're screwups. I think you need something I can't give you, and I hope that something is out here at the Triple Creek Ranch with Ray and Debbie. They're good people, so cut them some slack, yeah?"

I lean my head on the window and watch the mountains in the distance.

Cut them some slack.

When has anyone ever cut *me* any goddamn slack in this life?

I must fall asleep because suddenly, I feel the car stop, and when I open my eyes, I'm shocked to see a huge house in front of us. It's like something out of the movies. Something rich people live in, with log sides, and a porch that wraps around the whole place. Add in the mountains in the background, and it doesn't look *real.* Am I dreaming?

When we get out of the car, the older couple from the porch walk down to greet us.

"Ryker, Gideon, I want to introduce you to Ray and Debbie," Reggie says.

I step forward first and shake Ray's hand. His grip is firm, and he looks me steady in the eyes. He doesn't look mean. His mouth isn't turned up in a sneer.

But he's not smiling. He's sizing me up. So I keep my chin high and say with more bravery than I feel, "Hello."

Then, I'm suddenly caught up in a hug by the tiniest woman I've ever met in my life, and she's patting my back, rocking me back and forth, and it makes me want to cry.

Jesus. What is this place?

"I'm Debbie," she says and smiles up at me with the kindest eyes I've ever seen. I've been growing a lot lately, eating too much, according to the cook at hell house, but this woman is like a little fairy. I could put her in my pocket. "And you're too skinny. I'm going to put some meat on your bones. Do you like fried chicken?"

At just the mention of it, my mouth waters.

"Uh, yes, ma'am."

"Nope, call me Deb." She pats my cheek and then moves on to Gideon, giving him the same treatment, and his gaze meets mine over her head as he awkwardly pats her on the back.

I shrug.

I don't know, man.

Reggie sets our duffel bags at our feet. Everything we own is in these bags, and it isn't much.

"You'll be staying in the bunkhouse with the hands," Ray says, still looking us both over. "I have six hands hired for the summer, including Dusty, my manager. They'll get you situated. You all come up to the house every night for dinner."

Gideon and I both nod.

"I have one hard rule," Ray adds, narrowing his eyes, and then he gestures to Deb. "This is my *wife*. The love of my life. The only reason I do anything. No one sasses her on this ranch. You treat her with the kindness and respect that she'll show you. You'll get no second chances. If I find out that you even look at her sideways, you're out of here. Everything else we'll figure out as we go."

Deb rubs her hand up and down Ray's arm, as if to comfort him, and it makes my chest kind of feel funny.

"Yes, sir," I say.

"Yes, sir," Gideon echoes.

"Who are you?"

We turn as a girl with shiny blond hair and the prettiest smile I've ever seen rides over on a horse. She looks like she might be about our age.

"Oh, this is my niece, Willow," Deb says and gestures for Willow to climb off the horse. "She's here for the summer."

I want to learn to ride a horse.

"Willow, this is Gideon and Ryker."

"Hey," she says with that smile that dims the sun, and she offers us a little wave before flipping her blond hair over her shoulder.

Now my chest *and* my stomach feel funny.

"Hi," I reply.

"Hey," says Gideon.

"Same rule applies to Willow," Ray says sternly, and we both nod.

Nobody hurts the girls. Got it. I wish someone had clued the fuckers who used to kick the shit out of my mom in to that rule.

"You'll love it here," Willow says, bouncing on her toes. "I wish I could be here all year, not just in the summer. I mean, I live an hour away, so I visit sometimes, but I get to be here *all summer long* every year, and it's the best."

"They're not here to play," Ray reminds her. "They're here to work."

"Aw, Uncle Ray, they can't work every minute of the day." Willow kisses the older man's cheek, and his face softens as he smiles down at her. *Ray isn't an asshole.* "Can I show them around?"

"We'll both show them. Let's start at the barn, and you can put your horse away," Ray says.

"I'm headed inside to get started on that chicken," Deb says. "Welcome to the ranch, boys. Go get hungry so I can feed you."

I'm always hungry.

First, we're shown to the bunkhouse, where we each set our bags on a bed. I'm on the lower bunk, and Gideon is above me. It's pretty nice in here, with a kitchen and a living room with a big TV. It's clean, and the blankets and pillows on the beds look new.

I wonder if we can watch hockey when the season starts.

We head outside and are introduced to some of the guys in the barn, along with the horses. The afternoon goes by fast, and I sneak glances at Willow, who seems to be the *happiest* person I've ever met. I don't think she's stopped smiling once. She practically bounces when she walks, and she keeps touching me and Gideon as if we're old friends, pushing on a shoulder, hip checking us when she makes a joke.

I don't really like to be touched, but it's not so bad when she does it, as long as it keeps her smiling.

Then again, she's a princess who grew up on this ranch and has nice people raising her who don't beat the shit out of her. Of course she's happy. I'd be fucking thrilled.

"Hey," she says as she joins me where I'm standing not far from the house, looking at the mountains. "You don't look too happy to be here yet, but don't worry, you will be. I know—it's an adjustment."

"That's all life is," Gideon says from the other side of her, shoving his hands in his pockets. "Freaking adjustments."

"That's deep," Willow says, but she's nodding in agreement. "Who gave you the black eye?"

"Him," Gideon says, gesturing to me.

"And what did he do to you?" Willow asks me.

"Punched me in the dick."

Her eyes widen, and she looks back and forth between us. "So you're not friends."

"Hell no," I reply.

"Not even close," Gideon agrees.

"But what if I want to be friends with both of you?"

"It's a free country," I reply. "Doesn't matter."

Gideon just shrugs.

"You guys are going to be a lot of work," she says with a sigh as she pats us each on a shoulder and shakes her head. "It's a good thing I'm up for the challenge. We'll be the Three Amigos by the end of next week. Mark my words."

She's so pretty. So *bright*. Life hasn't sucker punched her.

I glance at Gideon. I hate that guy. But maybe for her, I can chill.

As long as he keeps his hands to himself and doesn't mouth off.

"Come on," she says. "Let's go get dinner. Deb's chicken is to *die* for."

"I think you're going to be nothing but trouble," I tell her as we stalk off toward the huge house for dinner.

"Who, me?" She bats her big baby blues at me. "Never."

Chapter One

Ryker

"That's right, motherfucker! Try that shit again, and I'll pound your ugly face into the boards!"

I laugh at Mac, my enforcer, and shake my head at him. Mac's an animal, which is good, given that it's his whole job to either pick fights or end them.

He's damn good at his job.

"Come on, Cap, we got this," Mac says to me as we skate to the bench. "One more period, and we can win this. We're only down by two."

We're not gonna win this.

It's the last game for us in this season. I know it. Coach knows it. Fuck, even the fans know it.

We've won the last two Stanley Cups in a row, but this year has been a rebuilding year since we lost some players after the last season and recruited some rookies, and frankly, I'm surprised we made it this far into the playoffs.

It was a mediocre season.

And that's okay. Everyone has them. I have no complaints.

But this is the last game for the Seattle Blizzard this year.

"James!" Coach flags me down, and I walk over to him.

"One more period," he says, echoing Mac's words. "Tie us up, at least."

"I'll do my best."

"You *are* the best," he reminds me and slaps me on the back. "Let's do this!"

I was *the best.*

For fifteen years, I've been known as *the phenom*. The best of the best. The GOAT. Better than Gretzky, having smashed his record for scoring in one season, and total scores in a career, and I've played for five years *less* than that legend.

He's also a friend and mentor of mine.

But am I *still* the best? Fuck no.

I'm thirty-five.

I've been beating my body up my whole goddamn life.

I'm tired.

But for the next twenty minutes on the ice, I'll fake it till I make it. No cringing when my knees feel like they're exploding. There is no pain. There is no messing up.

But shit, it's so much harder now than it was ten years ago. Even *five* years ago.

I do manage to score twice, much to the delight of the fans and my teammates, but so does the opposing team, and when it's all said and done, we lose, 4–2.

"James!" Dozens of reporters shout my name as I make my way to the locker room, and I stop to give interviews.

"What happened out there, Cap?"

Some of them call me Cap because I've been the captain of the team for ten years. I was recruited by Seattle my rookie year, and I've been lucky enough to stay here my whole career.

Aside from Montana, Seattle is my home.

"Hey, Mike." I swipe my forearm over my sweaty forehead and tip my head down so I can hear the shorter man ask me questions for the camera. The hallway leading to the locker room is loud as hell.

"What happened out there, Cap? Do you think there was anything you could have done to change how this one ended?"

I want to roll my eyes, but I simply shake my head. "You know, our guys really showed up tonight. Spencer had some amazing saves in the goalie box. I don't think we have anything to be ashamed of, and a great foundation for next year."

"So you think you'll still be in Seattle next year, with you being a free agent after this game?" Mike asks, his eyes shrewd.

Fuck you, Mike.

"Only God and my agent know that for sure." I smile at the camera, wink for Willow the way I always have, and turn to leave.

No more interviews tonight.

The locker room is somber, but not as sad as it gets if we lose during the Cup. *That* sucks ass. Tonight, we're disappointed, even though we saw it coming.

But I'm the captain, so it's my job to say a few words to lift their spirits.

"Listen up," I begin, getting everyone's attention. "I'm proud of every single one of you. You all worked hard this season. We knew that there would be a learning curve this year, and there's nothing wrong with that. You played your asses off out there tonight."

"Not hard enough," Mac mutters, and I reach out to pat him on the shoulder.

"You spent more time in the penalty box than on the ice," I remind him with a grin. "No pouting tonight. We made it into the second round of the playoffs, and that's nothing to be ashamed of. Now, we rest for a bit before we get back at it."

For me, that downtime will take place in Montana, with my dad and the animals, breathing in fresh air and listening to nothing but quiet. I need that.

But first, we're going on a trip as a team. The reservations, the plane, *everything* has been on standby to whisk us away whenever we're finished with the season. Whether that was tonight or after the Stanley Cup, we're going somewhere as a team.

Somewhere fucking warm.

With sand, sun, and hopefully plenty of scantily clad women. I haven't gotten laid in far too fucking long.

"But first, Bora-Bora!" Spencer calls out, and I grin at him.

"Damn right. We leave first thing, so don't get so drunk tonight that you pass out and miss the flight. We won't wait for your stupid ass."

Against a backdrop of snickers and smiles, I walk over to my locker and start to strip down to hit the shower. Now that the adrenaline from the game is over, my knees ache. My back is stiff.

I feel eighty.

As I joke with the guys—always keeping my hockey-star mask on—I get showered and then pull on my suit and tie.

The guys give me shit for always dressing up for game day, but it's habit. It's my image. Ray—or Dad, as I've called him since I was sixteen—always says that you need to show the world who you are.

I'm not a slob. I'm a professional, elite athlete, and I fucking look like it.

Reaching for my phone, I frown when the screen lights up and I see that I've missed ten calls and a shit ton of texts during the game.

Fuck.

Still frowning, I see the calls were from Gideon. Most of the texts, too, except for a couple from Willow. They started coming in when we were still warming up for the game, almost four hours ago.

Willow: I know you're playing but you need to call me ASAP.

Willow: Seriously, I'm so sorry, but we need you.

Gideon: I'm getting on a flight home now. Call me, bro.

My stomach is in knots, dread sitting heavy on my chest, as I immediately dial Gideon's number, but it goes straight to voicemail.

He's in the air. The flight from Washington, DC, to Montana is a long one, but he should be almost there by now.

I dial Willow's number, and she picks up right away.

"Ry!" I hear the tears in her voice, and I have to sit down. My chest aches. My breaths are already coming fast. *Jesus, what is going on at home?* "Oh, Ry, I'm so sorry. I know you're playing—"

"I'm never too busy for you, and you know it, Wills. What's wrong? Breathe for me, and tell me what's going on."

She pauses, and I hear her take a long breath.

"It's Ray." *No.* Goddamn it. "It's not good, Ryker."

"Is he still alive?"

"For now, but you need to get here as soon as you can."

"I'm on my way. I'll be there in three hours."

"Come straight to the hospital, okay? Gideon will be here by then, and I'll tell you everything when you get here."

"Three hours. Deep breaths, honey. We're coming. We'll take care of everything."

"Oh, God." She lets out a choked sob, and I want nothing more than to be able to teleport myself there, to be there for them.

"I'll see you soon."

"Okay. Thanks, Ry."

She hangs up, and I immediately make some calls, arranging for the team private jet to take me home, and then I turn to the guys.

They're already watching me with somber faces.

"How much did you hear?"

"Enough," Mac says. "Go home, Cap. We can postpone Bora-Bora."

"No, you guys go and have fun. You've earned it."

"Keep us posted, yeah?" Spencer says, and I nod as I swallow hard. *Fuck.* I need to get home.

"Thanks, guys."

I hate hospitals. I've spent my fair share in them after particularly rough injuries on the ice, but mostly I despise them because it was a place like this where I said goodbye to my mom after the last asshole she was with beat her so severely, it killed her.

I always think of her when I have to be in a hospital. I know she would hate that, but I can't help it.

I held her hand in places like this more times than I could count, and one day, she didn't get to go home with me.

"Ry!"

I look up to find Willow rushing down the hallway, her pretty face ravaged from tears, and then she's hugging me, holding on tight as I stare over her shoulder at Gideon, who walks toward us, his face grim. We're both in suits. We look like we're late for a wedding.

"Am I too late?" *God, is that my voice?*

"No," Gideon says, and when Willow eases back, he pulls me in for a hug. "But you need to get in there."

"You two go together," Willow says.

I slip my hand in hers and link our fingers, our palms pressed together. "You come with us."

She nods and holds on to me tight. Willow has been my best friend since I was fifteen. Since she managed to make Gideon and me brothers rather than enemies. We're the Three Amigos.

These two are my best friends. The people I can count on, ride or die, no matter what.

Having Gideon next to me and Willow's hand in mine is the only thing keeping me from losing my shit right now.

We walk into a dim room, where Ray, the only father I've ever known, is lying on the bed. He's hooked up to monitors, and he's sleeping. He's lost all his color. I've never seen him so gray.

"What happened?" I ask, my voice a ragged whisper.

Christ. That's my dad.

"Stroke," Gideon says. "We'll go over it all later. It doesn't matter now."

No, I suppose it doesn't.

I cross to him and sit in the chair beside the bed, then take his hand in mine and bring the back of it to my lips. Since that day that we stepped foot on the Triple Creek Ranch all those years ago, this man has been bigger than life itself. Strong. Tall. Proud.

But then we lost Mama two years ago, and it was as though Dad died with her.

I hardly recognize the man lying in this bed.

"Hey, Dad," I say, squeezing his hand. To my surprise, his eyes flutter open, and he looks at me, and it's a hit to the solar plexus. *I love him so much.* "If you wanted to get me to come home, you didn't have to be so dramatic about it."

Humor flickers in his eyes, but he doesn't say anything.

"He can't talk," Willow whispers.

"I'm here, too, Dad," Gideon says, joining me, and Dad's gaze shifts to my brother.

None of us are related by blood, but we're linked by something far more important. Years of respect and laughter. Hard work. And the devotion we all had for the love of his life.

Dad's eyes fill with tears. I can tell that he wants to say something, and he's frustrated, but he's also so weak and tired.

"We know," I assure him, and kiss the back of his hand again. Gideon lays his hand on Dad's shoulder and gives it a gentle squeeze.

"We love you, too, Dad," Gideon says.

"Thank you." I swallow the tears down. "Thank you for everything you did for us. For giving us Mom, and the ranch, and Willow. Hell, for giving us a *life*."

A tear falls from Dad's eye, and Gideon brushes it away.

"Hey," Gideon says, his gruff voice soft. "You go to Mom. We know you've been missing her like crazy."

"Just tell her we love her," I add, my own tears falling from my eyes.

"I love you too," Willow adds, leaning over so he can see her. "So, so much. Please kiss Aunt Deb for me, Uncle Ray."

Christ.

"We've got this," Gideon says.

Dad looks at each of us once more, and then he closes his eyes and sighs, and the machine makes a static, beeping noise, signaling that there is no heartbeat.

Dad's gone.

Chapter Two

Ryker

It's late, and the house is finally quiet as I walk into the living room and find Gideon sitting by the fireplace, watching the flames, a tumbler of whiskey dangling from his fingers. Aside from standing up with Willow and me to give Dad's eulogy, he hasn't said more than two words today.

I've just poured my own tumbler, and I sit across from him, take a sip of the expensive whiskey I sent Dad for Christmas—that he never opened—and then rub my fingertips over my forehead. *Christ, I'm tired.*

"Did the last of them leave?" Gideon asks me. He's been in here for a while. Gideon doesn't do well with a room full of people. It puts him on edge. He's the strong, silent type. He's not a talker, and definitely *not* a socializer. The most social this man gets is when he comes to watch me play.

We couldn't be more different if we fucking tried.

"Yeah. It's just us now. Willow's finishing up in the kitchen. I offered to help, but she told me I was in her way and to get lost."

It's just us now.

"Sounds about right."

I nod just as the woman herself walks into the living room and sits on the stone ledge in front of the roaring fire so she can look at both of us. She's still in her black dress, but she's barefoot, having shed her heels a while ago. Her blond hair is down around her shoulders, and although she looks as bone tired as I feel, she's still gorgeous.

"I need to leave soon. I have to get Aiden."

Willow has raised her teenage nephew, Aiden, since he was five years old and her half sister dropped the kid off on Willow's doorstep. So much changed for our friend that day. I've only seen her in person a handful of times since then because I've been traveling for hockey, and she has a kid to raise.

Christ, I've missed her. Texts and calls don't cut it like being near her does.

Have her blue eyes always shone like that?

"Is everything okay there?" Gideon asks, and I frown over at him.

"What do you mean?"

But Gid doesn't answer—he just watches Wills, and she bites her plump lower lip and looks at the floor.

"Is Aiden giving you trouble?" he persists.

I narrow my eyes but wait for her to answer. The three of us don't keep secrets from each other.

"He's a teenager," she says with a shrug and swallows hard. "Teenage boys are supposed to be trouble. You two caused your fair share, remember?"

"Yeah, and we had Dad to knock our heads together to keep us straight." I lean forward in my chair. Gideon and I were hell on wheels when we first got here, but Dad set us straight quickly and never hesitated to remind us to keep our shit to a minimum.

She shrugs again. "I don't know. He's been a handful. I don't like some of his friends. But it'll be okay. Today isn't for teenager drama. It's for us, grieving the only father the three of us have known."

I frown and drink my whiskey and then glance at Gid, who's also frowning. Why do I get the feeling she's evading?

My phone rings, and when I see that it's Andy, my agent, I reject the call and set my phone aside.

"For fuck's sake."

"What's wrong?" Gideon asks.

"It's Andy. He *knows* that I'm in Montana for my father's funeral, and he's still bugging the shit out of me."

"I've always hated that guy," Wills says.

"What does he want?" Gideon's voice is hard. It's always hard, just like the steel in his blue eyes. The way he sets his jaw.

Gid is a badass. And he has to be. He's in the Secret Service. He protects the most important people in our country.

"You know that my contract with the team ended at the end of the season?"

"Sure."

"He wants me to commit to another contract. I haven't listened to his messages, but I've seen the texts. It's about the money."

"He makes a shit ton of dough when you sign the next contract."

"Yeah, well, that's *if* I sign another."

That has him and Willow both raising an eyebrow in surprise. "Don't tell me you're thinking about hanging up your skates."

I tip my head back, rest it on the back of the chair, and sigh.

"Christ, I'm tired." I swallow and look over at Gideon, then at Willow. If I can't talk to these two about what's going on, I can't talk to anyone. "I *love* hockey. I'm not tired of the sport. The thought of not playing anymore, well." I shake my head. "It's like being told that I have to cut my own heart out."

"Then what is it?" Willow asks.

"I'm so fucking tired of being that man's ATM machine. He's shit when it comes to money, and he's always sure to tell me that he needs my deal to keep him afloat."

"What the hell?" Gideon scowls at me. "Hell no, man."

"It's not just that. It's the pressure of staying on top. I'm thirty-five. I'll never play like I did when I was twenty-five, but if I have an off game, I'm crucified."

"Fans don't get it." Gideon sips his whiskey.

"Not by the fans. By the coaches, by my teammates. Then, I have the constant work of endorsements. Don't get me wrong, the money's great, but it's constant. Then there's the shit side of it. People showing up at my house. The paparazzi. Random women being obnoxious."

"Yeah, I'm sure that fucking hot girls is a real chore for you."

Willow scowls at something over my shoulder, and it makes my stomach clench.

I smirk at Gideon. "I don't do that shit. No, I'm not a monk, but I don't hook up with every chick who looks my way."

Gideon laughs at that. "You'd have no time for hockey."

Willow looks more uncomfortable. *What's up, Wills?*

"I hate to complain because I have a life that, when I was a kid, I never would have dreamed was a possibility."

"I get that."

My eyes meet his again. "I know. You both do. That's why I can say this shit to you. I think it's time to retire and come home to the ranch."

"Oh, Ry," Willow whispers, shaking her head. "Don't do something rash."

"It's not rash. I've been contemplating it anyway. This is just the catalyst to get the ball rolling."

Blowing out a breath, Gideon looks back into the fire. "He let this place fall apart."

We've spent several days wandering around the property since Dad died, and it's evident that he did the bare minimum after Mom passed away.

"He fired Dusty."

Gideon nods. "He told me today. I had no idea."

"I didn't know either," Willow says, holding her hands up.

"Same here. I'll hire him back, if he'll come back. Dusty said that he still came by every day to feed the horses. Dad didn't want to sell them to Dusty, but he wasn't taking care of them."

"What in the hell was he thinking?" Gideon asks.

"He wasn't. He was sad, Gid. He missed Mom, and you and I were gone. I should have come home more to check on him."

"I should have driven out here more," Willow adds.

"That would have pissed him off," he says.

"So he would have been pissed—who cares? He might be alive right now." I push my hand through my hair in agitation.

"Don't do that. You don't know that, and all it'll do is tear you up inside. What's done is done. Dad was an adult, and he could have asked either of us, or anyone in town, for help, and he chose not to. The truth is, he missed her, man."

"Yeah." I finish my whiskey and set the glass on the floor by my feet. "I know. You'll stay long enough to help me clean out this house a bit?"

"That's the plan," he confirms. "I have four more weeks of vacation coming before I have to get back, and I don't have a return flight to DC until the night before I report for duty."

"I guess it pays to be a workaholic and never take a vacation," Willow says, and Gid grins at her. She rubs her hands up and down her thighs, as if she's nervous. *Why the fuck is she nervous?* "I'll help too."

"Who are you guarding right now?" I ask my brother, keeping one eye on Wills.

His lips twitch in a sneer. "You know I'm not supposed to tell you that."

I tip my head to the side and raise an eyebrow.

"I'm on Blackbird duty. The First Daughter. She's a pain in my ass."

Now I raise both eyebrows. "Why?"

"She doesn't do what she's fucking told."

"Ah." I nod slowly, watching him. "How old is she?"

"Nineteen."

I scoff at that. Willow laughs outright. "Come on, don't get me started on the shit we pulled when we were nineteen. It's a wonder Mom didn't kill us."

"We weren't the kids of a president. Our lives weren't on the line every day."

"I don't know, I really think Mom might have killed us if she heard about that time—"

"Yeah, yeah." He drags his hand down his face, obviously not wanting to rehash old stories. I don't know why not. They're damn funny. "You need to know that I'm not moving back here, Ry."

I frown at my brother as Willow watches us both. "I didn't ask you to."

"I'm just saying it, right now. I'll be back to visit, but I don't want to live here. I like my job in DC, and I'm not ready to retire."

"Hey, just because I'm ready for a change of pace doesn't mean that you are. I'm perfectly fine with that. I *want* to work the ranch. I have plenty of money to get things up and going again. I don't want you to feel any kind of way about that."

"Thanks to your finance-geek skills," Gid says, eyeing me as he tugs his tie loose around his neck, "I have plenty of money too. I can help. But I don't want to live here full-time."

"Understood. We'll take time over the next month to make plans for the ranch moving forward."

"Are you going to renovate the house, Ry?" Willow asks.

I blow out a breath. "I hadn't thought about it."

"You should. Just rip the bandage off and get it over with. This is your home now, and you should make it how you want it. If we're going to go through and clean it out, it's a good time to do it. I'll bring Aiden on the weekends, and we can both help. It'll be good for him to spend time out here."

I nod and reach over to squeeze her knee, and she stiffens.

I've touched this woman a million times before, and it's never been an issue. Never even a *thought.*

I narrow my eyes at her, and she visibly makes herself relax, and I pull my hand away.

"You okay, Trouble?" I ask her, and she nods, but she won't meet my gaze.

"Sorry, yeah. Just out of sorts. It's been a rough week, you know?"

But I don't believe her. I've known her forever. These are the two people I know the best in the world.

Something isn't right.

Because although I haven't spent time with Willow in person in years, I talk to her all the time. When life happened, and we all went our own ways, we didn't disappear from each other's lives.

But it's late, it's been a rough fucking day, and I have all the time in the world to make sure Willow's okay. I'll get to the bottom of it.

"When should we start on the house?" I ask the room.

"Might as well dig in tomorrow," Gideon says, and I nod in agreement.

"I'd better go. I'll be back before noon tomorrow." Willow stands, and I frown at her.

"Bring a bag for you guys and stay here for a few days at a time. Don't make that drive back and forth every day."

She bites that lower lip, which is plumper than I remember it being before, and shakes her head.

"I'll be working in the early mornings and evenings after we get home. Unfortunately, I still have deadlines, and Aiden has school. It'll be fine—I can make that drive with my eyes closed."

Wills is a voice actor and primarily works on audiobooks and video games.

She's fucking badass, and I couldn't be prouder of her.

But I wish I had a studio for her here so she wouldn't have to drive back and forth to her home in Missoula, which is an hour away. The trip is dangerous, as well as exhausting.

I can tell by the way her jaw tightens that there's no changing her mind.

Gid and I walk her to her car, and before she can get inside, she turns and hugs us both in turn. My brother whispers something in her ear, but I can't hear what it is. Willow smiles and nods and offers him a sweet look that almost has me feeling jealous.

I need some fucking sleep.

When she turns to me, she tugs that lip between her teeth, looking uncertain.

"Get over here, Trouble." I take her hand and tug her against me, wrap my arms around her and hug her close. She smells incredible. Like flowers and laundry soap. After a heartbeat of stiffening in my arms, she melts against me and lets out a long breath.

Maybe it's the sadness of the day that has her acting different. I hope that's it.

"I'm glad you're home," she murmurs. "Both of you."

"I knew you missed me." I kiss her head, and she laughs, which is exactly what I wanted, and then she pulls away, and I miss having her warmth, her softness, close to me.

This is Willow, man.

"I'll see you tomorrow," she says, but she looks so damn tired.

"Are you sure you won't stay?" Gideon asks, obviously reading my mind. "I'm sure Aiden will be fine with his friend tonight. I don't like you making that drive either."

"No, I need to get him." She shakes her head, her mind obviously made up. "I'll be okay."

"Let us know when you get home."

She nods, sinks into the driver's seat, and waves before heading off down the driveway.

Chapter Three

Willow

"Holy shit, Ry, I was just here two days ago, and this looks like a different house."

Ryker grins in that cocky way he always does that makes the butterflies attack my stomach lining. Good God, this man's smile should come with a warning label.

Smile will induce pantie melting from fifty paces.

He slings his arm over my shoulders, the way he always does, and we look around the living room. The old, faded furniture that should have been replaced more than a decade ago is gone. In fact, the room has been completely emptied, and there's a crew refinishing the original hardwood floors.

"They're going to paint when the floors are done. They should have done it before, but there was miscommunication," he says, but all I can think about is his rock-hard side, which I'm pressed up against. "The whole house is getting paint and the floors redone. Come on, you can clean up your room because it's getting the magic tomorrow, along with the rest of the second floor."

"My room is clean," I remind him with a smirk. "I'm not a slob like someone else I know."

"Hey, I was a teenager. I was supposed to be a slob."

He smirks and twists his baseball cap so it's sitting backward, and I'm pretty sure my vagina just did the hula.

He's your best friend, and that's it, Willow. Calm the hell down.

"You okay?" he asks, tipping his head to the side.

"Sure." I'm totally fine. Definitely not reacting to the way that gray T-shirt is molded against his torso and the sleeves hug his biceps. His body is just . . . *ridiculous.*

"Let me know if you need help," he says, once he seems satisfied that I'm telling the truth. "I'll be in the back guest rooms on the second floor. I'm converting the two rooms into one so I can have a gym."

And now I have visions of this man working out, and I need to get away from him before I do something stupid. Like lick him.

This is why it's always been better that we didn't live in the same place, and we just talked via the phone. Because where Ryker James is concerned, my hormones are in overdrive.

"Will do," I reply, trying to act as nonchalant as possible as I grab some garbage sacks and head upstairs to my room.

It's so weird to hear the noises of renovations echoing through the gigantic farmhouse. I practically grew up here. My mom was Debbie's sister. Mom loved to dump me off here so she didn't have to worry about me, and Aunt Deb and Uncle Ray never turned me away.

They treated me like I was theirs. Like I belonged with them.

Losing them hurt more than anything I've ever gone through in my life.

I walk into my room and take a deep breath. The full-size bed still has the same blue hand-sewn quilt draped over it that Deb made for me when I was ten. After college, I didn't stay out here often, but I was always reminded that I had a place here.

There aren't any mementos in here. No yearbooks or old clothes of mine. It looks like any other spare bedroom, but it always belonged to me. My safest place in this world. I spent countless summer nights sitting by that window, staring out at the mountains and the stars, daydreaming about Ryker. And I've never slept better in my life than I did in that bed.

It won't take me long to make sure everything is wrapped and covered so the furniture will be safe from the painters.

I've just folded up my sheets and blankets and am stuffing them into a giant plastic bag when I feel movement behind me. I'm bent at the waist, wrestling with the edge of this bag. I turn to look behind me and find Ryker's eyes pinned to my ass.

Embarrassment ignites over my face, and I jerk upright. Jesus, my ass is . . . not tiny. And he was just staring at it.

"Sorry," I mutter. "What's up?"

"Huh?" He's still staring at where my ass was and then seems to shake himself and meet my gaze. He licks his lips. "Oh, lunchtime. Come on down to the kitchen. We're making sandwiches and stuff."

"I'm not hungry."

My stomach decides now is the right time to make me a lying liar and lets out a loud growl, and Ry's grin slides into view.

"Not hungry, huh?"

"Okay, I'm a little hungry. I just have to finish stuffing this in this bag, and I'll be down."

"I'll help." He crosses over and picks up the edge of the plastic. "Here, you hold, I'll stuff."

With a nod, I join him, and we work together, getting it all secure, and then he tosses it on the stripped bed, and we haul the bed into the middle of the room and spread a tarp over the top.

"Thanks. I'm all done in here."

"Come on then. Gid always puts too much mustard on the sandwiches. I have to supervise."

He gestures for me to walk out ahead of him, and I slide past. I'm near the staircase when I glance back and once again find him watching my butt.

My steps falter, and I feel myself pitch forward. *Shit, I'm going to fall down the stairs.* I flail, but before I can fall, strong arms circle around me, and Ryker tugs my back to his front and plants his lips by my ear.

"Easy, Trouble. No hurting yourself."

I clear my throat and step out of his embrace. "Thanks. I don't know why I'm so clumsy today. What kind of sandwiches are we having?"

I'm halfway down the stairs when I glance back because Ryker hasn't answered me.

He hasn't moved.

He's just watching me with the oddest look on his face.

"Ry?"

He blinks. "Yeah?"

"You okay?"

His brows pinch together as he descends the stairs. He pats my back as he walks by and then leads me toward the kitchen. "I'm fine. We have turkey and roast beef. Out of ham."

Gideon is in the kitchen, already eating his sandwich, and offers me a closed smile when he sees me because his mouth is full.

"Hey, Wills."

"Hey, handsome." I kiss his cheek and ruffle his dark hair, the way I always do. Now *this* I can do. This is easy. "You're sweaty."

"I'm working," he says, his voice as dry as the Sahara. He's in his typical black tactical pants and T-shirt. I don't remember the last time I saw this man in jeans. He's such a military guy.

And honestly, it looks hot on him.

I also don't remember the last time I was in the same room with the two of them together, before our world fell apart and Ray left us.

Ryker didn't even make it home for Aunt Debbie's funeral roughly two years ago, which is something he truly beat himself up over, but he was in the middle of the playoffs, and no one judged him for that. He ended up winning the Stanley Cup that year, and I think he channeled all his grief onto the ice.

But last week, when Ry confided in us that he's retiring from hockey and taking over the ranch full-time, I had a moment of panic. Because that means that I'll see him often. Part of me, the best friend part, is excited at the thought of him being nearby.

The other part?

Well, she's been in love with this sexy hockey player since the day he climbed out of that car when he was fifteen and stole the breath from her lungs. He and Gid are both beyond handsome men. Tall, dark, and stupidly hot. Muscles for days. Gideon is my intense, gruff, quiet guy. The one who will kick someone's ass and burn the world to the ground for anyone he loves without blinking an eye, and will do it all while maintaining a straight face and without breaking a sweat.

Ryker is funny. A smidge arrogant, but that comes with being a super-famous, rich professional hockey player. Over the years, he's added an entire sleeve of tattoos to his left arm—his muscle definition should be illegal in all fifty states—and his chocolate-brown eyes . . . well, don't even get me started.

I love these two guys more than just about anyone, except Aiden. They are my family. My heroes. And I think of Gideon as my brother.

Ryker, on the other hand, I don't feel particularly sisterly toward.

I don't want to climb Gideon like a tree. The thought makes me slightly nauseated.

But Ryker? I would free solo that man in a heartbeat.

"Why do you have that weird look on your face?" Gideon asks, catching my attention.

"I don't have a look."

"You look like you just smelled something like rotting flesh," he continues.

"I wouldn't know what rotting flesh smells like, serial killer," I reply and get to work building my own sandwich. Ry's standing next to me, making his own as well, and he passes me the mayonnaise. Our fingers brush, and I swallow hard at the zing that shoots up my arm.

Ry pauses, and I feel his gaze on me, but I don't look up.

I need to have a serious talk with myself later. This is *Ryker*. My best friend. I need to get over this stupid crush. He admitted himself that he has all kinds of gorgeous women fawning all over him.

I am so *not* a puck bunny.

"I found this picture," Gideon says, tossing a photo on the counter. I cut my sandwich in half and set it on a plate before reaching for the picture, and I feel my smile spread all over my face.

"Oh, look at us."

I can't help but drag my fingertip over our faces. It's the three of us, all in swimsuits, with sopping wet hair, grinning at the camera.

"That's the summer we moved here," Ry says from beside me as he stares at the photo over my shoulder. I can feel his breath on my neck, and I pray to God no one sees my nipples react. "You were scrawny, Gid."

"Fuck you."

I laugh and shake my head as I walk around to sit on the stool next to Gideon and eat my sandwich.

"You two were *work*," I say before biting into my lunch. "So grumpy and surly and angry at each other."

"I think we were just angry at the universe," Ry replies with a shrug. "It worked out."

"I'll have copies made of this," I volunteer. "So we each have one."

"I thought the same thing," Gid says. "I'd like a copy."

"I'll make sure we all have one," I assure him and then bump his shoulder with mine.

"Found this one too," Gideon says, and then we're all staring down at a completely different photo, taken one year later. We're all dressed up, standing in a courthouse.

"Your gotcha day," I say with a soft smile.

"We're not puppies," Ry reminds me, and I can't help but laugh at that. We're all quiet for a long moment. I remember that day like it was yesterday. I *loved* that I got to be a part of their official adoption day.

Aunt Debbie cried like a baby when the judge signed off, and Ray held her tightly, the way he always did.

It was one of the most special days of our lives, and I can admit, I was a little jealous. I wish they could have adopted me as well.

"We'll need copies of this one too," I say after swallowing hard, and my guys both nod.

I turn to Gideon, needing to lighten the mood a bit.

"How are you? Are you going crazy being gone from work so long?"

"It's only been a little over a week," he reminds me, and I just lift an eyebrow.

I know my guys.

"Yeah, I've been checking in every day. It seems Blackbird doesn't only try to push *my* buttons. She's been difficult this week."

"What does she do that's so bad?" I ask him.

"She likes to run off. Evading us, sneaking away, is a game for her. She hates having security. Thinks she should have her freedom because she's an adult. But that's not how it works."

"I know the president has Secret Service for the rest of her life, but will her children also have them forever?"

"No. When Madam President's term is over, she and her husband will have a detail for the rest of their lives, but not their children. Only children under the age of sixteen."

"Interesting." I reach for the bag of chips that Ryker tossed on the island for us to share and pull out a handful. "How much longer in this term?"

"She's up for reelection. So it could be another five years or so," he replies, shaking his head. "Fuck my life."

"Can you get reassigned?"

"I could." Gid shrugs. "It's all good. At least it's not boring."

"That's true." I grin at him. "I'm proud of you, you know. You're pretty cool."

Gideon shakes his head, but I can see the pride in his eyes when he offers me a small smile. "Thanks, kiddo."

"I'm *one* year younger than you," I remind him, but he just chuckles.

"Still younger."

I glance up and find Ryker watching us, his jaw clenched.

"What's wrong?" I ask him.

He shakes his head. "Do you want another sandwich?"

"Nah, I'm full. Thanks, though. What can I do next? I need to leave in an hour or so to get Aiden from school. Are we cleaning out Ray's office? Their bedroom?"

We all frown at each other.

"No," Gid says, shaking his head.

"Agreed," Ry adds. "We'll shut those doors and leave them be for now. It's too soon."

I slump in relief. "I'm on the same page. But, Ry, you're going to need an office."

"I've already commandeered another guest room to convert. It's all good."

"I'll work on another room, then," I begin as I hop off my stool, but my phone starts to ring, and I scowl when I see it's the school.

Damn it.

What now?

"Hello?" I don't bother to leave the room. There's no point.

"Hey, Willow, this is Ms. Hileman at the high school."

"Hi there. What's up?"

Ryker and Gideon are watching me, not even pretending not to eavesdrop.

"I have Aiden in my office," the principal says with a sigh, and my stomach drops. "Are you able to come in for a meeting?"

"I'm about an hour away," I reply and rub my fingertips over my forehead. "But I can head that way, sure. Is he sick? Hurt?"

"No, he's not hurt. But he's in trouble, Willow."

I close my eyes and lean against the counter. "What did he do now?"

"Christ," Ryker whispers, and I do my best to ignore him.

"I think it's best if you come in, and we can all talk this out."

"I'd like to speak with him, please."

There's a pause. "Oh, well, you can speak with him—"

"Yes, I can speak with him *now*." I hear the ice in my voice, and I don't give a shit. This is my kid we're talking about.

"Speaker," Gid says next to me, and I do as he says, setting my phone on the counter.

"One moment."

"Wait. Why can't you hand him the phone? I thought he was in your office."

"He's just getting patched up by the nurse real quick."

I hover over the phone. "What in the hell, Melody? You just told me he isn't hurt. What is going on?"

"*Ms. Hileman.* He has a cut lip." Her voice is curt. "But he will be just fine. Let me get him for you."

I look up into Ryker's hot brown eyes and then glance at Gideon, whose hands are fisted.

We're all pissed.

"Aunt Willow." My boy's voice sounds so defeated, it makes my heart clench.

"Hey, sweetheart. Are you okay? Do you need me to take you to the doctor?"

"No, it's just my lip. It's okay."

"Buddy, I need you to be honest with me right now. Do you hear me?"

"Okay."

"Do you feel safe where you are?"

There's silence on the other end of the line, and that's all I need to know.

"I'm on my way *right now*. You sit and you keep quiet. Don't answer any questions until I'm there, do you understand? I've got you, baby."

"I understand. How long?"

"As fast as I can get there, but I'm at the ranch, so it'll be a bit."

"It's okay. You don't have to hurry. I'm safe."

I shake my head. I don't trust anything that I'm hearing right now. "It's okay, buddy. I'm coming. Just hang tight."

"Yeah, okay."

"I love you."

He ends the call without saying it back, which doesn't surprise me at all.

"Sorry, guys, I'm out. My kiddo needs me."

"Wills, what the fuck's going on?" Gideon demands, but I shake my head.

"I don't trust that woman, and I don't trust whoever hit my boy. I'll go straighten it out. He likely won't tell me what's going on, but if he's hurt, I don't want him sitting there."

"We can come with you," Ryker offers, and I want to cry.

God, it would be awesome to have help.

But this isn't their fight.

"Thank you, but it'll be okay. This isn't our first time in the principal's office." I offer them each a smile that I don't feel because I don't want them to worry, and then hurry through the house and out to my car.

I need to get to my boy.

"So he didn't start it, didn't throw the first punch, but he's the only one being suspended? Come on, Melody, that's not fair."

The other woman, with perfectly coiffed red hair, straightens her navy blue power suit and purses her lips. I've known Melody Hileman since we were in the third grade and she moved to town from Wisconsin. She's always been a jerk.

Now the jerk is the principal of my kid's high school.

"The other boy had to go to the urgent care," she says. "You're lucky I convinced his parents not to press assault charges."

I narrow my eyes at her. "No. *They're* lucky *I'm* not pressing assault charges, given that their kid threw the first punch, and *my* kid was defending himself."

Aiden shifts in his chair next to me.

"He's not suspended if the other kid isn't," I add. "And what are you going to do to keep my child safe while he's at school? It's obvious that boy is doing his best to get Aiden into trouble."

Melody shakes her head. "I can't talk about the other child with you."

"And you won't discuss my child's safety with me."

She simply holds my gaze, and I've never disliked someone as much as I do this woman.

"Good to know." I stand and glance down at Aiden. "We'll go home now."

"School isn't out for thirty minutes," Melody reminds me.

"And yet you kept him in here for the last two hours, didn't send him back to class, and you're worried that he's going to miss the last thirty minutes? He'll be here tomorrow."

She starts to say something, but I just raise an eyebrow until she nods.

"That's what I thought. Come on, Aiden."

He's quiet in the car ride home. Broody. Which is nothing new where my nephew is concerned. When I park in front of our little house, he walks inside, goes through to his room, and slams his door, and I let out a gusty breath.

We have to talk. And getting this kid to talk to me these days is like pulling molars.

When I knock on his door, he ignores me.

"We have to talk about this, Aiden."

He doesn't reply, so I try the handle, but it's locked. I hate that he's started locking his door. No fifteen-year-old should be able to lock his parent out of his room.

"Open up, buddy."

Still no response.

So I go find a hairpin and proceed to pick the lock. It's not easy, but the door finally gives.

When I open the door, I see that my boy is lying on his bed, his back to me, with his big headphones on, listening to music. He didn't even hear me break into his room.

"Aiden," I call out, but he can't hear me, so I walk over and put my hand on his ankle.

He flails, startled, and his sneaker-clad foot hits me right in the shoulder, making me fall back onto my ass.

"Ouch," I mutter, rubbing my shoulder.

"Aunt Wills," he says, tearing his headphones off and tossing them on the bed. "What the fuck? Why are you in my room?"

His green eyes go round when he sees that I managed to unlock his door.

"What did you do?"

"I came into the room that *I own* to talk to you about today," I reply, climbing to my feet. "You don't get to lock me out of here, Aiden."

"It's my room."

"And you'll speak to me when I tell you to. What is going on with you?"

He shakes his head, and seeing the injury on his lip makes me want to punch someone. I'm not a violent woman, but I'll do whatever needs to be done to protect my kid.

"I need you to tell me what's up with you, buddy. I can help you."

"I don't need help. I'm fine. I'll go to school tomorrow."

I sigh with disappointment. "You can tell me anything, Aiden."

No reaction.

"Okay. Well, I'll let you know when dinner's ready."

"Can I close my door?"

"If you promise not to lock me out."

His lips twist, but he gives me a curt nod.

I'm exhausted, and a little sore, when I leave his room. I wish he'd talk to me. I wish I knew what was up with my teenager.

More than anything, I wish I didn't feel so helpless where he's concerned. I don't know what to do with him.

"I don't want to go to the ranch."

I glance at Aiden in the passenger seat and then out the windshield. We've been on the road for almost an hour, we're only two miles away from the ranch, and he's just speaking up *now*.

"It'll be good for us. It's a beautiful day, and I'm sure there's plenty to do outside."

"Yeah, it's fucking awesome being free labor." He rolls his eyes, and I scowl.

"Watch your mouth, Aiden. I'm lenient with you, but you'll speak with respect, or you won't speak at all."

He growls and turns his head to look out the passenger window.

"Why are you so grouchy? You've always loved the ranch. You used to love hanging out with Ray—"

And then, it hits me. *Of course* he's upset at the thought of returning to the ranch since Ray has passed. He refused to come to the funeral, and I let that slide because we all grieve in our own way.

But Ray was the only grandpa that Aiden has known, and they loved each other.

"I'm sorry, buddy—"

"I don't want to talk about it."

I roll my shoulders. It's been a few days since I got Aiden from school after the fight, and he's been in the surliest mood ever since. Worse than usual. I've cooked his favorite meals for dinner, I've tried to tease him, and I've even offered to watch his horror movies with him, but he will not soften toward me even a little.

Finally, I turn onto the ranch road, and when I pull up in front of the house, I get out of the car, but Aiden stays put, his face drawn in hard lines.

Thankfully, there's no sign of Ryker or Gideon. There are plenty of workers bustling around, and even from out here, I can tell that there's been a lot of progress on the house since I was here a few days ago, but the guys are nowhere in sight.

Good.

I walk around the car and reach for the passenger door handle, but Aiden locks the car. He won't meet my gaze.

I have the fob in my purse, and when I touch the handle, the car unlocks, and I quickly open the door.

"Unless you want to lose every privilege in your life, you'll get out of this car and stop throwing a tantrum like a damn three-year-old."

"I don't want to be here." He sets his jaw and crosses his arms over his chest. "I'll wait for you in the car."

"Aiden. I won't warn you again. Get. Out. Of. The. Car."

"Fuck off."

That has me staggering back a step in shock.

"You want to speak that way to *me*, big man?"

I spin around and find Ryker at my back, his face mutinous, hands in fists, glaring at my boy.

When I turn back to Aiden, he swallows hard, but he still doesn't get out of the car, and he doesn't answer Ryker's question.

Ry takes my shoulders in his hands and gently moves me aside, and then, with his forearm resting on the roof of the car, he leans in and says something in such a low voice that I can't understand the words. Aiden shakes his head, and then Ryker says something else, and that has my nephew getting out of the car.

Aiden swallows hard and steps over to me. He won't meet my gaze, but he says, "Sorry I told you to fuck off."

God, he sounds so angry.

"Okay. Thanks for getting out of the car."

He shrugs, and then he's off, headed for the barn. Aiden's always loved the horses, and he knows how to ride, how to tend to them, so I leave him be.

Maybe he needs some animal therapy.

"Hey." Ry hooks his finger under my chin and tips my face up, and I'm fighting tears. "Are you okay?"

"Sure." I lick my lips and swallow the tears down. "He's just in a mood today."

"He tell you to fuck off often, Trouble?"

I shake my head and meet his gaze. "That's the first time."

"That's the *last* time," he says. "Come on, I'll pour you some coffee."

"I should go check on him."

"Leave him be. He's fine in the barn. I told him to go brush and feed the horses. He said Dad showed him how."

"He's great with the horses," I confirm, and Ry nods, takes my hand—sending sparks up my arm—and leads me inside. "What's on the agenda for the day?"

I stop short when we get inside.

"Holy shit, Ry. There's been so much done in less than two weeks."

"I think the crew hates the drive out here every day. Most of them live fifteen minutes away in Paradise Valley, but they don't even like *that* commute."

Paradise Valley is a small community a short drive away. It's the closest grocery store, schools, hospital, the whole nine yards. It's *much* closer than Missoula. But it doesn't surprise me that the workers don't even love that commute. At least it's spring and there's no snow, and I know for a fact that Ryker is paying them well.

I smirk. "It's pretty isolated out here. Makes sense they want to finish up quickly."

"The few repairs to the barn are done, and they're finishing the bunkhouse today." He pulls a mug out of the cabinet and fills it for me, doctoring it up just the way I like it.

How he remembers the way I take my coffee after all this time, I have no idea.

"That's great, Ry." I accept the mug, doing my best to ignore his fingers touching mine, and then take a sip. "Where's Gideon?"

"He's using my office for a while," he says. "Apparently, there's trouble in DC with the First Daughter. She's harder to deal with than Aiden."

I lift an eyebrow. "I'm sorry to hear that. I bet he's itching to get back there."

He leans his hip against the counter and crosses his arms, and I have to actually work at not salivating.

He's in that backward baseball cap again. Today's T-shirt is a black Seattle Blizzard one that sits perfectly on his biceps and hugs his abs, leaving nothing to the imagination. Add in the faded blue jeans, and he's every fantasy I've ever had in my life.

"Furniture's coming tomorrow," he says, pulling me out of my ogling of his body. "Things are wrapping up here, so if he needs to go back, it's okay."

"It's been good having him home." I sip my coffee and glance outside in time to see my boy ride his horse through the pasture.

"You want to talk to me about what's going on between the two of you?" Ry's lips flatten when I turn to him.

"He's angry," I reply. "And he won't talk to me about it. Maybe being out on the horse today will help."

To my surprise, Ryker leans closer and tucks my hair behind my ear, his fingertips lingering on my neck, and *holy shit*.

"If you need help, you come to me. I've always got your back."

I swallow hard. *Of course*. Because he's my best friend.

"Thanks, Ry. Now, what do you need me to do today?"

He doesn't answer. If anything, he leans closer, and he looks like he's going to kiss me, and my heart stutters to a stop. His chocolate eyes fall to my lips, and his hand slides back to my hair, but then there are footsteps coming closer, and Ryker drops his hand just as Gideon walks in the room, looking like he's about to spontaneously combust.

"You okay, handsome?" I ask him, trying to calm my system down.

"I'm going to fucking throttle her ass," he mutters, shaking his head, his face set in furious lines. Holy shit, Gideon is intense when he's pissed. Or is he worried? "She's a goddamn menace, and she's going to get herself and someone else killed."

He's pacing, and Ry and I share a look.

"Gid, things are pretty well under control here. If you need to go—"

"In a couple of days." Gideon pulls his hands down his face, looking rattled. "I want to go on that ride with you and Dusty around the ranch to make plans, and I want to make sure most of the work in the house is done. This is what I'm here for, and I won't bail on you."

These two have come a long way from that day when they came here as fifteen-year-old enemies, ready to tear each other apart.

They might not be related by blood, but they're brothers in every way that counts.

"It's your call," Ryker says. "I'm not kicking you out."

"Good."

"What are we doing today?" I ask them both, and they grin at me, but it's more of a sinister grin than a happy one. "What? I don't like those looks. I'm not doing anything gross."

"We're peeling the wallpaper off the walls here in the kitchen," Ry says.

"Ugh, that sucks." I eye the faded walls. The paper has apples and ducks on it. I have no idea why Aunt Deb chose it. It's . . . not pretty. And I think it's from the 1980s. "Why not just paint over it?"

"Because that's not the right way to do it," Ry replies, and his lips tip up in his cocky grin as he reaches out to tap the end of my nose.

"And you can't throw some of your many millions to the crew bustling around to get it off?" I prop my hands on my hips, already thinking about how sore my shoulders are going to be later.

"They're busy getting the rest of the house finished," Ryker says. "If we get this off the walls today, they can paint in here tomorrow, and then the crew is done."

I heave out another sigh. "Fine. Let's do it."

Chapter Four

Ryker

I have a thing for my best friend.

Jesus Christ, she's all I think about these days. The way she filled out those jeans the other day had my cock straining against my zipper. I wanted to strip her bare in that bedroom and push into her from behind and fuck her until she forgot her name.

This is *Willow*, and I'm suddenly so attracted to her, I can't see straight.

And her hair is fucking silk, and I want to wrap it around my fingers while she's on her knees—

Fucking hell.

When I heard Aiden tell her to fuck off, it ignited something primal in my chest. He's just a kid, but I wanted to teach him a lesson for speaking to her that way. Instead, I made sure he went to the barn to cool off.

This is Willow. I keep saying that to myself, but it doesn't seem to matter.

I can't get enough of her.

Gideon had to go back to my office for another call with someone in DC, and I glance over to where Wills is on the top of a step stool, reaching high above her head. The motion makes her arch her back, pushes her tits out, and puts that perfect ass on display. The woman's body was made for the leggings she's wearing today.

I'm going to hell for lusting after my best friend.

"Hey. You don't need to get the stuff up high. I'll do it."

"It's fine," she replies and catches her tongue in her teeth, stretching up to peel the paper, and the stool tips. Before she can let out a peep, I'm next to her, my arm wrapped around her middle, tugging her to me. "I wasn't going to fall."

"There's a reason I call you Trouble. Because you're always getting into it. I told you to work down lower."

"You're not the boss of me, Captain."

My dick twitches at her calling me that.

Let's be honest, my dick twitches whenever she's nearby these days, full stop.

I press my lips to her ear, still holding her against me, and I can't stop the grin that spreads when I feel her gasp. "You're in my house, Wills. That makes me the boss of you."

"Whatever." She tries to sound like her normal bratty self, but her voice is breathy, and when she steps out of my hold and smooths her hands down her shirt, there's no mistaking the way her nipples are puckered.

She's not oblivious to me either.

"Fine." She sniffs and turns away from me. "I'll start in the corner over here."

She bends over, and I have immediate regrets.

Especially when Gideon walks in and catches me ogling her ass.

Goddamn it.

He lifts a brow, and I shake my head and turn away.

"I do have to go," he says with a heavy sigh. "My flight leaves tomorrow afternoon."

"We can ride out with Dusty first thing," I reply.

"I'm sorry to leave early."

I shake my head and clap him on the shoulder. “Don’t be. You’ve been here for almost three weeks, man. The furniture comes tomorrow. The house is mostly cleared out. After tomorrow, things are pretty much business as usual around here.”

He nods, but I see the guilt in his eyes.

“Stop it. I’m a big boy. You don’t have to hold my hand.”

That has him rolling his eyes as he goes back to peeling the paper he started on before his phone call.

I glance between the two of them. Neither of them notices me. I love them both. We have a history, and we’re family.

But the way I’m feeling about Willow is . . . *more*. Can I have her without completely destroying what the three of us have?

I don’t know, and that’s what has me holding back. I know that I can’t simply fuck her and then move on and expect everything to be the same between us. Ruining our Three Amigos status isn’t an option for any of us.

Catching feelings for Willow only complicates things. And I don’t need any more complications in my life.

But keeping my hands to myself isn’t feeling like much of an option either.

Mornings on the ranch have always been my favorite time, even in the heart of winter when it’s twenty below zero and the wind feels like it’s cutting through you.

The sun hasn’t quite come up yet as I pour my coffee and take it out on the porch off the kitchen and sit on the steps, watching the mountains come awake. Spring has definitely sprung here at the ranch. I have grass to mow, and plenty of cleanup from winter now that the house is done. There are some dead trees that I need to take out, and I’ll use the wood for fires this winter.

I also need to speak to Dusty, who should be coming by later this morning to talk with Gideon and me, so I can get the working side of this ranch back up and going. I want to get beef cattle bought, fence lines repaired, pastures checked.

There's still so much to do out here.

This summer is going to be a lot of work.

And that's okay. I'm ready for it.

But for right this second, I'm going to sit here and enjoy the sun coming up over those mountains, and the way the sky looks like it's on fire. I've been all over the place, traveling for hockey, or just for fun, but I've never seen anything like the view before me.

This is home.

This is where I'm supposed to be.

"Mornin'," Gid says as he steps outside with his own coffee. He sits next to me and takes a sip. "Dusty coming this morning?"

"Yeah." We're quiet for a few minutes, and it's nice to sit with my brother in the early-morning quiet.

"Heard from Willow?" he asks after a bit, and I shake my head.

"Not since she and Aiden got home last night."

"You should probably stay away from her, you know."

I don't answer at first, because I'm sure that I heard that wrong. "What?"

"Willow. Don't go there, man."

I shake my head and sip my coffee. "I don't know what you're talking about."

"Fuck that." He scoffs. "I have eyes in my head. Shit, you could cut the sexual tension with a knife. But she's not a puck bunny you can fuck and then move on from. This is our Willow, and I'm not going to choose sides when it all goes to shit."

I blow out a breath and drag my hand down my face. "There's a lot to unpack there. First of all, insinuate that Wills is anything in the realm of a goddamn puck bunny again, and I'll bust up your pretty face."

"You can try."

"Second of all, no one's asking you to choose sides in anything because we're exactly what we've always been."

"You're a liar if you think that's true."

"It *is* true. I haven't touched her."

"I'm simply making an observation."

I shake my head. Christ, if Gid sees that I'm suddenly seeing Willow in a sexy light, I must have been obvious as fuck.

Because she is *sexy. There's no denying that.*

"I'm not trying to start something with her," I say just as a truck rounds the bend in the driveway.

Saved by the truck.

"Thought he was coming later this morning," Gideon says.

"Me too."

I wasn't expecting Dusty until a little later, but I'm glad he's here now.

"Ryker," Dusty says by way of greeting as he approaches the porch. "Gideon. Thought I'd see if you two were available a little early."

"We are. Come on inside, and I'll get you a cup of coffee." I stand and gesture for the older man to follow me, and when we step through the door, Dusty whistles.

"Shit, did I come to the wrong house?"

I shake my head as Gideon walks in behind us. "Gideon and I have gotten a lot done since the funeral. The house needed some freshening up."

"You two have busted your asses. Listen, I know I said so at the funeral, but I sure am sorry about your dad."

I swallow as I catch Gid's gaze, and I walk to the coffeepot to pour Dusty a cup, then refill my own. I don't usually drink more than one cup a day, but I have a feeling I'm going to need this.

I know how Dusty takes his coffee. I made it for him for years. During the school year, Gid and I lived here in the house, but in the summer, Dad put us out in the bunkhouse with the other hands.

We fucking loved it.

Dusty was our boss, and he was someone who, along with Dad, taught us how to be a man. How to do what needed to be done here.

Sometimes, he was a hard-ass, but he taught us a work ethic that has served us both well.

"Thanks," Dusty says when I set his mug in front of him and then sit across from him at the table cupping my own mug in my hands. Gideon sits next to me.

"When did he let you go?" I ask, jumping right into the reason we asked him here.

He stares at the mug, taps the table with the tip of his finger. "About six months ago. The only animals that were left on the ranch were the horses. He'd let all the other guys go at the end of the summer, and then he pulled me in here, in this kitchen, and told me he didn't need me anymore."

"That was bullshit," Gid says.

Dusty nods. "He was my boss."

"He was your friend," I counter.

"Yes, he was my friend, but he was also my boss, Ryker. If the man wanted to fire us all, that was his prerogative. He owned the land. I didn't have a say in that. But I kept coming every day to look in on the horses because by that point, he hardly left this house."

"Shit." The guilt just sits heavier and heavier. "What did he do in here all day?"

"He drank," he says. "Ate garbage. Missed Debbie. Losing her is what killed him."

"I know." I tug my bottom lip through my teeth, watching the older man. Gideon stands to pace. He's not good at sitting still. "I'd like to hire you back on, with a raise. Summer's coming up, and I'll be hiring others to help too. I need to buy cattle and get this place up and running."

"You're reviving the Triple Creek?" Dusty's face is full of surprise.

"Yes, sir."

"What about hockey?"

I blow out a breath and shake my head. "I haven't officially told anyone this, but I'm retired. This is my job now."

Dusty just stares at me. "Don't do that. Don't give up something that great for this ranch."

"I'm ready to retire, and I happen to *like* this place, you know. I knew I'd end up back here someday. Dad left everything to Gideon and me, split in half. I'll be the one living here, taking care of things, and Gid's a silent partner."

When we learned how much money Dad had in the bank, we were shocked that he didn't just hire more people to take care of things when he couldn't, rather than let it all go to shit.

The man was rich several times over.

"I guess I could come out of retirement for you," Dusty says slowly.

"We rehabbed the bunkhouse. It's pretty much new inside, so you'll be comfortable," Gideon tells him. "It's finished already."

He nods. "Thank you."

"When can you start?" I ask him.

"I'm here now," he replies. "I'll drive out to the bunkhouse, look around, and then stop in at the barn before I head into town to pack up my rental there."

Relief washes over me. *Thank Christ.* I don't know what I would do without Dusty.

"Thank you. But before you go pack up and move in, how do you feel about going out on horseback with us to make some plans before Gid has to head back to work this afternoon?"

He nods. "Sure. Whatever the boss men want. Let's get out there and figure it out."

We both stand, and the older man tugs me in for a hug, slapping me hard on the back.

"He loved you boys. He'd be damn proud of you."

He hugs Gideon too.

With a nod, we follow him out to the barn to saddle up and get to work.

Three hours later, with my head spinning with ideas, Gideon and I return to the house, and I'm pleased to see that the kitchen is painted and the work crew is gone. The furniture should arrive this afternoon.

"I'm taking an hour to work out in your fancy new gym before I have to go to the airport." Gideon claps me on the back.

"Technically, it's *our* fancy new gym."

"No, this is *your* home. I'll just use it when I visit."

"I'll be in my office for a while."

"Making me money?" he asks. "You've always been such a numbers nerd."

"This nerd has made you a shit ton of money, asshole."

I grin at him, and then I make my way back to my office. I'll work for a while, and then I'll get in a workout of my own.

Yeah, I like numbers. Watching the market, shifting investments, is my hobby. Hockey was my job.

I did it backward, and I don't regret even one minute of it.

I commandeered one of the rooms toward the back of the house, where I have a great view of the mountains, and set up shop in there with a new desk, a few chairs and bookshelves. It works great for what I need, and I dive in for an hour of numbers crunching.

I'm just about to turn off the computer and go to the gym myself when my phone rings.

At the sight of Willow's name, my stomach flips, and I have to tell my dick to calm the fuck down.

"Hey there, Trouble. What's up?"

"Hi." She clears her throat, and I lean forward. I don't like the sound of her voice. "Hey, can I come out and talk with you about something?"

I frown at the wall of windows before me. "You can come here anytime. You know that. Is everything okay?"

"I'd rather just talk to you in person. I'm leaving Missoula now, so I'll be there in an hour, if that works for you."

"Works for me. Gideon and I are around. Just drive safe."

"See you soon."

The day is looking up. One hour gives me time to get my workout in, and then I'll get to see Wills.

Chapter Five

Willow

I'm going to kill him.

What is he thinking?

He's not. That's what. I'm at my wit's end with my teenager. I hope that Ryker will help me. He will. Ryker's my person. He won't turn me away. He *told* me to come to him for help.

Honestly, I don't usually hate the hour-long drive from my house in Missoula to the Triple Creek Ranch, but today it feels like it's taking forever, even with the audiobook I have playing in the speakers. I don't always listen to books, since it's my whole job to narrate them, but today I thought a story might take me out of my head.

Right now, in this sexy Mafia romance that I'm listening to, the hero and heroine are *getting it on.* Jason Clarke is narrating the male point of view, and I love his voice. He's so growly, and the way he says *that's my girl* makes my toes curl.

Most people have an image of an actor or some celebrity in their head as the main character when they listen to books. For me, every single leading man is Ryker James.

Every single time. And it's been that way for *years.*

Because of this, listening to or reading the sexy parts is almost torture.

It used to be safe because I hardly saw Ry in person for years. He's always been so busy with hockey, and once Aiden came into my life full-time, I've been busy with him, so although I spoke with Ryker all the time via texts and phone calls, I was rarely in the same room with him.

"Calm down, Wills," I mutter to myself as I turn onto the ranch road off the highway. I've been saying that to myself for the past few weeks every time I'm around my best friend, and it's not working.

I can't seem to calm down when I'm around Ryker.

I park and start to climb the steps, but then I freeze in my tracks when the door opens and Ryker's standing there, shirtless, wearing only black sweatpants and sweat.

For the love of chiseled muscle.

"Uh, bad time?" I ask him.

"No, I just finished a quick workout. Your timing is perfect."

I haven't seen him shirtless in a long time. Ogling Ryker when he's in a T-shirt is hard enough. The muscles, the tattoos, the veins in his forearms . . . they wake up every nerve ending in my body and make my ovaries do the jitterbug.

But shirtless? I'm going to need a defibrillator. Why do his abs look like they're sculped from marble? And is that a tattoo over his ribs? When did he get that?

"Wills?" My eyes climb to his face, and he raises an eyebrow. "Wanna come inside? Gid's in the kitchen. He's leaving for the airport in a few minutes."

"Oh, I'm glad I caught him before he goes." I slide past him as he stands to the side, gesturing for me to walk through the door. The living room is ready for the new furniture, and it smells new in here, with the fresh paint and flooring. "I know I've been here through this whole process, but I still can't believe how different it is in here."

"Do you hate it?" he asks, and I can see that he's worried.

"Are you kidding? It's gorgeous. You live here now. It should be *your* space, Ry. It looks great."

His shoulders drop in relief, and he offers me that cocky smile that's been on his face since he was a teenager.

"Need something to drink?" he asks me.

"I'll take some water," I reply and follow him into the kitchen.

I see the paint was done this morning. I head straight for Gideon and hug him tight.

"You're leaving us."

"For now," he confirms, and kisses the top of my head. These guys are so tall, I fit right under their chins. "I'll be back before the end of the year."

"Christmas?" I hear the hope in my voice as I look up at him, and he grins at me.

"I'll try."

"Try *hard*." I poke him in the stomach, and he doubles over as if he's in pain. "Weenie."

"You're so fucking mean," he growls, but his gaze is playful. "I won't miss you at all."

Ry passes me a bottle of water, and I pop the cap and take a long sip. "Whatever. You'll miss me. Call me when you get home."

"I'll consider it." He walks over and hugs Ryker, pats him on the back, and then lifts his suitcase. "I have to get going. You okay, Wills?"

"I'm great. Safe travels today."

Gideon nods, and then, with a wave, he walks out the front door. Ry and I watch each other as we listen to the rental car fire to life, and then the tires crunch on the gravel down the driveway.

"I'm gonna miss him," I murmur.

"Yeah. Me too. So what's going on?" he asks me, and I'm reminded why I'm here.

Right.

"I need your help," I reply, and his eyes immediately narrow, that smile drops, and he crosses his arms over his chest, making his biceps bulge.

"Talk to me. What's going on."

"Uh." I swallow and clear my throat. "Can you put a shirt on?"

"Why?"

Because you're half naked, and I want to lick you all over.

I blink at him. "Because you're distracting me."

"Yeah? Why's that?"

"You have such an ego, Captain."

He smirks and holds up a finger, jogs up the stairs to his room, and I admire his ass as he goes.

You have got *to calm the hell down, Willow.*

Less than thirty seconds later, he returns while tugging a tight black T-shirt over his head and down those washboard abs, and I admit, I'm a little sad that they're covered.

"Better?"

Not really.

"Thank you."

"Okay, what do you need?"

I lick my lips and take in a deep breath. I *hate* asking for help. It doesn't come easy to me. It never has.

But I don't know what else to do. He knows that I'm having some challenges with Aiden—he doesn't know *how* bad it is. But he's about to.

"I need you to give Aiden a job here this summer," I say and watch as he pulls his eyebrows together in a frown. "We're struggling, Ry."

"Financially?"

"No, it's not that at all."

I pull out a chair at the table and sit in it, and Ryker sits across from me, watching me intently.

"It's time you tell me what's going on at home, Trouble."

I lick my lips.

"I know that a fifteen-year-old is going to push my buttons. Test boundaries. But he's so . . . *angry*. I just got an email this morning from the school. He's skipped school *seventeen times* this semester. He's missing so many assignments it boggles my mind. He's not doing any work, and he won't talk to me anymore."

I push my hands through my hair and cover my face for a second. "We've always gotten along so well. He's such a good boy. Sweet. Affectionate. But that kid hasn't had a nice thing to say to me in two years, Ryker. I don't know what changed. I don't know if there was something specific that happened, because he won't talk to me. He's completely frozen me out. And now, as you know, he's getting into trouble, and I'm failing him. I don't know what to do, but school's going to be out in two weeks, and I can*not* have him left to his own devices this summer while I work, even if I do work from home."

I shake my head and stand up to pace.

"I don't trust him. That's the part that sucks so damn bad. I don't trust my kid."

I'm a mess. I'm wringing my hands, and I'm on the verge of tears. I'm just so frustrated.

Ryker stands and simply pulls me into his arms and hugs me against his chest, and *oh my God*. It feels so good to lean on him. I wrap my arms around his middle and hold on, enjoying his heat and the sound of his heartbeat.

"Okay, we're going to figure this out," he murmurs and kisses the top of my head as his hands rub up and down my back, trying to soothe me. "I need help for the summer anyway, so he can work here and stay in the bunkhouse like Gid and I did when we were kids."

I slump against him, and I'm so relieved that the tears threaten to fall, and I have to blink fast to keep them at bay.

"You don't have to pay him—"

"I'll pay him," he says. "The same as the other hands, because he'll be working his butt off, and it'll give him some motivation."

"Honestly, I think just working with *you* will be motivation. I know he was a jerk last weekend, but he thinks you're super cool, what with the whole hockey thing."

"I *am* cool," he reminds me as I pull out of his arms. "Hockey or no hockey."

"You're okay."

He taps me on the nose. "Admit it. You like me."

"You're okay," I echo, making him grin. "I offered to put Aiden in hockey because he loves it so much, and we used to go to the rink to skate all the time, but he said no. I can't get him to do *anything* except hang out with kids he shouldn't be hanging out with. I know this isn't your job, but I don't know what else to do."

"I'm not complaining, and I already said yes."

"Thank you." I bite my lower lip and wish that I could hug him again. "School gets out in two weeks, and if you're open to it, I can bring him out here the next day to start work."

"That's fine by me." He nods and then leans back against the countertop, crosses his ankles, and looks like he should be in a magazine. "Hey, I haven't asked you, and I feel like an ass because I should have brought it up earlier. How's the audiobook business going?"

I grin at him. "It's great. I'm booked out about a year in advance with gigs, and I just finished some voice work for a video game."

"Wow." He tilts his head, watching me. "That's fucking amazing. I'm proud of you."

"Thanks. And speaking of work, I have to be in the booth today, so I'd better get home so I can get some work in before I have to pick Aiden up from school. I don't let him walk home anymore."

"You know that I hate that you drive back and forth from here to Missoula."

"I've been doing it for a long time. I could probably do it with my eyes closed." I smirk and walk to the front door. "But I won't."

"Text me when you get home."

"Okay. Thanks, Ry. I mean it."

"You didn't even have to ask, you know. Just tell me what you need, and it's yours."

You. I need you. Naked and sweaty and saying filthy things in my ear.

"You're blushing," he says, and I'm instantly mortified.

"I am *not* blushing. I probably got sunburned yesterday or something."

"Nope. Blushing." He steps toward me.

"I have to go." I hurry down the steps and wave at him before lowering myself into my car. "Talk to you later!"

He's grinning at me, and it makes the butterflies wake up in my stomach.

I start the car, and with another wave, I drive away, but he doesn't walk inside. I can see him in the rearview mirror until I drive around the bend and he's out of sight.

It's been the longest two weeks of my damn life. I've been buried in work, making up for the time I took off over the past month after Ray's passing, and needing to be more present at the ranch for Ryker and Gideon. I feel like all I do is sit in my booth. I've barely spoken to Ryker at all. We're mostly back to our normal texts and once-a-week phone calls, like it used to be.

And I kind of hate that. I got used to seeing him often.

Add on to that—and I didn't think it was possible—the way Aiden's attitude has gotten progressively worse with each passing day. He's so short tempered and has been pretty much giving me the silent treatment.

School got out for the summer yesterday, and at some point after I went to bed, Aiden sneaked out of the house, and is just now at six in the morning sauntering through the front door, his hair tousled, his clothes rumpled, and is that a freaking *hickey* on his neck?

When he sees me waiting for him, standing in the kitchen with my arms crossed, there's a quick flicker of guilt that flashes over his face, and then the scowl that seems to live there permanently takes up residence once more.

"Where the hell were you all night?"

"Celebrating" is all he says.

"You didn't answer your phone."

"Turned it off." He yawns and scratches his flat stomach. Aiden may only be fifteen, but he's *big*. He's well over six feet tall, and he's muscular. Weight lifting class is the only class he hasn't missed all year. "Going to bed."

"No, you're not. You can turn around and get in my car. Now."

"No way. I haven't even been to bed yet."

"Not my problem. Let's go."

His eyes narrow, and he steps into me, the way he's started to do when he's not getting his way and he thinks he can intimidate me.

I'd never admit this to anyone, but I'm starting to actually *fear* my kid, and that breaks my heart. It's one more reason that I'm sure taking him out to work at the ranch is the right thing for him.

"I said I'm going to bed."

I keep my chin lifted, not wavering in staring him down. "And I said get in the goddamn car, Aiden. Now."

He growls, and then, to my utter horror, he punches the wall by my head, busting through the drywall, before he stomps away, and I hear the car door slam.

Holy fucking shit.

He's *never* . . . What's happening?

With a shaking hand, I push my hair behind my ear and then grab my purse and walk out to the car, where Aiden's sitting in the back seat, fuming.

I guess he doesn't want to sit next to me. That's fine.

I don't say a word as I shoot off a quick text to Ryker to let him know we're on our way, start the engine, and pull out of the driveway. We're just leaving town when Aiden demands, "Where the fuck are we going?"

"You'll watch your mouth with me." I hate the tremor in my voice. "You'll see when we get there."

"I don't want to go to the freaking ranch."

I don't bother replying. I don't want to fight with him, especially when I'm driving. It's so early that the sun isn't fully up yet. I wanted to have him out there by six because the ranch gets going early in the morning, but we'll be late.

Aiden used to love the ranch when he was younger. He couldn't get enough of it. Now, he never wants to go out there.

It's a tense, quiet hour, and finally, I pull into the driveway and see that Ryker is standing on the porch, waiting for us. He's in old, worn blue jeans, a T-shirt with a flannel over it because it's cool this morning, and work boots.

"What the fuck," Aiden grumbles, and I sigh out a breath. My hands still aren't altogether steady after the altercation at home.

He's *never* done that before.

And frankly, it hurt my feelings.

"Hey, Trouble," Ryker says with a grin as he walks down the stairs, but then that smile falls when he sees my face. "What's wrong?"

I shake my head and wait for Aiden to join me.

"Say hello," I say to my boy.

"'Sup," Aiden says.

Ryker's eyes fall to Aiden's hand, which is swollen and bruised. A little bloody. And then he turns to me again and tips my chin up.

"What. The fuck. Happened?"

I swallow hard, caught in his gaze. "He wasn't happy about going out this morning. Punched the wall."

Ry's eyes narrow. "Where?"

"By my head."

The lethal rage that rolls through Ryker's eyes has me stepping back a pace, and he turns to Aiden.

"Did she tell you that you'll be working for me this summer?"

"No." Aiden glances at me, then at the ground.

"Well, you are. I have one rule. Are you listening to me? I'll only say this once."

"Whatever."

Ryker moves into Aiden's space, crowding him until Aiden looks up into his eyes. Ry is at least three inches taller than the teenager and is certainly stronger.

Aiden swallows hard.

"I'm listening," Aiden says, some of his bravado gone.

"Good. I have one rule on this ranch." He points to me but keeps his eyes on Aiden's. "No one fucks with her. You don't yell at her, you don't swear at her, you absolutely do *not* punch a wall anywhere near her. You treat Willow with respect. That's it. We'll figure everything else out as we go. You got that?"

Aiden's eyebrows pull together as if he regrets what he did, and then he licks his lips and offers Ryker a nod.

"Yeah. I got it."

"Good." He turns back to me. "Where are your bags?"

I shake my head. "I'll bring him in and pick him up every day."

Ryker scowls. "That's a lot of driving, Wills."

"Well, I'm not leaving him. Everyone else in his life has abandoned him, and I'm not going to ever do that." Aiden's gaze whips up to mine in surprise. "No matter how much of a brat he is, he's my brat, and he goes where I go. So I'll bring him every morning, and I'll pick him up at the end of the day."

Ry shakes his head and then sighs as he rubs his hand over the back of his neck. "Fine. He'll be done by around six every day."

I nod, and I want to reach out and hug my boy, but I know he won't allow that to happen, so I just pat him on the arm.

"I love you, buddy. You've always loved the ranch. You'll enjoy working out here."

"Right."

He hasn't said *I love you too* in years. It shouldn't hurt me anymore.

But it does.

"I'll see you this evening."

He nods, and I turn to Ryker.

"Thank you. Call me if you need me."

"That's my line." He grabs my hand and pulls me in for a hug, and then he plants his lips on my forehead and kisses me so tenderly, it almost brings tears to my eyes. "He'll be fine. Don't worry."

"Don't you know?" I laugh as I pull away and saunter to the car. "Worry is my middle name. Willow Worry. It has a ring to it."

I'm shocked to see that Aiden looks like he wants to smile, but then it's gone.

"Drive safe," Ry says.

"Have fun," I reply, and leave the ranch.

I really hope this works. I want my happy kid back.

Chapter Six

Ryker

Goddamn it, I want her to stay. I hate that she's driving back and forth, and I have a project going in the house as we speak that will make it possible for her to work here. But it's her choice. I won't force her.

When Willow's car fades from view, I turn to look at Aiden, who's suddenly taken a keen interest in the ground at his feet. His hands are in the pockets of his baggy jeans, and he shuffles back and forth on his sneaker-clad feet.

I see a lot of myself in him when I was that age.

Attitude.

Chip on his shoulder.

Ready to tell everyone to go fuck themselves.

But he scared Willow today, and that's never going to happen again. Christ, just seeing her shaken up an hour after it happened has *me* rattled, and this kid is standing there, looking like he doesn't give a shit.

And that pisses me the hell off.

"I haven't seen you much the past few years," I say, mirroring his stance by putting my hands in my own pockets. "You kept to yourself last weekend when Wills brought you out. I have a question."

He glances up and lifts his eyebrows.

"Why didn't you come to Ray's funeral?"

He shrugs, clenches his jaw. "I was busy."

"Nah, man. I don't buy that. Your Aunt Willow could have used you there, you know. It was a hard day for her."

He shakes his head. "She doesn't need me. She had you and Gideon."

I narrow my eyes at him. "Let's walk to the barn. Come on."

He falls into step next to me.

"So why'd you punch that wall today?"

He lets out a sigh. "She's always on my case. So what if I stayed out all night with my friends? Who the fuck cares?"

"She cares. Are you fucking some girl?"

His gaze snaps up to mine, surprised, and I gesture to the hickey on his neck.

He shrugs again. That seems to be his go-to mode of communication.

"So you were out all night, doing things you probably shouldn't with some girl, and you came home this morning and got pissed that Willow had plans for you today."

"I'm tired," he says, his voice hard with defiance.

"Tell me you're using protection. Don't get that girl pregnant."

He lets out a gusty breath, and his cheeks darken. "I didn't fuck her. We just fooled around."

My stomach loosens with that admission.

"Here's the thing," I tell him as we step inside the barn. The other guys are still at the bunkhouse, having breakfast. "Your aunt is one of my favorite people in the world. One of two, now that my dad's gone. Three, if we count you, but you're pissing me off today."

His lips twitch like he wants to laugh, but then he schools his features back into his signature scowl.

"You don't get to bully her."

"I wasn't—"

"Yeah, you were. You thought you could intimidate her into getting your way. Don't bullshit me—I've been you before. Shit, I was *worse* than you. But today's the last day you treat her like that."

"Sometimes, I just get so mad."

"It happens. Come yell at me or use my gym. Hell, I'll hang a punching bag out here, and you can go to town on it. But you won't take your shit out on the one person in this world who has stuck up for you and taken care of you. She loves you."

He blinks rapidly and turns away from me.

"Deal?"

"Yeah. I won't do it again."

"Great." I clap him on the shoulder. "I have some grass for you to mow today. Did you get some breakfast?"

"No, there wasn't enough time."

"Let's get you some food, and then on a mower. It's going to be a long fucking day."

I should make him miss breakfast altogether. It's his own fault for pulling the shit he did on Willow last night and this morning, but I've been hungry before, and I'll never intentionally withhold food from anyone.

We make our way to the bunkhouse, where Dusty's serving up some scrambled eggs, bacon, potatoes, and toast, and there's plenty for Aiden to join in. In the two weeks since Gideon left, I've hired five other guys from town, and it seems they're all getting along just fine.

I make the introductions and then point to Dusty.

"This is your other boss," I inform Aiden. "You'll do what he says, no questions asked. If I'm not around, he speaks for me. You won't sass him."

"Yes, sir," Aiden says with a nod, munching on his bacon.

Once everyone has eaten, we go our separate ways to get our chores done. We just got a shipment of cattle in, so Dusty and the other guys will be working with them today.

I'll have Aiden with me.

"Do I really have to mow all day?" he asks me.

"Yep."

"I'll get sunburned."

"You can borrow a hat," I reply and clap him on the shoulder. "You'll be fine."

I lead him to the equipment shed and show him where the riding mower, the Weedwackers, and all the tools he'll need are stored.

"Have you mowed a lawn before?"

He frowns over at me. "Of course I have. I mow our lawn at home, but it's just a push mower because the yard isn't that big."

"Same philosophy, different equipment."

I point out everything that I want him to mow—the entire area around the house, down either side of the driveway, and out in the east pasture by the tree line, where I plan to add some animals.

"That's ten acres, easy," he says with huge eyes, finally dropping some of the attitude.

"Roughly that," I agree, impressed that the teenager can eyeball that off the top of his head. "Did Ray teach you that?"

His face falls, and he shrugs a shoulder. "Yeah."

"I miss him too." I ruffle the kid's hair and pass him a hat before putting one on my own head. "While you mow, I'll be clearing brush and cutting down some trees."

Aiden nods and, to my surprise, jumps right on the mower and gets it started.

"You've done this before."

With a half smile, he takes off to start his job, and I watch him drive off.

He definitely helped my dad do this before, and that's good. I can see that he's grieving for the only grandfather he had in his life. I don't understand why he didn't come to the funeral to be around family, to take a little solace in us. He could have spent way more time with us over the past month, and it might have helped him feel better.

He's a complicated kid, but I'm determined to figure him out. I'm also determined that his days of hurting my Willow are over.

Three days later, we're inside for lunch. Aiden is sweaty and dirty, and I actually get a smile out of him when I toss him a can of cola before I make us a couple of sandwiches. This has become our daily routine, coming inside to make lunch, and he already feels comfortable enough to help himself to a fresh bag of chips in the pantry.

"Do you eat roast beef?" I ask him as he peels open the bag of BBQ chips.

"I eat anything," he replies with his mouth full, and I can't help but smirk. He frowns down at his can, as if he wants to say something.

"You can talk," I tell him. That's another thing he's started to do more of over the past few days. Talk. The first day, he barely said three words. By this morning, I couldn't shut him up. He's not telling me about what's going on at school, or why he's so pissed off at the world, but he *is* talking, so I won't complain.

"I don't want to ask weird questions or something."

"There's not much you can ask me that will surprise me." I pass him a sandwich and get to work building one for me. "Shoot."

"I want to know about hockey."

I raise an eyebrow, watching as he consumes a quarter of the sandwich in one bite. I slide the second sandwich over to him. He'll need it.

Building a third, I nod. "Okay. Ask away. I happen to know a lot about that sport."

He rolls his eyes. "Duh. People at school always try to get me to ask you for tickets, or jerseys, or whatever. It's stupid."

"They know we're family?"

He nods, stuffs more roast beef in his mouth. "Aunt Willow knows everyone, and they know that you guys grew up together, so that filters down to me. It's not a big deal. But people are weird."

"You can say that again." I take a bite, watching him. "Does it bother you?"

"No, I just tell them to get lost. I don't have that kind of pull."

"I would have flown you out for every weekend game, if you wanted to go."

His eyes widen and jerk up to mine. "Huh?"

"Willow and Gideon used to come to *every single* game," I continue. "Before he was with the Secret Service, back when it was early in my career, they'd follow me to every game, whether we were home or away. Then life sort of takes over, you know?"

"She got me and couldn't travel with you anymore," he says quietly, staring down at the last of his lunch.

Christ, this kid is smart.

"I don't think it was much of a sacrifice," I reply and reach over the island to ruffle his already messy dark hair. "She was happy to have you. Have you ever noticed that whenever I give an interview, I always wink at the camera at the end?"

"Sure. I figure it's because you're being cocky."

"I *am* cocky," I confirm, and then make the boy another sandwich because he still looks hungry. "But the wink is for Willow. She knows."

"That's why she always watches ESPN, looking for your interviews."

I pause with a slice of cheese in my fingers. "She does?"

"Yeah. She watches more sports than *me*. Hockey, anyway. She watches every game. We had a ritual where we wore our jerseys and she made us nachos, or pizza, or burgers, and we ate while we watched. She mostly did that by herself last year because I was out with friends."

He frowns and swallows hard but takes the new sandwich and bites in.

Willow watched every game.

I always hoped she did, but I knew she had Aiden to take care of, so I never assumed. She was always sure to call me to talk about the game, but she could have easily watched highlights to have talking points.

But she didn't just watch the highlights. She watched the games. And that has my chest feeling tight.

This does not help my growing obsession with this woman.

"She's kind of a sports trivia nut," he continues. "She can rattle off stats like nobody else. And sometimes, we'll be watching a game, and she'll start ranting about something, and then not thirty seconds later, the commentator dudes rant about the *same thing*. It's like she's psychic or something."

This is a side to Willow I don't know but I want to learn more about.

And now that the kid has diarrhea of the mouth, I don't want him to stop.

"Like what?" I ask him.

"Oh, I don't know off the top of my head." He chews thoughtfully. "Well, one time, you were playing, and we were watching as usual, and there was nothing on the screen hinting at the fact that you might be breaking a record that night. I hadn't heard anyone mention it in the pregame. I had no idea."

He takes a bite, and I cross my arms over my chest, listening.

This is *fascinating*.

"But Aunt Wills looked kind of nervous. She was pacing and biting her thumbnail, and she wasn't eating any of the nachos, and I was like, 'What's wrong with you?' And she said, 'He only has to score two goals to break it.'"

I have chills. Goose bumps all down my arms.

"And I said, 'Break what?' and she said, 'The all-time scoring record. They're not even talking about it, and he could break it tonight.' She was so mad that the commentator dudes weren't talking about it."

"They didn't want to jinx it," I murmur, remembering that night.

Christ, I was nervous. And I never get nervous on game night.

"And then, when you made that second goal," he continues, finished with his sandwich now and switched back to the bag of chips, "she freaking *cried*. It scared me because Aunt Wills doesn't cry. That woman is *solid*. And she just wept like a baby. I patted her back for a few, and then I was like, 'I'm going to my room.'"

Fuck me.

"Thanks for telling me that."

"Sure. She probably wouldn't like that I told you she cried, so let's keep that between us."

With a chuckle, I nod. "Okay. Was there something specific you wanted to ask me before we got off on the Willow tangent?"

"Oh, right. Do you think I'm too old to start playing?"

"I was your age when I started," I reply. "You're not too old."

He scratches his nose. "I don't know. I kind of want to. But some of the guys at school are assholes, and I don't want to hang out with them."

"Beat 'em up on the ice," I suggest. "That'll feel damn satisfying."

"I hadn't thought of that."

"Come on, let's finish up. We have a lot left to do."

Aiden is a hard worker. I can see that he's beat, since I worked him hard today, but he never complains. I don't have to ask him to do anything twice, and when he saw that I was struggling with a tree earlier, he jumped in to help me.

He's going to be an asset to the ranch this summer. This first week went really well.

And I can also see that Willow's right. He's a good kid. So why is he acting out and treating her so badly? What in the hell is going on with him?

I'll ask him over the coming weeks, and we'll get to the bottom of it because I hate seeing my Willow upset.

We're sitting on the porch with bottles of water when Willow comes driving up to the house. She climbs out of the car, and Aiden stands and turns to me.

"I guess I'll see you on Monday," he says.

"Get some rest tonight," I reply, and he walks down to where Willow's standing.

"I figured you'd be hungry," she says as she approaches, and I hear the hesitation in her voice as she speaks to him. Is she afraid of him? "So there are some burgers and fries in the front seat. I already had mine, so the rest is yours."

"Awesome, thanks."

Her eyes widen in shock as Aiden climbs into the car, unwraps a burger, and bites in happily.

"Holy shit," she murmurs.

"What's wrong?"

"He hasn't thanked me for anything in . . ." She swallows hard. "In a long time. I guess he must have had a good day."

"Yeah, we had a good day." I want to hug her more than I want to breathe, but I'm filthy, so I reach out and tuck her hair behind her ear. She's so damn soft. "How was *your* day, Trouble?"

"It was good. I started on a new audiobook for an author that I've worked with before, and I enjoy her books. This one is a football romance." She blows out a breath and shoves her hands in her pockets. "I should be able to have it done by Tuesday, if I work through the weekend."

"No days off for you?"

She shakes her head. "I have back-to-back projects, and I'm still catching up from last month. Not to mention, driving back and forth takes a chunk of time out of my workday."

I wish she'd stay out here. I hate that she has a long-ass drive ahead of her. They should be here, on the ranch. She should be with *me*. This week has taken a toll on her. I can see that she's exhausted.

"He didn't give you any trouble today?"

"Not at all. He did well."

Her shoulders drop in relief. "I'm so glad. Well, I'd better get him home, but we'll see you on Monday."

She watched all my games and cried when I set the record.

"Why are you looking at me like that?" she asks.

"Like what, Wills?"

"Like . . . I don't even know, but it's different."

I think I'm finally seeing what I've been missing all along. She's not just my best friend. But I don't know for sure if she feels what I do, and I have to tread carefully so I don't fuck up three lives.

"I just think you're pretty great."

She smiles softly and then frames her face and rolls her eyes. "I'm glad somebody notices." She smirks and walks to the driver's side. "Have a good weekend, Ry."

"You too."

Both of them wave, and then they're off, leaving me here alone, and I wish they'd stay. I want to talk about hockey with Willow and pick her brain. Listen as her sexy-as-hell lips rattle off stats to me. I never considered that to be hot before, but just the mere thought of it has my cock stirring.

With a shake of my head, I walk into the house and head straight for the shower.

Chapter Seven

Willow

"I bet I'll get to help with the cattle today," Aiden says. He's sitting in the passenger seat, and we just left the house, on our way out to the ranch after he had the weekend off. It's so freaking early in the morning, and I don't remember the last time I was this exhausted, but I've seen such a huge difference in my boy in the past week that he's been working out there, it's totally worth it.

He even smiled at me this morning. I'd do just about anything for that handsome grin to be pointed at me. Not to mention, I didn't have to coax him out of bed this morning. He spent most of the weekend sleeping, which I expected. He worked his butt off last week. But this morning, he jumped right up and was ready to go before I was.

He was waiting for *me*.

That never happens during the school year.

"Are they branding the cows?" I ask.

"Nah, they already did that, but we have to herd them to a different pasture where they'll be for about a month or so. And I think Ryker's getting some more head in next week. That's what he was telling Dusty."

I don't remember the last time we had a conversation this long. He was sullen over the weekend again, not saying much of anything, but now he's animated, and obviously excited to get to work, and it fills me with so much hope, I'm almost bursting with it.

It's amazing what one week can do for a person.

"I'm going to get some gas really quick," I inform Aiden as I pull into a filling station.

"I'll run in and get some snacks for later," he says, hopping out of the car.

"Do you need cash?"

"Nah, I have some money." He almost has a spring in his step as he walks inside.

When I've finished filling the gas tank, I pull into a parking space closer to the door to wait for my kid. It's taking him longer than I would have thought, but maybe he's agonizing over his snack choices. I can relate to that. Sometimes, it's hard to decide what you want.

However, when it's been more than ten minutes, I lock the car and walk inside, only to find my boy throwing a punch at another kid.

"Aiden!" With my heart in my throat, I run to him just as the boys turn in a circle, and the other kid's elbow catches me in the chin, making me see stars and my teeth clack together.

Ouch.

"Holy fuck," someone says as I fall on my ass.

"You son of a bitch," I hear Aiden say, but I hold up my hand.

"Stop." My voice is firm and leaves no room for arguments. "I mean it."

"I've called the cops," the person behind the counter says. "Should be here in a sec."

Aiden helps me to my feet, and I scowl when I see that he already has a black eye.

"Baby," I say, but he pulls out of my reach, and his brow furrows.

"*Baby*," the kid taunts, and I glare at him.

"Enough," I bark.

The cops have already pulled up outside. Where were they, down the street getting donuts for breakfast?

Quickly, I pull my phone out of my pocket and text Ryker, keeping one eye on the cops.

Me: Hey, running late. Got delayed at the gas station. Will be there ASAP.

He replies almost immediately.

Ryker: Just be safe. No rush.

I shove my phone in my pocket as the two officers walk inside, and they give my kid the stink eye.

All in all, it takes fifteen minutes for the officers to give the boys a firm talking-to and send us all on our way. The happy kid that I had in my car this morning is long gone, replaced by the broody, angry boy that I've become used to.

"Hey, it's okay," I tell him and wince when I see how swollen his eye is. "We'll get some ice on that."

"I'm fine."

"What made you guys throw punches, anyway?"

"It doesn't matter."

"Yeah, it does."

He shakes his head and looks out the window. "Why can't I just stay in the bunkhouse at the ranch, like Ryker suggested on the first day? It'll be easier for you. That way, you don't have to drive me and stuff."

I frown at him, but he can't see me, so I return my gaze to the road. My jaw hurts, and I'm going to need some ice myself.

"I like having you with me, buddy. I don't want to just dump you out there and leave."

The way my mom used to do to me when I was a kid. I loved the ranch so much, and I still do, but I also knew that my mom took me there because she didn't want me around. It didn't feel good.

He doesn't say anything at all to that, so I leave him be, and the car is quiet as we drive the rest of the way out to the Triple Creek Ranch.

Ryker's pacing on the porch when we pull in, and he hurries to my side of the car, opens my door, and pulls me to my feet. He immediately frames my face in his hands, his eyes skimming over my face, and he's scowling.

"Are you okay?"

"I'm fine. I got in the line of fire and shouldn't have stepped so close. Uppercuts are *not* fun."

"What the fuck?" He tips my head to the side, searching for injuries. "You should have called me. I would have come to you."

"We only talked to the cops for about fifteen minutes."

He scowls before kissing my forehead, which sends a shiver all the way down my spine, and then he shifts his attention to Aiden.

"Whoa. For fuck's sake. Come on, we'll get you both some ice, and I want to hear everything."

"I can go join the others at the bunkhouse," Aiden says, but Ryker shakes his head.

"I said get inside," he replies, and Aiden trudges in, his head hanging low.

Ry takes my hand, laces our fingers, and walks with me, surprising me. He doesn't usually hold my hand. Certainly not like this.

But I'm not going to complain, because it feels damn good, and I'm still shaken up.

After he pulls out two ice packs from the freezer and passes them to us, Ryker folds his arms over his chest and leans his hip against the counter.

"Someone tell me what happened before I lose my shit."

"We were at the gas station," I say. "I fueled up, and he went in for snacks for the day. Hey, you didn't get your snacks."

"It's fine." Aiden won't look at either of us. He just stares at the floor.

"When he didn't come back outside, I went in looking for him and found him in the middle of a fistfight. I ran toward them, the kids turned, and I caught an elbow to the chin."

Ryker's eyes burn with anger, but his hand is gentle when he reaches over and tips my head up so he can have another look. His simple touch is warm and soothing. "How do you feel now, Trouble?"

"Sore. I saw stars for a minute. How did you do that for a living?"

"I didn't get beat up every night," he says with that crooked smile that sets my heart on fire. "Only some nights."

Now he turns to Aiden.

"Who was the kid, and why did he deserve to have his ass handed to him?"

My boy's gaze whips up to Ryker's, and his cheeks go red, and I just want to hug him.

"He was running his mouth," Aiden replies.

"About what?" Ryker asks, holding up a hand to me when I would jump in, as if telling me to let Aiden talk.

So I do.

Aiden's eyes jump to me, and then back to Ryker. "I don't know."

"Sweetie—"

Ryker shakes his head and steps forward, sets his hand on Aiden's shoulder and gives it a squeeze. "What the fuck did he say? You can tell us. You're not in trouble."

"He said shit about Aunt Wills."

My heart stutters to a stop. "What? Me? Why?"

"And we don't disrespect her," he continues, watching Ryker closely, and I'm quite sure I'm about to have a stroke. "I told him to shut it, and he wouldn't. So I shut it for him."

"Good." Ryker nods, then turns to me and skims his hand from my shoulder to my fingers, and then holds on. "It doesn't matter what the kid said—he had your name in his mouth, and your boy was having none of it."

Without thinking twice, I hug Aiden. I just wrap my arms around his middle and squeeze him. It takes a few seconds, but then his arms come around me, and he pats my back awkwardly.

"I'm not in trouble?" he asks.

"No, you're not in trouble for the reason behind it. But you need to learn to walk away. You were in a public place, where people could have been hurt, Aiden. We need to talk about self-control. Not to mention, you should have told me what happened when I asked you. Don't be that kid that only opens up to men, Aiden. I raised you better than that."

I open my eyes and see Ryker grinning at us, but I'm suddenly so damn tired. I haven't been sleeping well because I'm afraid I'll miss my alarm. Driving four hours a day is exhausting, and I'm worried about Aiden, and I have so much of my own work to do. I'm overwhelmed.

Suddenly, I can't take it anymore, and I bury my face in Aiden's chest and start to cry.

"Whoa, don't cry." He pats my back a little harder, as if that will help. "I don't . . . you don't . . . *help*."

Ryker pries my hands apart from around Aiden, and then I'm in his arms, and he's holding me close, kissing the top of my head.

"Hey, it's okay. You're both fine."

"I know." I swipe at my tears. "It's just been a really crappy week, and I can't sleep well, and I'm *so tired*."

"I told you to just let me stay at the bunkhouse," Aiden says, his voice almost desperate. "I'll be fine out here. Honest, Aunt Wills, I don't mind at all."

I shake my head. "No. You need to be where I am at night."

"Okay, take a breath." Ryker frames my face in his hands and rubs my tears away with his thumbs. "Deep breath for me, Willow."

Willow. He hardly ever calls me by my full name. It's always Wills or Trouble.

I follow his directions, and when I've calmed down a bit, he surprises me.

"I want *both* of you to move out here."

I shake my head. "I would love to spend the summer here, I really would, but I have a job, and I can't work just anywhere. I need my booth and my equipment. I need my soundproofed room, Ry."

"It's time I showed you the project I've been working on since you came out here a few weeks ago and asked if I would give Aiden a job." He kisses my forehead so softly that it boggles my mind, and then he laces his fingers with mine and gestures for us to follow him. "Come on, both of you."

He leads us upstairs and toward the back of the huge farmhouse. This area of the house is mostly guest rooms with en suite bathrooms, but he converted one of the rooms into his own office, and then the next door he opens is at the end of the hall. He flips on a light, and I . . . stop.

"Whoa," Aiden murmurs, but Ryker's eyes are on me.

"Am I in an alternate universe?" I ask.

"When you told me that Aiden needed this job, I assumed that you'd both be staying out here," Ryker begins as I prowl the room. "He'll sleep in the bunkhouse, but he also has a bedroom here. You have your room, of course. And I had these two bedrooms combined into one, soundproofed, and made ready for you to move in and get to work."

This is the kind of booth that only a filthy rich former hockey player could come up with. He obviously did his homework, because I can see that it's entirely soundproofed. There's a smaller desk by the window for me to work at, but there's an *incredible* setup in the corner for my sound equipment, iPad, computers, and all the things I need to record. In fact, all I'll need to do is pack up a few things from my setup at home and move them over. It'll be easy.

"This is way better than the booth at home," Aiden says, looking around. "The one at home used to be a closet. It's tiny, and it gets so hot in the summer."

"You don't have AC?" Ryker asks me.

"I can't run it while I'm recording," I reply. "The mic picks up the sound. Wow, this is . . . incredible. You did all this for me?"

"I had the space, and I figured you'd need to work." He shrugs as if it's not a big deal, but he's wrong. This is a *very big deal.*

"Buddy, will you please give us just a second?"

"I'm out while you finish talking her into it," Aiden says and leaves the room. "I'm searching for snacks."

We listen to Aiden's big feet clomp down the hallway.

"We can change anything you don't like," Ryker says with a frown, but I ignore him and simply hug him. I've gotten more hugs this past month than in the past year combined. It feels so freaking good. "You didn't want to hug in front of the kid?"

"I don't want to cry in front of him," I reply, shaking my head as the tears come. "It upsets him, and I'm going to cry again."

As he rubs his big hands up and down my back, I feel his chuckle through his chest. "Does that mean you'll come stay with me?"

"I would be an asshole to say no after you built me this incredible home studio."

"I only want you to be comfortable and safe. It's not safe for you to drive back and forth to Missoula every day, twice a day. There are animals on the road, and it's not light out yet when you head this way. I don't like it. Not to mention, it's obviously taking a lot out of you, and I don't like that either."

"I don't want to sleep through my alarm," I admit, "so I wake up every hour to check the clock."

"That's not good enough rest." He takes me by the shoulders and pulls me away so he can wipe my face off and smile down at me. I miss the warmth of his hard body, but I don't resist.

Because he's being *brotherly* right now, and I'm fantasizing about this man's lips on me and how it would feel to touch his naked body. Holy shit, I want to lick his abs and that V that runs down into his pants, right to his—

"Wills?"

"Huh?" *Shit, I'm staring at his lips.* Maybe we shouldn't live out here. I'll spontaneously combust or make a complete fool of myself and ruin a twenty-year friendship.

That would suck ass. Big time.

"Whoa, you're overthinking something," he says. "Stop that. It'll be great."

He takes my hand and leads me out of my shiny new booth, and we find Aiden in the kitchen, eating a muffin he must have grabbed from the pantry.

"We're going back to Missoula to pack your bags," Ryker announces.

"Now?" I ask.

"Yep. I'll call Dusty and let him know that Aiden and I will join the others after lunch. Let's go do this."

"Let's *do it*," Aiden says around a mouthful of muffin and saunters to the front door.

Chapter Eight

Ryker

She's been nervous around me since we left the ranch, and I don't like it.

I drove us back to her place, and she was quiet in the car, leaving the conversation to Aiden and me. She's already packed up what she needs from her office and recording booth, Aiden has his bag ready to go, and he and I are in the kitchen, emptying the fridge, since she won't be back here for a little while, and there's nothing worse than spoiled food.

"We have those reusable grocery bag things," Aiden says and opens the pantry door.

"You load up the groceries, and I'll go see what's up with your aunt."

He nods, and I walk back to her bedroom and find her standing in front of her closet, just staring, as if she's deep in thought.

"Are you okay?" My voice is soft, but she still jumps and then presses her hand to her chest. "Sorry, didn't mean to startle you."

"It's okay. I was in my own little world, I guess. I don't honestly know how much to bring."

"I'd bring most of your summer stuff," I reply, stepping closer to her. "But we can come check on your place every week, if you want, so you don't have to bring it all at once."

She nods and walks into the closet, boosts up on her toes to reach a duffel bag, but she's too short, and her fingertips slip off the edge of it.

Moving up behind her, I press my front to her back, reaching over her, and easily grab the bag. Her warmth, her scent, is like a gravitational pull that I can't stay away from.

"Here you go." My voice is rough as I pass her the bag, and I haven't backed away from her.

Her breath hitches. She doesn't joke with me the way she would have years ago. She doesn't elbow me in the ribs and tell me to get out of her bubble.

No, Wills swallows hard, and her entire body tenses.

"Do I make you uncomfortable?" I ask her. Shit, if that's the case, I'll stay away. I'll do my best to go back to normal, to treating her like she's my sister.

It'll be fucking hard, but I don't ever want this woman to feel uncomfortable, especially not around me. She's too amazing for that shit.

"No," she says, shaking her head slowly.

"Then why are you suddenly nervous around me, Wills?"

She takes a deep breath before she opens the bag and starts to pull clothes out of the dresser that's in her closet.

"I'm not nervous. That's silly. You're my person, my best friend. I have no reason to be *nervous*."

"Right." I cross my arms over my chest and watch her for a minute, and then she skirts by me, careful not to touch me, and grabs some things out of her bathroom, then tosses that small bag onto the bed.

It smells so good in here. Like honeysuckles and laundry detergent. Like Willow.

I could bury my face in her closet and simply *breathe*.

But that might be creepy.

"Excuse me," she says, and I realize I'm still standing in the middle of the closet, blocking her way.

"You may not be nervous," I say, continuing the conversation, "but you're not acting normal, either, and I'd like you to tell me why."

"I haven't been around you like this in a really long time," she finally admits as she folds some shorts and tosses them into the bag. "I get texts, calls, and the occasional FaceTime, but I haven't spent significant time with you, in person, in *years*, Ry. So it's just different. It's something I'm still getting used to. That's all."

"That's not all," I insist, and she blows out a breath.

"It's just an adjustment period," she says softly, and when I step toward her, she doesn't tense up. She doesn't move away. "But I'm really okay, and I'm not nervous."

She frowns, as if she wants to say more, but then Aiden pokes his head around the door, interrupting us.

"I loaded the food into the car."

"Thanks, buddy," Willow says with a smile. "We're ready here too."

She zips her bag closed, and I lift it before she can, and we make sure the house is locked up tight.

"Hey, Wills?"

"Yeah?" she asks.

"I have to answer some emails. Do you mind driving back out? If you're tired, I'll do it."

"Nah, I don't mind." She smiles and circles around to the driver's side.

Aiden's already in the back seat, his AirPods in his ears, watching something on his phone, when we pull out of her driveway and head out of town.

Andy's emails are pissing me off.

We're thirty minutes from home when my phone rings.

Fucking Andy.

Why have we spent all this time emailing if he was just going to call me anyway?

"Hello."

"You've been avoiding my calls for almost a *month*, James!" He's pissed as fuck.

I don't care.

"But we've been emailing all day. I didn't go off the fucking grid."

"You know I prefer to talk over sending messages."

"And *you* know that my dad died, and I've been taking care of my family and everything going on here." I sense Willow casting a quick look my way. "The season is over, and I'm under no obligation to you right now. The team has told me to take care of things, and there's no rush to discuss anything else yet."

"Well, they're starting to ask questions. They want a commitment. They've already sent me the paperwork for a two-year contract, with more money than the last one, and you'll get to stay in Seattle where you belong. We need to get this signed."

I shake my head. "No, we don't."

"Listen." I hear him take a breath, and his voice calms, as if he's trying to talk to a wild animal. "I know you've had a lot going on in Montana. I understand that. But the team needs answers. Hell, the *fans* are starting to wonder if it's the team's fault that you haven't committed, accusing the Blizzard of not offering you enough money. Once you sign the new contract, all the hype will calm down, and you can do whatever you need to do until training camp starts."

"I'm not signing another contract." He starts to swear on the other end of the line, but I talk over him. "I'm retiring, Andy. I'll come to Seattle for a press conference, and I'll keep the commitments we've made for sponsorships, but I'm not signing anything new."

"You ungrateful piece of—"

I hang up on him and blow out a breath.

"You're *retiring*?" Aiden asks from the back seat.

"You're listening?" Willow counters in surprise. "I thought you were watching something on your phone."

"I can do both. I can multitask," Aiden says. "So are you really gonna retire, Ry?"

"Yep. The ranch is my job now."

"I thought that Andy works for you," Willow says. "Not the other way around."

"What are you getting at?"

"I don't like the way he speaks to you." Her voice has an edge to it that makes my dick twitch. "What a colossal jerk."

"I'm severing ties with him," I reply. "I'll still need an agent moving forward because there will be guest appearances and stuff, but I don't want to work with Andy anymore."

"Good." She reaches over to pat my thigh, and I snatch her hand up in mine, keeping her close.

Her eyes leave the road long enough to look at me, but I still don't let go. I want to touch her. I want to keep her close.

And I'm done fucking fighting it.

"If I ever go to the NHL, I'm not hiring Andy," Aiden says from the back seat.

Willow's eyes widen, and she looks at her nephew in the rearview mirror. "If you've already decided that you're going to the NHL, does that mean that you want me to put you in hockey, buddy?"

"Yeah." I glance back in time to see him shrug. "It could be good, I guess. Ry says I'm not too old."

She presses her lips together, and then they tip up in a small smile. "I don't think you're too old either."

Wills squeezes my hand, and for the first time since I saw her this morning, her shoulders relax.

"Thank you," she whispers.

"I didn't do anything."

She just squeezes my hand again and shakes her head once. "Thank you."

Chapter Nine

Willow

Now that I don't have to worry about sleeping through my alarm every morning, you'd think that I would sleep like a baby in a milk coma.

But no. Not me. Not this girl.

I've always slept well in this room, and I know my boy is safe out at the bunkhouse. In the three days we've been living here, I've managed to get so much work done in my new studio, I'm giddy about it. I feel at home here, and I'm not uncomfortable at all.

But can I sleep?

No.

And why, you ask?

Because of the hot hockey player two doors down.

Make that *former* hockey player. I'm so damn proud of Ryker for standing up to Andy and telling him off. I wanted to reach through that phone and punch that guy's nose. I've met him a couple of times through the years, and I never liked him. I never believed that he had Ryker's best interests at heart. Andy has always been all about the money, and sometimes that meant too much work for Ry.

I hate that guy.

But even that isn't why I can't sleep. I don't know what to do about all this lust I'm feeling. I think he feels it too. He hasn't said so, but we've had moments when he touches me, when I think he wants to kiss me, and I know he's not oblivious to the chemistry.

But if he admits to himself that he feels it, he's holding back.

And that makes me want to hold back, too, because I'd be absolutely fucking mortified if I made a move and he rejected me.

I don't think I could come back from that. I don't know if our friendship would survive, because . . . how do you get over that?

So, instead, I ogle the sexy man and have these stupid daydreams about what it would be like if he railed me all night long, and I get myself so worked up, I can't sleep.

I've never been good at getting myself off, so I'm simply perpetually keyed up.

"There's some ice cream downstairs," I mumble to myself and push the covers off my body. I'm in a thin tank top, because my usual pajama top is in the wash, and a pair of sleep shorts that have seen better days.

Not that sneaking downstairs to eat Cherry Garcia out of the carton is worthy of a fashion show.

Besides, Ryker's asleep.

Soundlessly, I open my door and pad down the hallway and descend the stairs. Ryker had little night-lights installed throughout the house, so it's not pitch black, and they help me find my way to the kitchen, where I turn on the light over the stovetop, retrieve a spoon from the drawer, and then open the freezer and pull out the pint of ice cream.

I pop off the top and take a spoonful, moaning as it melts in my mouth.

That's good.

Ice cream always satisfies.

I hop up on the island, facing the window that looks out to the property, and let my feet dangle as I take another spoonful. I like it when the house is quiet and dark. Even through the window, I can see that it's a cloudless night, and there are a billion stars shining tonight. There's no light noise out here in the middle of nowhere.

Suddenly, the air shifts, and I feel Ryker walk into the room behind me.

"You okay?" he asks from the doorway. His voice is low and a little rumbly, and just as sexy as the rest of him.

"Sure." I don't look back at him, just hold the pint out. "Want some?"

He takes it out of my hand and lifts my spoon to his mouth, taking a bite, and then boosts up onto the countertop next to me, almost touching me, and I can feel the heat coming off him.

I almost choke when I glance his way.

He's shirtless.

Because of course he is.

And he's in gray sweatpants.

Because of course he fucking is.

He passes the carton back to me, and I lift the spoon to my mouth and hope that it's dark enough in here that he can't see the way my body is betraying me, or how my breathing has picked up.

"Couldn't sleep?" he asks.

I shake my head and scoop up more ice cream. "You?"

"No. Must be a full moon or something."

I glance at the window. "I don't see any moonlight out there."

"Hmm."

He takes the carton from me, scoops up a bite, and then passes it back.

"What's on your mind, Trouble?"

You. Me. Naked.

I can't say that.

"All kinds of things, I guess. You?"

"Nothing and everything," he replies.

"Yeah, that's a good way to put it." I lean against him, wanting just a little physical contact, and let out a small sigh.

To my surprise, he jumps off the counter and starts to pace.

Ryker's always been a pacer. Whenever he's deep in thought, his feet are moving.

"Thank you again for my booth," I say, needing to fill the quiet with something other than my desire to reach out and touch his smooth skin. "It's seriously amazing, Ry."

He nods and pulls his hand down his face, as if he's agitated. "You're welcome. I feel better having you here."

"I know. I hate the drive too."

"No." He props his hands on his hips and shakes his head. "It has nothing to do with your drive. I just *feel better* with you here."

I bite my lip, watching him.

"Why does that make you mad?"

With a humorless laugh, he faces me and steps forward, nudging his way between my knees, and tingles spread all over my body. His hands drift up my bare, goose-bump-covered thighs to my hips and stop there, just holding me in place, and that's our only point of physical contact.

But his dark eyes are on fire.

"Are you okay?" My voice is a whisper.

"Yeah. I'm okay, Wills."

I swallow hard and offer him the carton of ice cream. "Do you want another taste?"

His eyes fall to my lips.

"Yeah, I fucking do."

I offer him the spoon, but he takes the melting ice cream out of my hands and sets it on the counter.

"That's not what I want."

His hands lift to my face, and his lips cover mine in the gentlest of kisses. I plant my hands on his bare sides, making little circles with my thumbs and reveling in how smooth and warm his skin is as he deepens our kiss with a moan in the back of his throat. "You taste so damn good."

He changes the angle and covers my mouth once more, licks the seam of my lips, and I open for him. His tongue tangles with mine as my hands skim up his back and down his shoulders.

I want to touch him *everywhere.*

I want *him* to touch me everywhere.

His magical hands drift down to my breasts. His thumbs brush over my nipples, through my thin shirt, and I arch into his touch as electricity zings down my spine, making me gasp. I can feel his hardness pressing against my center through his sweatpants, and *holy shit*. There's a reason why this man gives off big-dick energy. He grinds into me, rubbing against that sweet bundle of nerves that want nothing more than for him to make me come.

God, I need him to make me come.

"Ry." Is that *my* voice? So raspy and full of need.

But suddenly, he pulls his lips away and rests his forehead against mine as his body stills, breathing hard, his eyes closed.

"Ry?"

Finally, he licks his lips and pulls away, leaving me feeling cold without his touch.

"Go to bed, Wills."

I frown as I cross my arms over my chest, feeling rejected and ridiculous. I want to question him, ask him what in the hell is going on in his head, but before I can, he opens his eyes and pins me in his tortured gaze.

"I need you to go to bed, Willow." He licks his lips slowly, as if he can still taste me there. "Please."

It's the *please* that does it. I hop down and walk away from him. When I get to the doorway, I look back and find him with his head hanging down, his hands on his hips.

He looks . . . forlorn.

And I want to comfort him.

But he rejected me.

Now I know where I stand with him. He doesn't want me, or won't let himself want me, and I need to get over this stupid lust-crazed crush I have on him because he's too important to me for me to screw it all up.

I'm an adult. I'll be okay.

But there are tears in my eyes as I march up the stairs, and when I walk into my bedroom, they fall. What is it about me, and this ranch, that makes people I care about want to . . . *leave*? Mom dumped me here at every opportunity and left without a backward glance, even in the early days, when I'd beg her to stay.

And now, it's Ryker turning his back on me.

I would have let him fuck me down there.

And how pathetic is that?

But now, here I am, back in the same old bedroom that was always my safe haven, and I crawl under the covers, keeping my tears silent so I can listen for Ryker's footsteps outside my door. If he goes back to bed, I don't hear him.

And I don't fall asleep for the rest of the night.

Chapter Ten

Ryker

I didn't fucking sleep. How could I, when I've finally had a taste of the sexiest woman on earth, had her pressed against me, her hot little pussy grinding against my cock, and then I turned her away?

The look on her face was . . . *devastation*.

"I'm a grade A prick," I mutter as I set my mug under the coffee maker. I'm not confused. I want her.

Christ, I *need* her.

And based on how she responded to me last night, she wants me right back, and that is the best fucking feeling in the world.

But Gideon's right. I should stay away from her. If I ruin our friendship, the three of us will never be the same, and I can't be responsible for that.

And yet the thought of never touching her again, never tasting that sweet mouth, makes me want to punch holes through the walls.

I hear footsteps behind me, and when I turn, I see Willow shuffling in, her eyes half closed, hair a mess from her pillow, and she's scratching her head as she yawns widely.

I can't help but smile. She's fucking adorable.

But when she sees me, she stops short and scowls.

"I'll come back later." She turns to leave, and I panic.

"No! Don't go."

She stops walking but doesn't turn around.

"I'll make you some coffee, Trouble."

After a moment, she spins on her heel and pins me in a glare.

"You're pissing me off, Ryker James."

To be honest, I'm pissing myself off too.

"You're sending me so many mixed signals. One minute, you're touching me, holding my hand, kissing my forehead. The next, you go back to being my buddy. Then, last night, you kiss the hell out of me on that island, make me feel things, and then, you reject me and send me off to bed." She lets out a frustrated growl. "And now, you *want me here*? Why, so you can torture me?"

"I don't want to torture you."

"Well, you are." She crosses her arms over her chest, pushing her tits together and up, and that little tank top does *not* hide anything. "My eyes are up here, Captain."

I swallow hard. "Look, I'm sorry that I'm being an asshat, but I *do* want you. Christ, woman, you make me lose my mind. I didn't expect to move home and suddenly have these feelings for you."

"What feelings?" It's a challenge. She tilts her head to the side with sass and taps her foot, and I want to bend her over, spank her ass, and fuck her hard, just to teach her a lesson.

"I thought my hard cock pushed up against your hot pussy made those feelings pretty obvious last night."

Her cheeks darken, but she doesn't look away from me.

Good girl.

"I didn't say no," she reminds me.

"Maybe you should have."

"See? This right here. Mixed messages, and I'm over it, Ry. If you don't want me, that's okay, but you don't get to touch me and confuse me anymore."

Not touch her? Fuck, I don't like that.

"Maybe I just need a little time to get my head on straight," I reply and push my hand through my hair. "I don't want to fuck this up. I can't lose you, Wills."

Her eyes soften just a bit at that. "You haven't lost me. I'm right here. But you need to figure your shit out and make up your mind, because I don't enjoy feeling like I'm being played with. I don't deserve that. You'd punch someone else out for doing that to me."

"I'd destroy them." *I'd fucking kill them.* The thought of anyone else putting their hands on this woman makes me homicidal.

"Then you don't get to do it either."

I nod and blow out a breath. "That's fair. I won't touch you."

She looks almost crestfallen at that, and it only makes me feel like an even bigger asshole.

"Fine."

Well, shit. Now, I want to hug her. This is all fucked up.

"I'll come back for coffee," she says and turns to leave.

"Wills?"

She pauses, sighs, and then looks back at me. "Yeah?"

"It's only because I respect you and care for you, and I need to be careful."

She swallows hard. "Figure your shit out. Okay?"

I nod, and then she's gone.

"Fucking hell," I grumble while staring at my computer. My eyes are killing me. I've been stuck at my desk all day, working through my investment portfolio, along with wrapping things up with my agent, who is on my last damn nerve.

He won't stop trying to push me to sign another contract. We already informed the team of my decision to retire. I'm not backing out on that.

But he's doing his best to badger me into it. We've been emailing back and forth all afternoon, and now my phone is lighting up with his name on it.

"What."

"You're being unreasonable," Andy says. I can hear the edge in his voice.

"No, Andy, you just don't like being told no." I dig my fingertips into my forehead. "I'll be in Seattle next week for the press conference."

"We'll be announcing your new contract at that press conference," he snarls.

"No. We won't. I'm not signing another contract with Seattle or anyone else. I'm retiring. From everything. I'll do appearances now and then, but I'm not working for ESPN. I'm not taking on new endorsements. I'm done, Andy."

"This is bullshit," he mutters. "After everything I've done for you—"

"You can stop right there. I made you a wealthy man, and we both know it. It's not my problem that you have a gambling addiction and can't keep a quarter in your pocket."

"You don't know—"

"Oh, I know. You've made it clear that the money you get from me is the only thing that keeps you afloat, and I'm drying that up on you. Again, not my problem. I hope you get help for the addiction, but you and I are through. Even if I chose to stay in the sport—which I'm not—I would seek out a new agent. I'm not your meal ticket, Andy."

He hangs up on me, and I set the phone down before I throw it against the wall. I'm not excited to go to Seattle next week, but I need to say goodbye to my team, and I need to sell my house.

When I'm finished there, my life will truly be settled here in Montana.

With a sigh, I turn off the computer and stand, roll my neck and stretch my back, and then follow my nose to the kitchen.

"What's for dinner?" I ask when I see Willow standing by the sink.

Christ, she looks good in this kitchen. Yeah, it may be a little misogynistic, but it's true. It's been a few days since I found her in here, eating ice cream. I'd been thinking of her, had already taken a shower and fucked my hand with thoughts of her running front and center, and still, I couldn't shake her.

And then I walked in here, and she was sitting there in practically nothing, like a goddamn wet dream.

And I took it too far. Since the next morning, after our talk, she's tried to act normal, but there's an edge to her that's driving me nuts. Now that I know just how amazing she tastes, how hot she is, I want more of her.

"Meatloaf," she says, pulling me out of my thoughts. "With potatoes, salad, and corn on the cob."

"Awesome, thanks for making it." I want to hug her from behind. Wrap my arms around her and pull her against me, bury my face in her neck, and then fuck her against the countertop.

To ensure I absolutely do *not* do that, I open the cupboard for the plates to set the table, and Aiden walks into the house through the back door.

"You're filthy," Willow says with a laugh. "Go get a quick shower before dinner."

"I can shower later," he says, but she's already shaking her head.

"No. You're not sitting at the table like that. Go clean off that grime, and then you can eat."

Aiden rolls his eyes, but he doesn't sass her further and heads to his bedroom to shower and change. He spends the night out at the bunkhouse with the other hands, but he comes to the house every evening for dinner.

Just like Gid and I did when we were kids.

Willow and I take turns making dinner each night. We've settled into a nice routine.

Except I'd like that routine to include me buried inside her at every opportunity.

I'm not confused. I don't need more time to think about it. Not touching this woman is driving me out of my fucking mind.

"Are you okay?" Willow asks me, and I turn to her with a frown. "You look tense. Honestly, you look kind of pissed off. Who peed in your Cheerios?"

I blow out a breath and set the table. "I *am* pissed off. Andy's a dick."

"I've been telling you for years that Andy's a dick. You should have shaken him off a decade ago, but you're too loyal." She shakes her head, those blond curls of hers falling over her shoulders. She's so fucking beautiful in her black tank top and denim shorts. Wills has legs for days, and her feet are bare, and all her perfect-as-fuck curves are on display. "Right?"

Christ, what were we talking about?

Right. Andy.

"He's not taking the retirement well," I reply and ignore the way she's bending over to pull the meatloaf out of the oven.

I lied. I'm not ignoring it at all.

I bite my fist and hold my breath. Jesus, her ass should come with a warning label. And the way she's bent over, those shorts ride up, and I can almost see butt cheek. I could slide my hand up her thigh, and—

"I'm hungry," Aiden announces as he bounds back into the room, and I have to turn away so I can calm myself the fuck down.

"That was the fastest shower ever," Willow says, eyeing him.

"I'm *hungry*," he repeats, making her laugh. "And your meatloaf is my favorite."

"Well, it's ready," she replies and starts passing bowls to us to set on the table. When we're all seated, we dig in, heaping food on our plates, and Aiden eats as if he's never seen food before.

Or as if he's a fifteen-year-old kid.

"You didn't come out with us today," he says as he shoves a heaping forkful of potatoes in his mouth.

"I was in my office all day. I'll be out with you guys tomorrow."

He nods and then turns to his aunt. "What kind of book are you working on?"

Her fork stills halfway to her mouth, and she stares at Aiden in surprise. "I'm sorry, are you talking to *me*?"

Aiden frowns as he puts more food on his plate. "Yeah. Are you still working on the football book?"

"No, I finished that one." She sets her fork on her plate and blinks at the boy. "I'm working on a romantasy book now about dragons and witches."

"That's cool," he decides.

I'll enjoy listening to that one. I listen to all her books. For years I did it just so I could hear her voice when I couldn't talk to her. Then, it got to where I actually enjoyed the books themselves. Willow's excellent at what she does. I admit, she's damn good. When she acts out the sex scenes, I have to make sure I'm by myself so I don't humiliate myself in public. And she's great at accents, which surprised me at first.

"Do you take dialect training?" I ask her, grabbing her attention.

"I did," she replies. "Sometimes I have to brush up on accents, if I haven't done one in a while. Some are harder for me than others."

"What's the hardest for you?" Aiden asks.

"Irish," she replies, and resumes eating her dinner. "British is the easiest for me."

"That's really cool," Aiden says, and I notice she pauses eating again.

The teenager has opened up quite a bit in the last week, talking more at dinner and asking questions, and I know she's not used to it. It hurts my heart for her because I know how much she loves her nephew.

When Aiden reaches for thirds, Willow's eyebrows climb into her hairline. "You must be burning a ton of calories. I've made this a thousand times, and I've never seen you eat this much."

She's laughing, obviously not bothered at all, and Aiden grins at her.

"I told you, I'm *hungry*."

"Well, eat up. I'd rather you were full than we have leftovers."

When we're finished eating, Aiden offers to help with the dishes, but we both shake our heads.

"Go on out and relax," Willow says, reaching up to ruffle his still-damp hair. "Sleep well, okay?"

"Okay. Good night."

He pats her back and offers me a high five, and then he's off to the bunkhouse.

"He's almost *jovial,*" Willow says after the door closes behind him. "And he asked me about work. He's honestly never done that."

"This ranch is good for the soul," I reply and help Willow load the dishwasher. "I heard a rumor about you."

"It's probably true." She shrugs and then snickers. "Okay, what was it?"

"That you know your sports trivia."

She narrows her eyes at me. "I see my kid has been telling my secrets."

She's not wearing any makeup tonight. Her face is clean and fresh and the most beautiful thing I've ever seen. She lights up this whole house. She lights *me* up.

"Who's the greatest of all time?"

"Here you go with your ego again."

I laugh and shake my head. "Between Jordan and James."

"*LeBron* James?" she clarifies, and I nod. "Oh, we're going the basketball route, I see. I thought you wanted me to feed your already ridiculously huge ego."

"That's not all that's huge, sweetheart."

She flushes, but then makes gagging noises, which only makes me laugh.

"This is a stupid question," she begins. "Obviously, Jordan is the GOAT."

"James beat his thirty-points-scored-in-a-single-game record not long ago."

"Yeah, and he had to play seven seasons *longer* than Jordan played to beat that record. And do you know that if LeBron were to beat Jordan's forty-points-in-a-game record, he'd have to play for another forty seasons based on his average? Basically, if Jordan got thirty in a game, he likely scored forty as well."

Yep. She's unbelievable, and hearing her rattle off stats is making my dick sit up and pay attention.

I can't stay away from this woman any longer. Fuck being careful.

"Now, yes, James does hold the record for the highest scorer of all time, and that's incredible. But again, Jordan is number five of all time, *to this day*, and he played far fewer seasons than James. Jordan has six rings. I wish I'd seen those games live. What a rush that must have been."

I'm moving closer to her. I can't help myself. She's animated, her hands move as she talks, and she's wiping down the counter with a rag, and then she turns to me, and her eyes are bright, her cheeks flushed because she obviously loves this conversation, and I've never wanted anyone the way I want this woman.

My Wills.

My Trouble.

"I'm going to kiss you again," I whisper, surprised that the words aren't just in my head.

Her pretty blue eyes widen, and then she pushes up on her toes and quickly presses her lips to mine before pulling away again, and that's all the invitation I need.

"I-I'm sorry. I shouldn't—"

"The hell you shouldn't," I growl and move in. One hand fists in her hair at the nape of her neck, and the other slides around to cup her ass, pulling her flush against me, and I sink into her. She groans, and her hands grip onto my shirt at my sides. When I lick the seam of her lips, she opens to me, and I'm completely lost in her. She feels like heaven against me, and when her hands move under my shirt to skim along my skin, it takes everything in me not to strip her naked and fuck her hard and fast against this counter.

"Ry," she whispers against my lips.

"Yeah, Trouble." I bite at the corner of her mouth, and with my hand still in her hair, I tug her head back so I can skim my teeth down the side of her throat. "You're so fucking delicious."

"Does this mean you've figured out your shit?"

Should I do this? Probably not. But damn it, I can't stay away from her. I *need* her in a way that I've never let myself need anyone else before. And the way she's kissing me back and touching me tells me that she wants me just as much.

"Figured it out."

"Thank God. Take this off." She's tugging the hem of my shirt, and I waste no time yanking it over my head and casting it aside. Her hands glide down my sides as I frame her face and go in for another life-altering kiss.

I boost her up onto the countertop and step between her legs, just like I did the other night, and she lifts her tank over her head and tosses it to the floor, and then makes quick work of her bra.

I can't help it. I have to step back to take her in. I've never seen her like this, bare from the waist up. Her tits are fucking *magic.*

"You're killing me." I meet her eyes and see that she's just as turned on as I am. That she wants this just as badly as I do. "If you need to stop this—"

"I'll smother you in your sleep if you stop now."

Chapter Eleven

Willow

Ryker grins against my mouth. *Grins*, in that cocky way he does. His hands are on my ass, pulling me against him, and I can feel his hard cock as he nestles it against my cleft and leans in to kiss me some more.

What started out as crazed lust has simmered down to longing. To exploring. To savoring.

And I am here for it.

"Your lips are fucking magic," he whispers before brushing his mouth over mine again and then sinking into me, exploring my mouth with his tongue, and he groans so loud, I can't help but tighten my thighs around his hips and rub against his hard length.

I can't stop moving my hands up and down his sides, over his back and across his shoulders. His skin is warm and smooth, and he's so freaking muscled, it boggles my damn mind.

"You're—" I can't complete the thought because his talented mouth has drifted to my neck again, and that seems to be the sweet spot that makes my whole body flush with unadulterated lust.

As if it wasn't already before.

My tingles have tingles. I can't catch my breath.

"I'm what, sweetheart?" he asks as his thumb grazes over my nipple, making it harden and strain for more. "Tell me."

"I don't even know."

He chuckles, and then I'm airborne. My legs wrap around his waist, and he's carrying me effortlessly up the stairs.

"Bedroom," he mumbles against my lips. "If I finally get to have you like this, it's going to be in my bed."

"What do you mean *finally*?" I ask him.

"Later." He lowers me to my feet, and with a flick of his wrist, my shorts pool around my feet. "Fuck me, you're not wearing underwear."

I press my lips together. Instinct has my arm coming up to cover me, but he moves fast, grabs my wrist and lifts it to his lips.

"Don't." He kisses the inside of my wrist, right over my pulse point, and threads his fingers through mine, making my stomach flutter. He's so freaking *hot.* "You're beautiful. So fucking incredible."

With my free hand, I reach for his jeans, and with his hot brown eyes on mine, I unfasten them and lower the zipper, and they fall to the floor.

Ryker quickly removes his boxer briefs, and then we're standing here, in the middle of his bedroom, both naked, and taking each other in, only connected by our linked hands.

He wasn't joking earlier when he said his ego wasn't the only huge thing about him. Sure, I felt it the other night, but seeing it is another thing entirely.

"Once we do this," he says as I lick my lips and my gaze flicks back up to his. "There's no going back, baby."

Baby. Sweetheart. I've had fantasies about this very scenario for *years*, and I never could have conjured up anything this freaking good.

"Did you hear me?"

"I heard you," I reply and step forward, and without a second thought, I drag my fingertips down his abs, relishing every ridge of hard muscle, before wrapping my hand around his length and stroking him up and down. "I'm not afraid of this, Ry."

Unless you reject me again. I'm going to hope for the best because the look in his eyes tells me he's *in*.

"Thank fuck." He lifts me again and moves me to the center of his giant bed, then settles his elbows on either side of my head, kissing me as if he wants to consume me.

He works his way down my neck, sending those tingles through me again that make me whimper, and then he's nibbling on my nipples, and his hands—dear God, those hands—are working magic on my hips and sides.

"Your skin is so fucking incredible," he mutters before rubbing the tip of his nose in a circle around my belly button. "And the sounds you make are . . . *goddamn, baby*."

"Ry." My hands are in his hair, urging him down almost desperately, but he resists me. He grins up at me, and my core tightens just from that crooked smile alone.

"What do you need, Trouble?"

"You."

"Perfect. I'm right here." He licks over my pubis, and I gasp, which only makes him chuckle and do it again. "What do you need me to *do*?"

"Everything. Anything. All the things, Ry, just *do it*."

He spreads my legs wide, and the look he sends me when his gaze returns to mine is full of sexy intent that has my stomach tightening in anticipation.

"This gorgeous pink pussy is soaked, baby."

"Shocker."

He bites the inside of my thigh and then licks over the sore spot before his mouth journeys to my slit, and he licks me, from my entrance to my clit, and my hips lift up off the mattress.

"Holy hell."

"You taste like candy," he says before repeating the motion, and I see stars. "This is my new favorite meal. I'm going to eat this every goddamn day."

Okay—Ryker James, hockey sensation turned cowboy, likes dirty talk. Sign me the fuck up.

He *feasts* on me. He doesn't just taste or sample—he devours my pussy as if it's his only job in life and he's aiming for a promotion.

And then he adds two fingers to the mix, and I'm done for.

"Ryker, I'm gonna—" My hands are fisted in his hair, my hips are moving of their own accord, and I'm going to explode with the craziest orgasm I've ever had in my life.

"Come all over my face, sweetheart. Make a mess of me." His fingers brush over that spot that makes me wild, and then I'm flying through the stratosphere. "That's my girl. God, you're so damn beautiful, baby."

Turns out, I have a praise kink.

He's kissing and licking his way up my torso, and then he takes my hands and pins them above my head with one of his and cups my face with the other as he kisses me. I can taste myself on him, and it only makes me want him more.

I want all of this man. The funny boy I crushed on, the man that I'm so proud of, the one that I trust more than anyone in this world.

I want him.

"Please," I whisper against his lips. "I need you, Ry."

He tips his forehead to mine and moves his hips, dragging his length against my sopping wet slit.

"I need you, too, but we have a problem."

"We'd better *not* have a problem. If you reject me again, I swear to God—"

He exhales and shakes his head. "I don't have any condoms."

I blink at him and frown, but then a smile spreads over my face.

"Why do you look happy about that?"

"Because that means you weren't planning to fuck a bunch of random women out here."

He blinks in surprise, and then his eyes narrow. "Would you be jealous if I did?"

"Psh. Yes." I lift up to kiss his chin. "I'm on the pill, and it's been a long time for me, so please finish what you started."

He releases my arms, and I wrap them around his neck as he buries his fingers in my hair, watching me. "Did I hear you right? I get to take you bare?"

"Please do."

"I promise," he says with a swallow, "I've been tested. I'm good to go."

"I trust you, Ry."

I don't have to tell him twice. He immediately presses the crown inside me, and I suck in a sharp breath as he lets out a low groan.

Holy shit. I'm sopping wet, but he's big, and I haven't had sex in a really, alarmingly long time.

"Breathe, Trouble." He nibbles my lips and brushes my hair off my face. "Take a breath for me."

I do as he guides my leg up higher over his hip, and he pushes in farther, then pauses.

"You're so fucking tight." One hand drags down to my breast, where he grazes my nipple with his thumb, but those hot dark eyes are pinned to mine. "You feel *incredible*. Fuck, your pussy is hugging me so hard."

I take another breath, and he pushes in the rest of the way, bottoming out, and we stare at each other.

I've never felt so close to another human being in my life.

"Ryker." I frame his face and kiss his lips, and then he starts to move. Long, deep, hard strokes that feel like he'll break me in half, and like he's claiming me. Branding me as his. "Oh, God."

"Not yet." His voice is hard and demanding now, and his hand circles my throat, but he doesn't cut off my air. "Look at me, Wills. You won't come yet."

Oh, I like bossy Ryker. I like him a lot.

"I don't know if I can stop it."

He pulls out all the way, and my muscles clamp down on *nothing*. "Hey!"

"I said not yet." He bites my lower lip, sending another jolt down to my pussy. "You can give me your sexy-as-fuck sass all you want, but you won't come until I say you can."

"Please."

"I like it when you ask nicely." Skimming his lips down my jawline, he whispers, "Ask me again."

"Please, Ry, make me come?"

He pushes in, all the way, and as my walls clench around him, he growls, "Come, Willow. Come for me."

Thank God. I couldn't hold back if I wanted to, which I don't. And as I fall apart, tears filling my eyes, my legs shaking, incoherent words falling from my lips, Ryker comes with me, rocking into me and spilling himself inside me.

He doesn't move away as soon as he's finished. He holds me to him, peppering kisses all over my face and neck, dragging his hand up and down my side as if he's comforting me.

"Your body is supernatural," I inform him after I catch my breath. His head pops up, and he lifts an eyebrow. "Like, I knew you were ripped and stuff from the hockey, but God, Ry, you're just . . . I don't have words."

He rests his head on his palm and offers me a smug grin as he drags his thumb over my bottom lip. "So you're saying I'm hot."

"Need your ego stroked?"

Sobering now, he brushes his fingertips under my eye. "By you? Yeah. I do, baby."

It's not often that Ryker is vulnerable. He shields himself fiercely from anyone getting too close to him. Maybe it's from his shitty childhood, or it's the cost of fame, but I love that he's continuing to open himself up to *me*, especially during a moment that could have turned awkward fast.

"I think you're fucking hot as hell." I fold him into my arms and hug him close. "Everything about you is amazing, Ry. Your body is just an extension of that. But shit, it's a really good body."

He laughs, and the mood lightens, and then he's tugging me from the bed.

"Hey, where are you taking me?"

"To the shower. I'm going to clean you up, and then I'm going to fuck you against the tile."

"I like this plan."

"I thought you might."

I surface out of sleep slowly, feeling disoriented. There's no alarm today, but the sun is already up and shining on my face, and when I crack an eye open, I'm quickly reminded that I'm not in my bedroom.

I'm in Ryker's room.

And he's already up and gone.

Every delicious moment from the night before flickers through my mind, making me shiver with happiness.

We had shower sex. Then we had bed sex again, and before we fell asleep, we changed the sheets so no one had to sleep on one of the wet spots. And when Ryker wrapped me up in his arms, I fell fast and hard into a deep, dreamless sleep.

"Holy shit," I mutter to myself as I roll and bury my face in his pillow, breathing in the scent of him. God, I'm sore. Muscles I didn't even know I *had* weep from all the exercise I got last night. "I had sex with my best friend."

Was that such a good idea?

I roll onto my back and stare at the ceiling.

The sex itself was a brilliant idea. I've never been . . . *worshipped* . . . like that in my life. The fact that some women go through their entire lives never being sexed up the way Ryker can sex a girl up is criminal.

Not that I'll share him. They can find their own Ryker.

Yeah right, he's irreplicable.

However.

He's my person. My best friend. And Aiden and I are living out here with him, all with the purpose of helping my boy, *not* with the intention of my having a hot affair with the sexy former hockey star. And when this is over, when he decides that it's time to move on to someone else, well, that's going to *kill me*. We may have only had one night together, but I'm good and attached already.

Give a girl roughly half a dozen orgasms in one night, and she'll get clingy.

"Shit." I scrub my hands over my face and decide to go take a shower and pull myself together. I pad through his bedroom and open the door, listening. It sounds like I'm alone, so I scurry to my bedroom, close the door, and immediately walk into my en suite bathroom to turn on the shower.

Thirty minutes later, after I've washed and shaved and scrubbed all the things, including my hair, I pull on my usual pajama top, which happens to be an *old* James hockey jersey, and a pair of panties. If everyone is out working, I can walk downstairs like this long enough to make myself some coffee, and then I'll come back up to dry my hair and put on some makeup.

As I make my way through the house, I hear a whirring noise coming from the home gym, and when I peek in, I see Ryker on the treadmill facing the windows, his back to me. He's running faster than I ever have in my life. His earbuds are in, and he's sweating buckets.

How long has he been jogging?

At some point, he shed his T-shirt, so he's only in jogging shorts and sneakers, and his back flexes as he moves, and my mouth goes dry. At some point, he added tattoos there too. He has the sleeve, the one over his ribs, and ink down his back that is simply delicious.

I'm standing here salivating.

Was it a bad idea to start up a physical relationship with my best friend? Possibly.

Probably.

Am I sorry?

Fuck no.

After giving myself a shake, I walk downstairs to the kitchen and pop a pod into the coffee maker to brew a cup, then open the fridge for my creamer and wait for the mug to fill.

I'm humming, swaying back and forth to sort of stretch out my sore inner-thigh muscles—*damn, I'm so sore*—and then I get goose bumps, and I feel him. He hasn't said anything, but I know he's standing in the doorway behind me.

"How long have you had that?"

I frown over my shoulder, and my breath catches.

Yep, he's still shirtless.

And sweaty.

And breathing hard.

His dark eyes are narrowed and pinned to my back.

"Had what?"

"My jersey."

"Oh." I turn as I look down at it. "This one is really old. Maybe from your first season? It's my sleep shirt now. I have others that are more appropriate to wear in public."

He's walking toward me so slowly, like a cat stalking its prey.

"You're wearing my name on your back, sweetheart."

With a smirk, I turn to pull my mug away from the coffee maker and put my creamer in, but his arms suddenly surround me, and he's licking up the side of my neck.

I sigh in relief, and he stills.

"What was the big sigh for?"

"You're not running away. Or telling me to go, like you did a couple of nights ago."

He kisses my neck once more, and I shiver in his embrace.

"No, sweetheart. I told you last night, there's no going back from this. Only moving forward. And right now, you have my name across your back."

"Like that, do you?" I ask as I lean back against him.

"Fuck yeah. I'm going to show you just how much I love seeing my name on you."

Chapter Twelve

Ryker

I don't know if I've ever had such an immediate, visceral reaction as I did when I walked into this room and saw my girl in my jersey and nothing else, her hair wet, smelling like shampoo and *Willow*. It was like a punch to the fucking gut and the hottest aphrodisiac, all rolled into one.

"You've seen me in your jersey plenty of times," she reminds me, her voice breathy as she pushes back against me and reaches up to cup my cheek when I kiss her neck.

"It's been a while." My hands glide up under the jersey, but I don't pull it off her.

No, I'm going to fuck her while she has it on.

I cup her breasts and pluck at her nipples, making her gasp, and then I plant my lips near her ear.

"You're going to lean forward and grab onto the countertop for me. Right now, baby."

Without needing to be told twice, Willow steps back from the edge of the countertop, leans forward, and braces herself on her hands, and that little move has the jersey pulling up, offering me a spectacular view of her round ass.

Hooking my thumbs into her little blue panties, I tug them over her hips and down her legs and squat behind her, spreading her lips.

"Christ, you're wet. How did you get so wet so fast, baby?"

She whimpers, but she doesn't say anything, so I smack one cheek, nice and loud.

"Answer me, Wills."

"I saw you."

I lift an eyebrow, intrigued. "Saw me doing what?"

"Running." She gasps when I brush a finger through that wetness and groans when my digit comes out soaked. "In the gym."

With a smug grin, I lean in and bite her left ass cheek. "You liked that, did you?"

"I told you you're hot, you egomaniac."

I laugh and then reward her by dragging my tongue from her clit to her opening and then back down, and she reaches back to tug on my hair, but I dodge her hand and smack her again.

"I said hold on to the countertop. I won't tell you again."

"Christ, you're bossy during sex."

And I love her sass.

"Don't worry, you'll like what I have planned." I push my tongue inside her, fucking drunk on the taste of her juices. I add two fingers as I suck on her swollen clit, and just when I feel her start to tremble, when she slaps one hand on that countertop because she's about to come apart, I stand, push my shorts down, and replace my fingers with my cock, bottoming out and growling in satisfaction. With the jersey clenched in my fist at the small of her back, I fuck her, hard and fast, losing myself in her.

"Ry!"

"That's my girl." I bare my teeth, staring at her profile as she tries to look back at me. "You drive me out of my goddamn mind."

"Sorry."

I growl again and grip onto her chin and pull her up so I can kiss her delectable lips.

"Never be sorry. You're everything I've ever wanted. Christ, you're a wet dream, sweetheart."

She's trembling as she cups my face, and her pussy is clamped down on me like a vise, and when she resumes her position, hands on the counter, and I see my name and number on her back again, I know I'm going to blow my load.

"Go over, baby." Her pussy tightens, and I bite my lip. "Fuck yes. Come on this cock, while you're wearing my name. Jesus fuck."

I follow her over, the intensity of my climax surprising the shit out of me, and when I regain the strength in my arms, I pull out of her, then turn her around and tug her to me so I can hug her close, bury my nose in her damp hair and give myself a moment to calm down.

"Ry?" She wraps her arms around me.

"Hmm?"

"I've been wearing this jersey every single night for about a decade."

I fist my hand in the wet hair at her nape and tug her head back so I can nibble her lips.

"You like being wrapped up in my name?"

She smiles against my lips. "Look who's catching up."

"Are you trying to get me to fuck you again already? Jesus, you're insatiable, Trouble."

She huffs out a laugh and tips her forehead down to rest on my chest. "I'm simply sharing the information."

My phone rings from somewhere on the floor, and when I see the screen, I sigh.

"That's Dusty. I have to get that."

She steps back and then surprises me by boosting up onto her toes and kissing my chin.

"I have to get to work," she says. "I have a full day in the booth."

I tug on my shorts and lift the phone, and then turn back to her. "I want you to go in there and record that filthy book while my cum is dripping down your thighs."

Willow chokes on her coffee and then lets out a surprised laugh. "Holy shit, Ry."

"Don't you dare clean yourself up, baby."

"I'm going to need an ice pack for my vag." She chuckles and then winces when she stretches side to side. "You might have broken me."

"Not sorry." I wink at her, and her cheeks heat, and that's the image that sticks with me as I saunter out of the kitchen. I need to change into work clothes. There's no sense in showering now because I'll need another one when I come back in later.

Once I'm dressed and I'm ready to head out with the guys, I call Dusty back.

"Hey, boss," he says. "We're out in the farthest north pasture with the new cattle that came in last week."

"Is everything okay out there?" I ask as I grab a hat and my keys, then head out to the barn to saddle up my horse.

"Everyone seems fine," he replies. "Aiden noticed one of the cows is limping, so we're keeping an eye on that one."

The kid has a good eye.

"I'm on my way out there. ETA is about thirty minutes. Do you need anything from the barn?"

"Nope. We were about to start riding fence. There's some mending to do out here."

"I'll see you soon."

I end the call and then get busy saddling up my horse, Billy. He's a big boy, but he's also gentle, and he nudges my shoulder with his muzzle as I slip his bridle on.

"Hey, buddy." I kiss his nose and then get to work saddling him up. "We'll go out with the others for a while. What do you think of that?"

He snorts and nods his head, making me smile.

I've missed working out here in the summertime. When I was between seasons with the team, I'd try to get out here for a little while each year, but it was never for long enough. I always had a packed schedule with appearances and pretty much every little thing that Andy could toss at me. If it paid a dollar, he wanted me to do it.

If I'd told him to piss off sooner, I could have spent more time out here with my dad. He'd roll his eyes at me and tell me to stop sitting in regret when I can't go back and change anything, but I can't help it.

I should have made more time for him.

I should have made more time for Willow and Gideon too.

"Come on, let's go do some work." I hop up into the saddle, and Billy and I head out to the north pasture. I didn't get much sleep last night, and I worked my ass off in the gym this morning. I wanted to wake Wills up with my face between her legs, but she didn't get much sleep either, and she was so beautiful, resting so peacefully, I didn't have the heart to wake her. So I went to the gym to work off the sexual energy with weights and some time on the treadmill.

Now I'm glad I let her sleep because it led to that amazing fuck in the kitchen.

It's only been twelve hours of being intimate with her, and I know I'll never get my fill of her. It will never be enough.

She's mine.

If she needs time to come around to that conclusion, that's fine. I'll prove to her that we're meant to be together. Because no one else in this world was made for me the way she was, and I'll kill any other bastard who tries to touch her.

Mine.

When Billy and I ride over the small hill that leads to the pasture where the others are, I see them gathered in a circle, talking. They're on their horses, and Aiden is telling a story, his face animated and his arms outstretched, as if he's discussing the size of a fish or his dick.

The others laugh.

"What did I miss?" I ask when I join them.

"We were just going to pair up and ride fence line," Dusty says.

"I'll take Aiden," I tell him, and the others share a look.

I have men of all ages here. Some have worked summers out here before, and others are younger and new, but Aiden is the youngest at fifteen.

"Problem?" I ask, raising an eyebrow.

"No, boss."

They shake their heads, and I notice one guy, Spike, clear his throat.

"Hey, boss," he says, "Can I go with you today? I need to talk to you."

"I'll take Spike." The man's head nods in thanks. We pair off, and Spike and I ride for a couple of miles without saying a word.

We find a spot in the barbed wire that needs to be fixed, so we hop off the horses, and I grab the supplies out of my saddlebag.

"How's it going, Spike?" I finally ask him when he continues to keep quiet.

"I've got a situation, boss."

I nod and pass him a pair of pliers. "Okay, let's talk about it. What's up?"

He wiggles an old nail out of the post. "I don't know what your old man told you about me."

I frown as I pass him a new nail.

"Dad always had good things to say about you." He glances at me in surprise. "How long have you been working out here?"

"About ten summers, I guess," he says.

Spike sighs and stands up, tips his hat back so he can wipe the sweat off his brow. He's about my age, but the years haven't been kind to him. He's overweight, his hair is thinning, and his skin is like leather. But what I said is true; Dad never had a bad thing to say about Spike or his work ethic.

"I've been going through a bitch of a divorce," he says as he looks out at the pasture. "Been dragging on forever because we have a kid, and she doesn't want me to see him. Thinks it gives her power to keep my boy from me."

Shit. I shove my hands in my pockets and listen.

"I didn't think I'd get to see him much this summer. Even though we have a court-ordered parenting plan that says I get him every weekend, she never abides by it."

I raise an eyebrow. "But?"

"But now she has a boyfriend." *I see where this is going.* "And she wants Micah to live with me this summer."

"How old is Micah?"

"Sixteen." He blows out a breath. "He's a good kid, and I'm excited at the prospect of spending the summer with him, but I need this job."

"Bring him."

That has Spike blinking, and his eyes cut over to mine. "Just like that?"

"There's room in the bunkhouse," I reply. "And I'll pay him to work for the summer. The two of you can be together. It's a win-win for all of us."

Spike swallows hard. "I thought that with Aiden working out here, you might say that, but I was worried."

"Aiden and Micah just might end up as friends," I add with a nod. I like the idea of that. I don't think Aiden has many friends. "I know it's not any of my business, but how's the court battle going?"

With a sharp breath, he kicks at the dirt under his boots. "Slow as hell, and I can't afford the attorney anymore to keep fighting it."

I narrow my eyes. I don't like bullies.

"You can now. I'll make some calls, and we'll see if this can get wrapped up for you. But if there's something I should know, something about your past, like you were an abusive fuck, or an asshole to your wife and kid, I want to know now before I put my name on the line for you."

Spike scowls. "My only sin is that I ain't rich. I've never raised a hand to her or my boy, and I take care of what's mine."

I nod, happy with both the reaction and his words. "Good. Bring your boy out here for the summer, Spike. He's welcome here."

"Thanks, boss."

"No need to thank me."

Spike shakes his head, and we climb back on the horses. "Aiden kicked my ass at poker last night."

"How much did he take you for?"

"Twenty bucks."

I laugh. "Good for him."

"This was good." Aiden pats his flat belly and leans back in his chair.

"I guess so. You ate a whole pizza by yourself," Willow says with a laugh.

"Homemade is my favorite."

"I thought my meatloaf was your favorite?" she counters, and Aiden snorts.

"If it's food, it's my favorite."

Willow stands and walks around the table so she can hug Aiden around the neck, and she plants her lips on his head. She can't see it, but Aiden's smile slips, just a bit.

Based on my own childhood trauma, I can see that this boy has food issues, and he doesn't love to be touched.

But he tolerates it for his aunt because he loves her.

"You're at that age," she says as she continues to hug his neck, "where your legs are hollow, and you want to eat everything in sight. I remember when Ryker and Gideon were the same way."

His eyes shoot over to mine. "Really?"

"I'm still that way," I confess with a shrug. "We burn a lot of calories, man."

"Yeah, I guess," he says. Finally, Willow lets him go, and he sighs in relief. "Why are you all mushy and stuff?"

"Because you're my kid and I can be." She makes like she's going to hug him again, and Aiden holds his hands up.

"No more! Ew. Gross."

"I will *smother you* in kisses, you little ungrateful brat." They're both laughing when she kisses his hair again. "I love you, buddy."

"Yeah, yeah, I guess I love you too."

She freezes. Her face falls, and her eyes mist up, and she immediately scurries into the kitchen.

"I'm going to start cleaning up," she calls out, as if nothing at all is wrong.

A couple of weeks ago, she said that Aiden hadn't thanked her for anything in a while. I suspect he also hasn't told her he loves her in a long while either.

"I'm headed out." He's oblivious to the meltdown happening in the kitchen.

"Go take Spike for another twenty at poker."

He lets out a loud laugh and then heads for the door. "It's too easy. See you."

When the door closes, I jog up the stairs to my bathroom and the soaking tub inside. After I get the water hot enough, I pour in some salts and then walk back down to the kitchen to collect my girl.

She's standing at the sink, looking out the window, wiping tears from her cheeks.

"It's okay, sweetheart."

She doesn't turn to me. She just wipes another tear away.

"I don't remember the last time he said that to me," she confesses. "It just hit me out of nowhere."

I kiss her head and then loop my arm around her shoulders and lead her to the stairs.

"I have to clean the kitchen."

"No, that's my job tonight. You need to get in the bath. I know you're sore, and you're emotional, and I want you to just relax for a while."

Once I lead her into the bathroom, I see that the tub is full, so I shut off the faucet and turn to find her staring up at me with those wide eyes.

"You get in and get comfy. I'll bring you some wine, if you want it."

"Yeah." She blows out a breath. "I think I want it."

After kissing her forehead, I step away, but she catches my hand in hers and links our fingers.

"Ry."

"Yeah, baby."

She offers me a watery smile, and I lean in to kiss her on the forehead again. I can't stop touching this woman. "Thanks."

"Anytime. Now, get naked and in that water before it goes cold."

I close the door behind me and head downstairs to fetch her wine.

Chapter Thirteen

Willow

With my voice work all wrapped up for the day, I save the audio files for the Mafia romance I'm currently working on and then shut everything down securely and move to my desk so I can check email and social media.

I always save the admin work for the last part of the day, when my voice is growing tired and I can catch up on other things.

I work with several production companies, and they're often checking in with me for availability in my schedule or to see if I can shift projects around. I also get requests to do live recordings to help promote books for authors, in addition to live streams on social media.

Being a successful narrator doesn't stop with the recording. It's a business that I have to promote and work hard at so I stay relevant in an ever-changing market.

I freaking love my job.

After I check my schedule and work in an Instagram Live video, along with a Christmas novella that sounds like fun, I close up shop for the day but keep my phone with me, just in case. It's become my new routine to head out for a nice long walk late in the afternoon, to get some exercise and fresh summer air before I cook dinner. Some nights,

Ryker's already in the kitchen cooking by the time I get back, beating me to it, but I want to be there for that too.

Seeing a sexy Ryker cooking is something to behold.

It's been almost two weeks since Aiden and I moved out to the ranch, and I think it's safe to say that we're both beyond happy with the situation. My boy is all smiles when he comes in for dinner at night, usually filthy and dead on his feet as well, but I haven't seen him this happy in years.

Since Ryker and I started having the best sex in the history of the universe, I haven't slept in my own bed. Before I can even suggest it, the man whisks me off to his bedroom, where he worships my body and makes me feel . . . *alive.*

You like that, don't you, Trouble? You love feeling my cock filling you so full, making you scream my name.

I shiver at the memory and set off on the path that meanders into the woods.

I know the Triple Creek Ranch like the back of my hand. I've spent most of my life in these woods, but I always bring bear spray with me, just to be safe. I don't need to surprise a mama bear and end up on the evening news.

My phone pings with a text, and I grin when I see that it's one of my favorite producers, Katie.

Katie: Hey friend! I am looking at your calendar, and I need to squeeze in a cowboy romance next month. Any wiggle room for me?

I smirk and bring up my calendar as I continue to wander down the path.

Me: I have these four days, the thirteenth through the sixteenth, and the rest is full. How long is the book? Is this enough time?

The dots bounce on the screen as she replies.

Katie: That's actually perfect! I'll take it. It's on the shorter side, and shouldn't be an issue.

Me: Then it's yours.

While it's true that I am usually booked out about a year in advance, there are always cancellations, or authors who run late to deliver, so the schedule has to have a little wiggle room for moments like this.

With that taken care of, I tuck my phone in my back pocket and look around. The trees are thick in this part of the woods, with a lot of brush, making it virtually impossible to veer off the path. And just through these trees is my favorite clearing.

It's full of wildflowers, so much yellow and red, with a smattering of bluebells, and it's impossible not to hear the buzzing of bees as they float from flower to flower.

It's a great spot, and it's exactly one mile from the house, so I usually come out here, then head back to the house after resting for a few minutes.

But this time, as I turn back, I notice black clouds forming in the distance, and my stomach clenches.

Summer storms in Montana are legendary. They come out of nowhere, and they're *brutal*. So much lightning and loud thunder, and they never fail to terrify me. One summer, the lightning hit a tree not far from the house and started a fire that we all worked *days* to put out before it spread to the house and the rest of the property.

I hate the storms. A Montana thunderstorm is one of the few things out here that truly scares me. I'd rather come across that mama bear I mentioned earlier than deal with being outside in a storm.

In the summer, it's rare *not* to have an afternoon thunderstorm, complete with rain. Usually they don't last long. But some days, cell after cell will blow through, and it's an all-day-and-night event.

Those are the days I hate the most.

Picking up my pace, I jog through the woods, making noise so I don't startle any wildlife, but I'm not fast enough to get to the house before the sky opens up and starts to dump huge droplets of rain. Lightning flashes overhead, making me scream, and then three seconds later, thunder cracks around me.

Shit.

"I hate this, I hate this, I hate this," I continue to chant as I run to the house, and when I bound up the steps, the door flings open, and Ryker is waiting on the other side.

"I didn't know you were going out in this," he says as he wraps his arms around me, not caring at all that I'm sopping wet, and tugs me against him. "You're wet, baby."

"It was blue skies and clear when I went out there." Thunder cracks, and I shiver, but it's not from being cold. "I fucking hate storms, Ry."

"I know." He was there that summer too. He kisses my head and leads me upstairs. "Let's get you dry, and we'll make dinner. This one should blow over pretty fast, but I told Aiden to stay at the bunkhouse for dinner. I don't want him walking in a lightning storm."

"Thank you. I don't either." I quickly strip out of my wet clothes, and Ryker has a fluffy towel waiting for me to wrap up in and dry off with, and then he passes me one of his team T-shirts, which I pull over my head.

He is obsessed with seeing me in his team gear. It's kind of cute.

The house rattles with a clap of thunder, and I close my eyes, swallowing hard. I am not prone to panic attacks, but storms give my heart a workout.

"It's okay." Ry steps up behind me, loops his arms around my chest, and pulls my back to his front. "I've got you."

"Let's just get to work on dinner and talk about something else," I suggest. "It'll keep my mind off it."

"I can do that." He links his fingers with mine, and we walk downstairs together. "How about burgers and fries for dinner?"

"Yum. I'll cut up the potatoes."

He kisses me on the sensitive spot just under my ear and then opens the fridge to pull out the ground beef.

"How was work today?" he asks me.

"Productive. That booth is the best, Ry. I'm so spoiled in there. I don't know how I'll go back to my tiny setup back home at the end of the summer. I got a new gig this afternoon, so now next month is completely booked solid. Here's hoping I don't get sick or anything. Because there is *no* wiggle room."

Lightning flashes through the windows, as if it's enveloping the house, and then thunder crashes, and I jolt, slicing my finger with the sharp knife.

"Fuck."

"Whoa, come here." Ry takes my hand in his and leads me to the sink, his face dark as he stares down at the cut. "No more knives for you today."

"It's not that bad." I sound so grouchy, it's almost laughable. "I can still help with dinner."

"Nope." He hooks my chin and makes me look at him. "I'm not asking, Wills. I'm telling you."

"Bossy in the bedroom is fine, but I don't need—"

"You're hurt," he counters, just as thunder strikes again and I jump. "Hey. No sharp instruments for you when you're jumpy. I don't need you severing a finger or something. Let's get this bandaged up, and I'll cook dinner."

"My plan worked." I'm trying to lighten the mood here. "I got out of dinner duty."

"Next time, just tell me you don't feel like cooking." He sighs and fetches the first aid kit from below the sink and bandages me right up, then places a sweet kiss over my little wound. "There. How about some wine?"

"I won't turn that down."

"You sit, I'll pour."

"I'm not an invalid, you know."

He lifts an eyebrow, daring me to talk back again, so I fold my lips together and sit my ass on a stool while he opens a bottle, pours, and then slides the glass over to me.

"Thanks. How was work for you today?"

"It was good. Nothing is injured, and everyone seems to be settled in just fine. Spike's son, Micah, moved into the bunkhouse yesterday, and so far so good there."

"I hope the two teenagers get along okay," I say before taking a sip of the crisp white wine. Thunder claps, but I manage not to jump this time, and I can tell that the storm has moved on, as the sound is growing fainter.

Thank God.

"Aiden was showing Micah the ropes in the barn this morning, and neither of them looked ready to kill the other, so I'll take that as a win."

He winks at me, and my heart stills. It's the same wink he'd give the camera after every single interview.

The wink just for me.

I won't even admit to how many times I'd find interviews on YouTube, just so I could rewind and watch that wink over and over again.

"Have you noticed that Aiden doesn't like to be touched?" Ryker asks.

Frowning, I sip my wine. "He's always been that way. I know he tolerates me hugging him, and once in a while, I'll press my luck and kiss his head, but no. He doesn't like to be touched."

Ry scowls and leans on the counter. "Do you know why?"

"I assume because Sabrina was a shit mom who had men coming through their lives constantly, and who knows what that poor kid was subjected to?"

Ryker swallows hard.

That describes his own childhood.

"Ry—"

"I'm fine," he says, shaking his head. "I know you've told me the story before, but lay it out for me again. What the fuck happened?"

He's rinsing off the potatoes and shaking the colander so they drain.

"Well, you already know that Sabrina is my bio dad's daughter from a previous relationship. I'm younger by a few years."

"Never met her," Ry reminds me.

"And you never will. She died a couple of years ago from a drug overdose."

He fully faces me now, his face falling. "Christ, Wills, I'm sorry. I had no idea."

"I didn't, either, for almost a year after she died. I hardly knew her. We didn't grow up together, as you know. Hell, you and Gid were more siblings to me than Sabrina ever was."

He circles the island and tips my face up, then settles in to kiss me long and slow, igniting every cell in my body.

"I'm not your brother, baby."

"No." I blow out a shaky breath. "But you know what I mean."

His eyes narrow, he wipes his thumb across my lower lip, and then he backs away. "Go on."

"I didn't even know she'd had a baby," I continue. "I hadn't seen her in a long, *long* time. Mom had died, and I was doing my own thing, as you know."

He nods and forms burger meat into disks. "I don't like to speak ill of the dead, but your mom was a bitch."

"It always shocked me how different my mom and Debbie were. Like two sides to a coin. And let's be honest, Ray and Deb raised me in all the ways that matter. Mom couldn't wait to dump me off here on the last day of school every year so she had the whole summer away from me."

"Christ," he mutters and glances at me. "She told you that?"

"It was written all over her. You should have seen how gleeful she was. As the end of school approached, she got giddy. Told me all about her fun plans for when I'd be out of her hair."

"I'm never violent with women," he says. "But I'd like to punch her out."

"Yeah, well, other men took care of that for you. Never while I was around, surprisingly. It was weird how she seemed to have morals about not bringing guys home when I was there, but then as soon as school was out, she ditched me and probably slept her way all up and down the West Coast."

"Did you not want to be here?" He looks stunned as he asks the question. "I always thought you liked it here."

"I would have lived here full-time if I could. Aunt Deb asked Mom to let me just be here with you guys, but Mom refused. Anyway, that doesn't matter."

"It fucking matters," he grumbles, but I keep going.

"Gideon and I traveled with you to Toronto for a game—this would have been about ten years ago or so. We always went with you."

"We won that game, two to zero. I remember, Wills."

I lick my lips. "Yeah, well, when I got home, Sabrina was waiting in front of my apartment with Aiden. She had a suitcase packed for him, told me she didn't want to be a mom anymore, and to have papers drawn up and she'd sign them. And then she left. We never saw her again. But I had to take Aiden to the hospital that night because he was *so sick*, Ry. He had bronchitis so bad, he could hardly breathe, and he was burning up with fever. And she just left him."

I shake my head, feeling the tears want to come.

"He was the cutest little guy. A little small for his age because I'm pretty sure she didn't feed him enough. He was quiet. Withdrawn. He'd do exactly what I told him to, without saying a word. For the first two weeks he was with me, I didn't know if he *could* talk." I brush a tear off my cheek. "But then he started to come out of his shell. He started to feel better. I'll never forget the first time he laughed. It caught me so off guard, I just cried and cried, and he was so worried that he'd done something wrong."

I'm crying in earnest now, and Ryker hurries around to me and hugs me close.

"We've known our fair share of shitty parents," he murmurs against my hair.

"It's why I couldn't leave him out here without me. I couldn't do it."

"I get it." His hands rub up and down my back, soothing me. "He's lucky to have you, sweetheart."

"We're both lucky. Sabrina did us both a favor the day she left him with me. It was *so hard*, but I'd do it all over again in a heartbeat."

"Because you're so amazing." He kisses my cheek. "And so brave." His lips move to my lips, and he brushes back and forth lightly.

My stomach growls, making us both smile.

"Feed me, Captain."

The bedroom lights up with a flash, and then a loud boom sounds around us, and I'm suddenly cradled in Ryker's strong arms.

"Holy shit," I whisper. That clap of thunder woke me up out of a dead sleep.

"Another storm's rolling through," he murmurs. "Don't worry, I've got you."

He's behind me, wrapped around me, and I can't help but rotate my hips against him, brushing his growing erection with my ass.

"Is that the distraction you need, Trouble?"

"Mm-hmm." Reaching back, I cup his cheek, and his hand journeys down my stomach and over my clit, then down farther to guide my leg up and over his thigh, giving him better access.

His fingers find my center once more, and lightning strikes.

"Fuck, I can see you when the room lights up," he whispers against my ear. "I've never seen anything more beautiful than you."

His finger slips through my already-soaked slit, and his chest grumbles against me.

"You're so fucking wet."

I push back against him. "And you're so fucking *hard*."

"I'm always hard when I'm around you." He nudges the head of his cock against my opening, and when lightning strikes again, he pushes inside, circling my bundle of nerves with his fingertips, whispering the filthiest words in my ear. "That's right, fucking take it. Goddamn, this pretty pussy was made for me. Only for me."

"Ry."

"Say it."

"Only you."

He's licking and biting my shoulder, my neck, and moving in long, steady strokes as the storm rolls around us. Rain pelts against the windows, and then lightning strikes again.

"Taste yourself, baby." His fingers brush over my lips, and I open, taking them in and tasting myself on them as he starts to thrust so much harder. His hand circles my neck, and I fucking relish it.

I love being at his mercy.

Because this man would *never* do anything to hurt me.

"I want you to let go," he says, tightening his hold on me. "I want you to come for me, sweetheart."

"Ry."

"That's right." He licks up my neck and then blows on the wet trail, and that's all it takes to send me over. When the next round of thunder roars around us, I explode into stardust, screaming out his name, and then he rolls me onto my stomach, his knees planted on either side of my thighs, and with one hand braced on my low back and the other gripping my shoulder, he fucks me *hard*. "You're mine, Willow. Do you fucking hear me? Mine, goddamn it. Fuck, you're so goddamn beautiful."

He thrusts three more times and then rocks into me as he comes, crying out with his climax, and then he collapses on top of me, pushing me into the mattress.

I don't even care if he smothers me right now.

But he rolls to the side, and I turn my head to smile over at him.

"That's one way to ride out a storm," I say as he drags his fingers up and down my spine.

"Might be my new favorite thing." He kisses my arm and then rolls away. "Stay here. I'm going to clean you up."

"I can—"

"Stay." He points at me, and I can't help but smile at him. "Be a good girl, and I'll keep distracting you."

"Promises, promises."

I hear the water run in the bathroom, and then he's back with a warm, wet rag, and he cleans me up.

"If the storms persist like this all summer, we're going to get worn out really fast."

He snorts. "Storms or not, I plan to be inside you as often as possible. I'm addicted to you."

"That might be the nicest thing anyone has ever said to me."

With a smirk, he tosses the rag into the hamper and then smacks my ass hard enough to make me yelp.

"I'm not done with you."

"Lucky me."

Chapter Fourteen

Willow

He held me all night. Made love to me, distracted me with spine-tingling kisses, and then simply wrapped those strong arms around me and held me. Despite several more storms blowing through, I slept relatively well and didn't freak out.

If I'd been alone, I never would have rested.

When I woke an hour ago, the bed was cool where Ryker had been, and the sun was streaming through the windows. Everything outside looks calm.

But I don't trust it.

Because I was smart and checked the weather app, and we're getting more storms this afternoon, and I want to make sure I get all the recording time in that I need today before there's a chance that I could lose power.

So now that I'm showered and armed with both coffee and breakfast, I make my way to my studio.

For several hours, I lose myself in the work. Record, stop, back up, rerecord. Make notes. It flows well, and by the time noon rolls around, I'm working at a good pace, not willing to take a break to grab something to eat.

I'm in the zone.

But then, the power flickers.

And I panic.

"Shit, did I save that?" I'm hitting keys, checking documents, relieved that everything seems to be there, and rather than press my luck, I double-check that everything is secure and then shut down altogether.

I'd like to keep working, but it looks like the storms are starting to roll in, and this time, the electricity is going to join in the party.

I open the door to my studio just as thunder rolls overhead. My soundproof booth kept the noise out, and that was amazing.

"It's okay." I take a deep breath and go back in for my noise-canceling headphones. "Wear these, crank the music, and do some stress cleaning."

That's how I usually deal with summer storms.

The power flickers once more and then goes out altogether, and I blow out a breath.

Great.

I know that the house has a generator, but I have no idea how to get it going. I don't want to text Ryker and interrupt him because I'm sure he's still cleaning up from yesterday's storms.

If the power's still out in an hour, I'll shoot him a text and ask him to guide me through starting the generator.

With that decided, I raid the cleaning supply closet in the laundry room and fill a bucket with glass cleaner, toilet scrub, brushes, sponges, and plastic gloves, and then make my way to the primary en suite bathroom.

With P!NK blaring in my ears, I get to work, starting with the shower. Halfway into scrubbing, I get too hot, so I shed my T-shirt and continue working in my bralette and shorts.

Of course I notice the flashes of light through the windows, but I do my best to ignore them, safe in my music from the thunder.

When that bathroom is finished, I work my way down the hallway to the one off my old room and get busy in there. When I turn to the vanity, I get lost in going through my makeup, deciding what's old enough to toss and what I should keep.

But then there's a noise I can't ignore. Even through the noise-canceling headphones and the music, I can hear it.

Or it's the rumble making its way through my body that I recognize, and that has me pulling the earphones off, and I gasp.

Holy shit.

The rain! It's coming down in sheets, no droplets anywhere in sight.

And then the thunder starts again, and my stomach climbs into my throat.

Shit, this is a bad one.

Without overthinking it, I rush down to my studio and close the door, and it blocks out all the noise, and I huddle in a corner, pull my knees to my chest, wrap my arms around my legs, and pray that the storm passes quickly.

Chapter Fifteen

Ryker

Last night's wind blew so many trees down over my fence line, and cows got out, got lost in the woods, and it's been a goddamn clusterfuck all day.

"More storms blowing in," Spike says, lifting his chin at the clouds on the horizon.

"Yeah, I know." I want to know if my girl is okay, but I haven't had time to text her, and there's definitely been no time to go to the house to check in with her. "How's that southern border coming?"

"We got the fence patched and the cows back in the pasture," he says. "But the north side is a fucking nightmare."

Wincing, I brace my hands on my hips, looking out to where Dusty's wielding a chainsaw, working to get trees moved.

Aiden and Micah are both on horseback, guiding cows back into the pasture.

"I don't like the boys being up that high with lightning coming."

Spike nods. "I'll get them off. I think those are the last three cows we lost."

We ride over to where the others are, and I start barking out orders.

"Those clouds look nasty, and there's a lightning warning for this whole area," I tell them. "Let's patch this fence and barricade what we can't fix, and then I want everyone to head to the barn and get the horses put away before this storm hits. Spend the rest of the day safe in the bunkhouse."

They nod, and we work together to patch the fence. Thunder rolls over us as we ride back to the barn, and just as we're getting the horses brushed and put into stalls, the sky opens up in the loudest downpour I've ever seen.

I glance at Aiden, and he looks nervous.

"Are you okay?" I ask him, setting my hand on his shoulder.

"*I* am," he says, shaking his head, "but Aunt Wills won't be. She hates storms, and this will freak her out."

I nod, already feeling like shit that I'm not with her.

"As soon as I finish putting Billy away, I'll go to the house," I assure him.

"I've got Billy," Aiden replies. "I'll take care of it."

He licks his lips and watches through the door as more rain pelts down.

"Thanks. I'll head in. You go to the bunkhouse, you hear me? Go ride this out with the others."

"I can come to the house to check in on Aunt Wills."

"I've got her. If anything's wrong, I'll call you."

He doesn't look happy about it, but he nods. "Yeah, okay."

I quickly check in with Dusty, and then I'm running for the house in an all-out sprint, through rain that feels like it's trying to tear the skin from my body.

My poor cattle.

By the time I run up the stairs and onto the front porch, I look and feel like I've been swimming with my clothes on. I'm fully drenched. My jeans are heavy as fuck, but I don't give a shit.

"Wills?" I call out as I burst through the front door. I stop to listen, but the only sound is my heart hammering in my chest. So I try again. "Wills?"

Nothing.

I run back to the kitchen, but she's not here, and it's dead quiet because it occurs to me that the power is out.

Shit, I have to get the generator running, but not until I find my girl.

I rush through the downstairs, and when I don't find her, I take the stairs two at a time and poke my head into every room.

When I get to the bathroom off her old bedroom, I find a bucket with a bunch of cleaning supplies. Obviously, she was in here cleaning, but there's no sign of her now.

"Willow!" I hurry down the hall and check our room. The bed is made, and the bathroom is sparkling and smells like cleaner. She obviously scrubbed this one first.

But no sign of her.

I rush back out and notice her studio door is closed, so I walk inside, and at first I don't see her, but then movement in the corner catches my eye, and my chest feels like it cracks open and my heart stumbles right onto the floor.

She's crouched in the corner, rocking, hugging her legs to her chest. Her headphones are on, and she's mumbling with her eyes closed.

How am I supposed to get her attention without scaring the shit out of her?

I squat about three feet away from her. Everything in me wants to scoop her against me and hold her tight, consoling her.

But she's shaking, in only a bra, and there are tear tracks on her cheeks, and I don't want to startle her. Before touching her, I go find her a shirt and then return to the room, squatting before her once more. She hasn't moved, and her bottom lip quivers.

Jesus, she's breaking my heart.

Gently, I reach out and slip my fingers into hers, and her eyes open. She doesn't jump or startle, so I pull her to her feet, quickly tug the T-shirt over her head, and then scoop her into my arms and carry her to my office next door so I can sit on the couch along the wall and cradle her in my lap.

I take her headphones off, set them aside, and then cup her cheek.

"Hey. I've got you. You're safe. I'm so sorry, sweetheart."

"This storm isn't your fault," she whispers, but she clings to me, buries her nose in my neck. "I was fine until the rain got so loud."

"Crazy, isn't it?" I glance to the window, where the rain continues to dump, although a little lighter than before. "I don't remember the last time it rained this hard."

Pressing my lips to her hair, I breathe her in. I'm soaked, and I'm getting her wet, too, but she doesn't seem to care.

Or maybe she just hasn't noticed.

"The power's out. I didn't know how to start the generator."

"I'll show you in a minute." I kiss her forehead and then her nose before she buries her gorgeous face back in my neck. "I need to hold you first."

"No complaints here. Shit, this makes me feel so weak. It's so stupid. The storm isn't going to hurt me. I *know* that, but—"

"You're not weak or stupid." I hook her chin on my finger and make her look at me. "Do you hear me? Don't talk about my girl like that. You're one of the bravest people I fucking know. So you have a thunderstorm phobia. We all have something we're scared of."

"What's your thing?" she asks, not taking her eyes from mine, and I swallow hard.

I don't want to admit this.

But she's already being vulnerable with me, and I need to give some openness back to her.

So I take a breath. "I have a couple. One, the thought of something happening to you makes me lose my shit."

She blinks rapidly.

"Always has, since we were teenagers. It's one of the reasons I always stuck to you like glue, and I made you and Gid travel with me."

"Wait." She's ignoring the sound of the storm now, frowning up at me. "I thought you just liked having the Three Amigos together."

"Sure, that was part of it, but I had to have you close by because I didn't want something to hurt you when I couldn't be near you. I know it's irrational."

"Ry." She shakes her head. "I didn't even live in Seattle."

"I know. I told you, it's irrational. I was going to buy you a condo in Seattle so you'd be closer, but then everything happened with Aiden."

"Do you know what that's called in dark romance novels?"

Of course I do.

"Obsession," she says before I can answer her.

Was I always obsessed with Willow? I've listened to all her audiobooks over the years, but I attributed that to being homesick and wanting to hear her voice. Is it really because I've been completely gone over her since the day I stepped foot on this ranch?

It's possible.

All I can do is shrug at her.

"Okay." She blows out a breath. "What else?"

"What do you mean?"

"You said there were a couple of phobias. What else?"

"That's not enough of a confession for you?"

She narrows her eyes, waiting.

"That's all you're getting for today. Feel better?"

"Yeah." She stands and pushes her hands through her hair. "Come on, I'll make us some food. I skipped lunch."

"For you to do that, I have to show you how to get the generator running. It's easy."

With her hand in mine, I lead her out to the garage and over to where the box is mounted on the wall.

"This is not what I remember from when we were kids."

"I know. It's solar." I open a panel. "I had it installed last month but haven't needed to use it. You just flip this switch."

I show her, and her whole face lights up as we hear the house whir to life.

"It's attached to the *whole house*? Not just the fridge and stuff?"

"Whole house," I confirm. "I'm fancy, remember?"

"You *are* fancy."

We return to the kitchen, and Willow pulls out ingredients for what looks like spaghetti.

"Hey, speaking of Seattle," I say, leaning on the counter. "We're going in a couple of days."

She pauses what she's doing, and her gaze darts up to mine. *"We?"*

"Yeah, *we*. I have to go to wrap things up with the team, give a press conference, all that stuff, and I'm not willing to be away from you for that long."

"How long will you be gone?" she asks.

"*We* will be gone for about four days."

"Ry, I have to work."

I shake my head and step closer to her, pull her against me as I wrap my arms around her waist. "Are you telling me that we can't figure something out, sweetheart?"

Her hands slide up my chest to my neck, and I want to growl. I fucking love it when she touches me.

"I guess I could see if I can juggle some things. Work longer days before and after, if it's that important to you."

"I don't want to be without you that long." I press my lips to her forehead.

"Okay—Seattle, here we come."

"You're going to Seattle?"

Our heads jerk to the side, to where Aiden's standing in the doorway, wet from the rain still coming down, his eyes full of hurt.

"We were just talking about it," Wills says, trying to pull out of my arms, but I hold firm.

We are not a fucking secret.

"Oh, cool. Glad to see you're okay. I'll head back out to the bunkhouse."

He turns to leave, but I call out, "Stop."

He doesn't turn around, but he does stop walking.

"We're *all* going to Seattle," I add. "The three of us."

Now, he does turn back. "We are?"

"Yeah. I have some business to see to, and we'll have some fun too."

His eyes drop to where I'm still holding his aunt.

"Are you two—" He swallows hard. "Uh."

"Yeah," I reply, just as Willow rests her forehead on my shoulder with a little moan. "It's new, but yeah. Is that okay with you?"

"Sure." He frowns.

"What would you like to say?"

"Nothing."

I kiss Willow on the top of her head and then gently push her away. "I'll be right back."

I cross to where Aiden is and then gesture for him to join me in the living room. When we're alone, I cross my arms over my chest and face him, man-to-man.

"What's on your mind, kiddo?"

Aiden runs his hand through his hair and scowls at the floor. "I like you, Ry, but if you hurt her—" He shuffles his feet, and my respect for the kid has just intensified by about a thousand percent.

"Now you know how I felt that day that you punched the wall."

He swallows hard. "I'll punch more than the wall if you hurt her." He firms his chin and looks me in the eyes. "Even though you're bigger than me, and you can kick my ass, I'll get some swings in first."

"Fair enough. So do you want to go to Seattle or not?"

He lets out a breath. "Yeah, I wanna go."

"Good."

Chapter Sixteen

Ryker

"This doesn't look like it does on TV," Aiden says with a frown as he looks out onto the ice.

"That's because this isn't where we play games." I pat him on the shoulder and pull Willow into my side as I show them around the Blizzard Iceplex. "This place is for practices. It's where our headquarters is, where we talk to the media. It's also open to the public, so leagues play here, and people can rent it out for parties. They can even come watch us practice a few times a week."

"That's pretty cool," Aiden says with a shrug, trying so hard to not look impressed, but his green eyes are wide as he takes everything in. "There's a restaurant in here."

I nod, seeing this place through the eyes of someone who's never been here before. "And a merch shop, in case you want to pick anything up."

I'll be buying them a shit ton of stuff.

Particularly for Willow, because seeing her in my team gear turns me on at the drop of a fucking hat.

Checking the time, I sigh.

"Go," Willow says, rubbing her little hand up and down my chest. "We'll wander around and probably buy out the merch shop. We're fine."

"I don't want to leave you alone."

"Hey, guys," Mac Reynolds says with a wide grin as he joins us. "Dude, go to your meeting. I'll show these guys around. Buy Wills a jersey with my name on it."

I lift an eyebrow. "Only if you want to lose your hand."

"He's so testy," Mac says and pulls Willow in for a hug. Mac's been here as long as I have, both of us having been drafted our rookie years and spending our whole careers in Seattle. He's one of my best friends on the team and has met Willow many times, especially back in the day. "Hey, baby girl. You look delicious."

"I. Will. Kill. You."

He smirks at me over her head and then lets her go. "Are you saying your girl *doesn't* look delicious?"

"Yeah, Ry?" Willow bats her eyelashes, and I snarl just as Aiden finds his tongue.

"You're Mac Reynolds." The kid looks starstruck.

"Guilty." Mac holds his hand out to my boy. "And you're Aiden. I've heard a lot about you. Let's ditch this guy so we can talk about him behind his back."

Aiden and Mac are already talking as Willow turns to me and lifts up on her toes, offering me her lips, but she's still short as fuck.

It's adorable.

"Have a good meeting," she says. "And we'll see you at the press conference in a little bit."

Framing her face in my hands, I lower my lips to hers and gently nibble at the corner of her mouth. "I'm so glad you're here."

"Are you nervous?" She frowns up at me. "Ry, if you're not ready to retire—"

"That's not it. I'm just *really* glad you're here with me today. It's an important day. You were here in the beginning, and you're here at the end, and I'm fucking grateful."

Her sweet face softens as she steps into me, rests her cheek on my chest, and hugs me tight.

"There's nowhere else I'd be. I won't miss it. Go have your meeting."

I press my lips to the top of her head, take a deep breath, and then step away.

"I'll see you in a little bit."

Willow offers me a wide smile and a *wink*, then hurries off to join Aiden and Mac.

Mac may give me shit, but he'll take good care of them while I'm busy with this meeting. As I walk through the facility, fifteen years' worth of memories swamp me. Practices. Injuries and therapy in the medical pavilion. Team meetings. Media conferences.

It was a damn good ride.

I make my way into the conference room next to the owner's office and find everyone already here.

The ownership, led by Barry Jefferson. My coaching team. My trainers.

Everyone that helped me be a success in Seattle is in this room.

Except Andy. He wasn't invited here.

"Cap," Coach says, holding out his hand. They all stand for me, shake my hand, clap me on the back. Mr. Jefferson hugs me, patting me on the back.

These people are an extension of my family.

"I'm so sorry about Ray," Mr. Jefferson says, and I nod in return.

"Thank you."

After we take our seats, I sigh and lean on the table, folding my hands together. "I need to thank you." My eyes move around the room. "All of you. You gave me a life that I never could have dreamed of."

"We didn't *give* you anything," Coach says, his voice as gruff as always. "You fucking earned it, kiddo."

I lick my lips. "I should have reached out to you all myself, rather than letting Andy handle it."

"It's the offseason," Mr. Jefferson reminds me. "And you were dealing with the loss of your father."

These guys get it, but my agent was a prick about it.

"Now," Mr. Jefferson continues, "we would be happy to extend your contract and offer you a fuck ton of money to stay for two more years."

I grin at him. "I appreciate that. I already have a fuck ton of money."

He nods. "I figured you'd say that. I just didn't want you to make a big decision like this while grieving."

"We want to make sure you won't regret it later," Coach adds.

I sit back in the chair and push my fingers through my hair. I'm in my usual suit and tie, which I haven't worn since Ray's funeral. It's not exactly comfortable.

"I was already considering retirement," I admit. "Hockey is a brutal sport, and I'm thirty-five."

"You have to hurt," one of the trainers says with a knowing wince.

"Daily," I confirm. "And I need to work the ranch that my father built. I need to retire before I'm so crippled up from hockey that I can't do that anymore."

"We're not closing the door," Mr. Jefferson says. "You may not play anymore, but we'll include you in alumni games and invite you for special events. I hope you'll consider coming. You are a part of our family."

"I wouldn't miss it. Thank you for including me."

"In addition," Mr. Jefferson continues, and I see Coach's face droop, as if he's sad. "We'll be retiring your number."

That doesn't shock me. In fact, I'd be surprised if they *didn't* do that. But hearing the words puts an ache in my chest.

"Thank you."

"No, thank *you*, for taking us to seven Stanley Cups, winning us two of those, and being a damn good example of what it is to be an elite athlete, on and off the ice. You're extraordinary, James, and I'm fucking pissed that we're losing you," Mr. Jefferson says, as the rest of the room nods in agreement.

"It's been my honor."

I mean every fucking word.

"Let's go to the pressroom," Coach says as we stand. "And get this over with."

We all file into the media room, and I'm surprised to find it's full, with standing room only. As I look to the back, I see my entire team standing there, watching. Even guys who don't live in Seattle during the offseason are here, and it makes the ache in my chest spread.

Christ, I'm going to miss this.

But then my eyes skim farther, and I find Willow smiling at me, tears glistening in her pretty blue eyes, and I know without a doubt that she's where I want to be.

She's where I *need* to be.

There's commotion outside the door we just entered, and I scowl when I see Andy trying to bully his way in, so I excuse myself for a moment and walk out into the hallway.

"What the *fuck*," Andy demands. "You were just going to do all this without me?"

"I don't need you for this. There are no contracts, nothing for you to do."

"I've been by your side for everything, and this is how you pay me back?"

I push the man old enough to be my father against the wall and get into his face. "I don't owe you shit. You made a *lot* of money off me. What you did with it isn't my problem. I don't want you here today. You've shown me over the past couple of months exactly who you are and what you want for me, and I'm done with you, Andy."

I turn to the security guard who was keeping him out of the media room.

"Escort him out."

He nods and reaches for Andy's arm, but Andy jerks it away, his face scarlet with rage as he scowls at me. "Fuck you, James."

"You're not my type."

With that, I return to the room, and everyone quiets down. Mr. Jefferson gestures to the seat next to him.

Rather than standing at a podium today, we're seated across a long table because we're likely to be here for a while, answering questions.

"I'm going to immediately pass this over to Mr. James, so he can make his statement," Mr. Jefferson says.

I look at Willow and clear my throat. She smiles even as she brushes a tear off her pretty cheek. God, she's beautiful in her blue summer dress, her hair falling around her shoulders. She's wearing makeup today, and she's done something to make her lips glossy.

Aiden's next to her, listening raptly, and he's actually holding his aunt's hand.

That's probably one of the reasons she's crying.

"I'll just dive in," I say. "I'm announcing my retirement, effective immediately."

The room erupts with voices. Questions. And so, for the next hour, I talk about why I came to the decision I did, how much I love my team and my teammates. How it's time for me to move on to the next thing.

When it's time to go, I stand to leave, but someone calls out, "Ryker!"

I stop and raise an eyebrow. "Yeah?"

"No wink? Are you already forgetting how you do this?"

There are chuckles, and I give him a crooked smile before my eyes dart to my girl.

"No need to wink today," I tell him. "She's in the room."

And with that, I walk out and wait for my girl to join me. She launches herself into my arms, and I hold her tight, kissing her for all I'm worth.

"Okay, lover boy," Mac says, clapping me on the back. "Let her go for two seconds. There's going to be a party tonight at Sport."

I pull Aiden in for a hug, pound him on the shoulder, and then turn to Mac. "What time?"

"Seven. There will be food. Beer. The usual."

"I'll stay at the condo with Aiden," Willow says, and I scowl down at her.

"Bullshit. You're both coming with me."

"Uh, I'm not taking my kid to a bar, not even for you, Captain."

Mac snorts.

Aiden rolls his eyes.

I cup the back of her neck and lean in to whisper in her ear. "Call me that again in this building, around my team, and I'll find an empty room to fuck you in. You and Aiden are coming tonight. They'll close it down for us, and besides, it's a restaurant. He'll be fine. You know I won't let anything happen to him."

She licks her lips as I pull away.

"We don't want to know," Mac says to Aiden, who just shakes his head.

"So can I go?" Aiden asks, and I lift an eyebrow at my girl.

"Yeah. We're going."

Chapter Seventeen

Willow

Ryker was right. They shut Sport down for the team to celebrate Ryker's retirement tonight. The place is packed full of anyone and everyone associated with the team, and the press was absolutely *not* invited.

I love that the guys can let loose a little bit and enjoy each other without the stress of wondering if something's being recorded or will be reported on.

Mac and Aiden have their heads together. The two of them hit it off right away, and even I can admit that Mac's way cooler than me.

My boy is drinking a soda, and Mac even joined him, ordering an iced tea and then winking at me, letting me know that he won't let anything bad happen tonight, and it made me feel good.

I wish Gideon would get here already.

I check my phone, but there's no message from him. It's a surprise for Ryker that Gid's coming tonight. He tried to make it for the press conference, but he got stuck at work longer than expected, and he's determined to get here for this.

Just when I'm about to call him, I glance to the door and see Gideon stride inside, his serious gaze scanning the room. When he sees me, he grins and saunters my way.

"Hey, handsome." I hug him close, and suddenly Aiden's here, too, getting in on the Gideon action.

Gid raises an eyebrow at me in a silent question. *Is this the same kid?*

I just smile and then look around for Ryker, who's laughing with his goalie and a coach. Before Ry can see us, I gesture for Gid to bend down so I can whisper in his ear.

"What's up?" he asks.

"I need to tell you, in person, before everything else, that Ryker and I are . . . um . . . together."

His eyes narrow on me. "Are you okay?"

"Never better."

"And he's okay?"

"Seems to be."

He turns to Aiden. "How about you?"

"It's gross, and fine, and I don't think about it."

"If he hurts you—"

"I already threatened him," Aiden says with a shrug. "He's been warned."

Gid's lips twitch up into a half grin. "As long as we understand each other. Where the fuck is he?"

I point to the other end of the bar just as Ry's eyes scan down, looking for me, and when he sees Gideon, his eyes widen, and he hurries over, wraps his brother in a hug, and starts to laugh.

"You're here!"

"Tried to get here for the announcement," Gid says. "Sorry that I didn't make it. I watched, though."

"You're here now," Ry says just before Gideon punches him in the stomach. "What the fuck was that for?"

"For hitting on my sister," Gideon says. "Don't fuck it up. Now, I need a beer."

Ry's eyes shift to mine, and I shrug. "Surprise."

Gideon is greeted the same way I was. With happy hugs and handshakes, and plenty of reminiscing.

My eyes find Ryker again. He's not in a suit tonight. He's in dark jeans and a blue button-down with the sleeves rolled halfway to his elbows, showing off the tattoos on that arm. The collar is unbuttoned, and when he swallows his beer, his throat works, making me squeeze my thighs together.

Literally everything the man does is a turn-on.

There are puck bunnies running around here. They flit around the room. Some are already attached to the single players, flirting outrageously.

There's been one that hovers around Ry, watching him, *wanting him*.

I'm not jealous of her, because he only has eyes for me, but I keep my eye on her.

"How you doin', baby?" Ryker asks as he slips his arm around my waist and leans down to kiss my temple.

"I'm great." I smile up at him and sip my own soda. As long as I have my kid with me, I won't drink alcohol. "It's good to see everyone."

He nods but suddenly looks so serious.

"What's wrong?"

"You got Gid here."

"I'm kind of surprised you didn't invite him yourself. He's your brother, Ry. He's been around for as much of this as I have."

"He's been working a lot."

I snort. "Whatever. He's happy to be here. Oh, look, a puck bunny has taken a liking to him. Shocker."

We glance over to see Gideon listening to something a woman is whispering in his ear. He doesn't smile. Gideon doesn't give his smiles away easily, unlike Ry, who smirks at the drop of a hat.

But he does widen his eyes just a smidge, and that makes me giggle.

"Wonder what she said."

"We probably don't want to know," Ryker replies.

"That one over there has her eye on you," I say, gesturing to the brunette with my chin.

Ry doesn't even look her way. With his eyes on mine, he leans into me. "Who the fuck cares, baby?"

"Not me. Just wondering if she's a problem."

"If she's bothering you, I'll have her escorted out. This party isn't for her."

Gripping his shirt in my fist, I pull him down so I can kiss him, and he sinks right into me, not giving two fucks who sees. His hands plunge into my hair, and he devours my mouth, right here in the middle of his party.

"Staking your claim?" he asks against my lips when he comes up for air.

"Just kissing my man."

His eyes darken, and he's about to say something, but we're interrupted.

"Cap! Come tell these assholes that I'm right. We totally beat Denver at home three years ago, when . . ."

Ryker lifts an eyebrow, silently asking me if it's okay if he leaves me here, and I nod.

"Go."

Taking a moment, I glance around. Gideon's no longer talking to the woman who was on his arm. He's talking with a couple of Ry's teammates.

Aiden and Mac are laughing at something on Mac's phone.

Ryker has a group of guys around him listening raptly as he tells a story.

This is *so fun*. I've missed nights like this. We used to do this all the time in the beginning of Ry's career, so I'm relieved that we're here tonight. It feels like old times, back when things were simpler.

The bartender passes me another soda and gives me a smile before moving on to the next customer. I didn't even ask for it, but he must have noticed that my glass was almost empty.

I realize, since I had two glasses before this, that I seriously need to use the restroom, so I set my drink next to Aiden.

"Hey, buddy, watch this for me, okay? I'm headed to the restroom."

"By yourself?" he asks, and it sounds like he's *worried about me*. Is this *my* kid?

"It's right there." I point to the hallway not even twenty feet away. "I'll be right back."

"If you're not back in five minutes, I'm coming after you," he says. "There's a bunch of guys around who have been drinking."

"She's good," Mac assures my nephew, his face not joking now. "No one will hurt her. We're good people *and* she's Cap's girl. Nobody here would dare."

She's Cap's girl.

Damn right I am.

With a reassuring pat on Aiden's back, I walk to the restroom. *Of freaking course* the bitch who's had her eye on Ry all night is in here.

Because I couldn't have better timing.

Her eyes skim down my body as I walk into a stall to do my business. When I cross to the sink to wash my hands, she's still here, but now she's leaning against the sink, her arms crossed, waiting for me.

"He's a good lay, right?" she asks. "Been there, done that."

I don't give her a reaction. Nothing about this surprises me. My man has been a chick magnet all his life. He's gorgeous and charismatic, and I know that he was not celibate before he and I got together.

Without saying a word, I dry my hands. When I turn to walk away, this bitch gets in my way.

"I'm talking to you," she says.

"I don't have anything to say to you."

"You think that just because you have his attention *for now* that you're better than me?"

"I don't have anything—"

"He'll cast you off," she spits at me. "He'll fuck you sideways and then won't give you the time of day."

"I'm sorry that he hurt your feelings." I cross my arms over my chest, and I don't back down. Finally, she spins on her heel and marches away without another word.

Part of me feels bad for her. I understand how it feels to pine after Ryker James. But it's not my fault that he doesn't want her.

I exit the bathroom, but before I can leave the hallway, I'm cornered.

What in the hell is up with these people?

"Well, aren't you a pretty one?"

Looking up into sinister green eyes, I feel my heart go still. The jealous woman I can handle.

A man well over six feet tall with muscles for days and evil in his eyes? This could get dicey.

"Excuse me."

"Now, don't be like that," he says and drags his knuckles down my cheek, but I yank my head away from his touch. "I just wanted to get a closer look at the great Ryker James's whore."

Who the fuck is this guy?

"Move." My voice is hard and leaves no room for argument, but he just smiles at me.

"You're adorable when you're angry. I bet you fuck good when you're all worked up, too, don't you?"

"Get away from her."

At the sound of Aiden's voice, this asshole simply turns his head and chuckles.

"And what are *you* going to do about it, kid?"

My sweet kiddo yanks this asshole off me and punches him in the jaw, sending him back against the opposite wall.

"Aiden!"

"I've got this, baby."

Ryker and Gideon rush past me. The asshole has his fist cocked back to hit Aiden, but Ryker hits him first, and Mac's there to pull Aiden back, out of the line of fire, while Ry and Gid proceed to beat the man senseless.

Holy shit.

Chapter Eighteen

Ryker

Patterson.

My fist connects with his nose, sending blood down his chin, as we push him against the opposite wall.

"You motherfucker," Gideon growls as he puts pressure on Patterson's windpipe. "You fucked with the wrong girl."

"You touched what's mine," I add and slap him across the face, humiliating him as I sense more teammates huddling around the end of the hall. Gideon vibrates with fury, but he lets me get the hits in.

"She was begging me to fuck her," Patterson wheezes out, barely able to speak thanks to the way Gid's holding his neck.

I'm going to kill him.

"Hey," Mac says in my ear, patting my shoulder. "Go comfort your girl and your kid. I've got this."

"I'll ruin you," I say in Patterson's face. "Your career is fucking over."

Knowing that Mac and Gid will take care of the piece of shit, and needing to see that Wills and Aiden are okay, I hurry over and pull them both to me.

"Are you okay? Did he hurt you?"

"Just wanted to scare me," Wills says, shaking her head, but her hand trembles as she lifts it to my face. "And mostly he pissed me off. Then, Aiden came to my rescue."

I turn to the teenager, and without a second thought, I kiss him on the head. "Good man. I'm proud of you."

"You're a worthless piece of shit," Patterson spits out at Aiden as he walks past, and I let them both go, then yank Patterson out of Mac's grip and punch him in the nose again.

"Say one more word to my kid, and I'll fucking end you."

"Come on," Mac says, picking Patterson up off the floor. "Let's get you out of here before I let Cap murder your dumb ass."

Other teammates step in to help Mac, and Gideon turns to us.

"Is everyone okay?" he asks.

"We're fine. Well, that was . . . exciting," Willow says with a little laugh. "It's not a party until someone gets a broken nose."

"Hockey," Aiden says with a shrug. "It happens."

How did I get so lucky?

"I'll take you both home."

"Absolutely not," Willow says, shaking her head. "Gideon just got here, and it's a party to celebrate *you*. We're having fun, and now that the asshole is gone, we can resume having fun. We're not going to let that ruin tonight. He didn't hurt me."

I search her eyes, looking for any indication that she's just putting on a brave face, but she smiles, and it's genuine.

"If you're sure."

"I'll buy a round of sodas," Aiden says, puffing out his chest. "I've been earning a shit ton of money this summer."

"It's an open bar, squirt," Gideon says, pulling Aiden into a headlock.

"Even better," Aiden says with a laugh as they head over to the bar.

I pull Willow against me and hug her tight. "Are you really okay, sweetheart?"

"Yep. He wanted to scare me because he doesn't like you. Who is that asshole?"

"Patterson. He's only been on the team for about three years, and he thought that because he was a college hotshot, he'd come in here, be captain, and rule the team."

"Oh, so he's young and stupid."

"Very. He doesn't like to be told what to do. I don't care. I heard today that now that I'm gone, he still won't be captain."

She looks up at me with those gorgeous blue eyes. "Who will?"

"Mac." I grin and kiss her forehead. "I'm sorry he took his shit out on you."

"I had a bunch of strong men come to my rescue. But I was about to use the self-defense moves that Gideon taught me. Stomp his foot, knee him in the balls, hand to the nose."

"That's my strong girl." With my arm slung around her shoulders, I lead Wills back out to the party. The woman who was flirting with Gideon earlier is back at it, sitting in his lap, now, whispering in his ear.

His hands are *not* on her. And she must say something that he definitely doesn't like, because he respectfully takes her by the waist, lifts her off his lap, and sets her aside.

Her face is mutinous as she storms away.

"Breaking hearts, as usual," I say as I move up beside him.

"These girls get bolder and bolder," he says, shaking his head.

"Or we're getting older and older."

He scoffs, but he doesn't deny it.

Ten years ago, we were all about this scene. Different girls, lots of booze. Okay, too many girls and too much fucking booze.

But now, all I want is the woman at my side. She checks every box for me, and I can't wait to get her home later. To curl up with her, hold her.

Love her.

Because shit, am I ever in love with her.

"Cap!" Mac's waving me down from across the table. I tip up an eyebrow. "Three on three tomorrow at the ice house."

The idea of being on the ice again with some of my teammates sends a surge of energy through me.

"You're on. Prepare to have your ass handed to you."

"Fuck that. We're on the same team."

I smirk at him and then glance over at Aiden. "You wanna play?"

His eyes widen in alarm. "What? No. I can't."

"Why not? You know how, right?"

"I mean, yeah. Sure. But I'm no pro or anything."

"It's a scrimmage, not the Stanley Cup." I ruffle his hair. "You'll play."

I glance down and see Willow blinking fast, trying not to cry.

"You're such a softy, Trouble."

"You should play," Aiden says to Gideon as we finish up our breakfast at the ice house. It's midmorning, because after getting home last night well past midnight, no one wanted to get up early to hit the ice. Aiden stuffs an entire slice of bacon in his mouth. "Don't be a pu—er, a wimp, Gid."

Aiden side-eyes his aunt.

Gideon's eyes narrow on the kid. Most people would be terrified of that look.

Not our boy.

Aiden grins.

"Are you scared, man?" Aiden shrugs a shoulder. "I get it. You probably haven't skated in a long time. Maybe you're worried that you'll look like a fool out there, with the rest of us being awesome."

I bark out a laugh, unable to hold it in. Aiden is a *shit talker*. I can't wait to see how he does on the ice today, because if he's good, he'd make an excellent hockey player.

"I don't want to hurt you," Gideon finally replies, holding Aiden's gaze as he takes a bite of his protein waffle.

Who the fuck eats protein waffles on vacation?

Gideon James, that's who.

"As if you could," Aiden scoffs, and then he laughs and leans over to high-five Gid, who's smiling at the kid now. "Come on. It'll be fun."

"Someone has to sit with Willow," Gideon replies. "It's our thing. We sit and watch."

"I can sit alone," Willow offers, but then Gideon's work phone is ringing, and he's scowling.

"Fuck my life," he mutters as he answers and then holds the device to his ear. "James." His brows lower. "When? How many?" His whole body goes perfectly still. "Say that again."

"Shit," Willow whispers, and her hand drops under the table to grasp my leg. "He's going to leave."

Gideon's stormy eyes have gone ice cold, his face hard. The fun-loving brother from a moment ago is gone, and in his place is quite literally a killer.

That look even gives me pause.

"ETA is seven hours," he says and then ends the call.

"You're leaving," Aiden says, sounding disappointed.

"It seems Blackbird is . . . well, yeah. I have to go." He shovels in the last of his waffle.

"Twelve hours was not long enough," Willow says, and the sadness in her voice has me leaning over to kiss her head. "The Three Amigos need more time than that."

"I know." He sighs and drinks his juice as he taps on his screen, I assume scheduling a flight back to Washington. "I'm sorry, you guys."

"I'm grateful that you came at all." I stand when he does and circle the table so I can hug him.

Once upon a time, I hated his guts. We used to beat the shit out of each other.

I love it here on the ranch more than I thought I would. It's only been a month, and the summer is close to being over, and I hope with everything in me that we don't have to go back to hell house.

Because now that we've been here, with these people and animals and the clean air, I can't imagine going anywhere else. I can't imagine being without them.

We find out tomorrow if we get to stay. I know that Deb and Ray have petitioned the state to keep us here. They've been honest with us every day.

And that night, last week, when they asked us if we would like to stay permanently? Well, it felt like I was kicked in the stomach.

But in a good way.

And later that night, I heard Gideon sniffle up in his bunk. And maybe I had a hard time keeping the tears away too.

Because this is more than I ever dreamed of.

I can't sleep, so I walk outside the bunkhouse to sit on the back porch and listen to the crickets and watch the stars.

But when I get out there, I realize that I'm not alone.

Gideon's already sitting out here.

"Sorry," I mumble when he turns to me in surprise. "Didn't know you were out here."

"Whatever," he says, lifting his shoulder. "You can sit if you want."

It's been kind of decent to have the ceasefire between us since we both met Willow. She's a firecracker, and she doesn't take any of our shit. If we start to fight, she tells us to get over it.

And neither of us wants to disappoint her.

We haven't thrown a punch since we got here, and that's gotta be a record of some kind.

"Do you think they'll let us stay?" Gid asks, his voice quiet in the dark.

"I dunno. I'm not sure how any of that works." I let out a breath, and we both watch an owl swoop overhead, looking for a midnight snack. "I don't see why not. No one's going to come looking for me. My mom's dead, and I don't have any other family."

Gideon's quiet for a minute. He never says too much. "No one's coming for me either. Deb and Ray are decent."

"Yeah."

"And everyone else seems good too."

I nod in agreement. "They're good."

He glances my way, and I meet his gaze, my brown to his blue. "If they keep us, that will make us brothers."

I thought of that, too, but I didn't know if I should say something. "I guess so, yeah."

He doesn't even blink, he just holds my gaze, his face so serious that I wish he'd tell me what's going on in his head.

"If we're brothers, we can't keep fucking with each other, because that'll mean that we have to have each other's backs. If you're my brother, I won't let anyone dick with you."

I nod slowly. "Same goes, I guess. I mean, you'll probably still piss me off all the time, but I'm the only one that gets to smack you around."

His lips twitch in the corners. "I want to stay."

"Me too." I let out a breath and watch that owl again. "I'm so sick of being scared, of being hungry, of not fitting in anywhere. This fits, you know?"

"Yeah. It fits. But Ry?"

I lift an eyebrow.

"Even if they don't let us stay, I think you're okay. I'd still let you be my brother."

I can't talk over the lump in my throat. I just hold my fist out for his, and he bumps it. We sit in silence for two more hours, taking in the night around us, lost in our thoughts.

And the next day, we get the news that we can stay. It was the best day of my life.

Now he's my best friend. My brother in every way that matters, including in our last name. And I miss the fuck out of him.

"Be careful," I tell him.

"Every day," he confirms. "I'll go back to your penthouse to grab my shit and then straight to the airport."

"Gid." Willow nibbles on her lower lip. "Can't someone else deal with that so you can be here for another day?"

Gideon wraps his arms around her and murmurs something in her ear that I can't hear, but it has her sagging against him, and she nods.

"I know," she says and smiles up at him. "Go be badass, then. Call me when you get there."

"You're such a mother hen," he tells her, and Aiden nods.

"Now you know what I live with," Aiden says, earning a scowl from his aunt. "Not that I mind or anything."

"Right, you brat." She ruffles his hair.

Gideon heads out, and I lead Aiden and Willow to the rink.

"Take him to the locker room," she says with a knowing nod. "I'll be fine over here. We're on this rink?"

"Yep. We'll be out in about fifteen or so."

"Take your time."

As she wanders out to find a seat, I take Aiden into the team's special locker room, and his jaw drops.

"Wow," he says.

It's the offseason, so it's pretty empty in here right now. My name is still above my locker, and I'm glad they haven't taken it down quite yet.

Mac, Spencer, and two more of my teammates are getting dressed, and between all of us, we get Aiden suited up in one of my jerseys and find him skates that fit him.

He looks nervous as fuck as he takes his stick and follows me out of the locker room.

"We're just playing around, kid," Mac assures him. "There's no right and wrong. Just have fun."

"Says the guy making millions to have fun," Aiden says with a smirk.

"Oh, hey," I tell Aiden. "Since I have you alone, I need to tell you that I'm taking your aunt out on a real date tonight, so you'll be at the penthouse by yourself."

I'm going to wine and dine her, romance her.

Sink inside her.

And I can't fucking wait.

"What am I, chopped liver?" Mac asks.

"Why are you coming to my penthouse?" I ask him.

"Because we're playing video games. Duh." Mac looks at me like I'm stupid, and Aiden laughs.

"It makes sense that you're bonding with the high school kid." I shake my head at him.

"He's cooler than most of the people I know," Mac replies.

I'm grateful to him for making my boy feel welcome and included. He doesn't have to do that. But Mac's good people.

"Okay, here's how this is gonna go," Spencer says as we all take the ice. I keep my eyes on Aiden, but he skates right out there, as if he does this every day. No wobble in sight.

Spencer lays out the rules, and I glance toward Willow, who grins right at me.

It's damn good to see her in the stands again. Wearing my sweater. Smiling at me.

My girl.

"Ready?" Mac asks us as we line up on the ice.

"Let's smash 'em," Aiden says, making me laugh.

The kid is good. He's out of practice, but he has an instinct for the puck, and he's perfect on his skates. Fast. And once we started playing, it was like he forgot to be nervous.

"I'm calling him the smasher," Mac says after I score a goal. "Jesus, Aiden, do you want a fucking job? We'll take you today."

I skate past Wills, and I pause by the glass to blow her a kiss.

"Badass," she yells out at me, and I wink at her before joining the others, and then we're flying down the ice again, and this time, Aiden scores a point.

"I'll take that job," Aiden says, raising his stick over his head as he does a little dance.

I don't remember the last time I had this much fun on the ice.

Chapter Nineteen

Willow

Ryker James, my man, the one who makes me laugh and sigh and turns me on with just a look, had a dress delivered to the penthouse. For me. It was waiting on the bed in the primary suite when I got home after the scrimmage.

He bought me a dress. And shoes. The kind with red soles.

How in the hell did he manage to do that? We've been on the go, pretty much nonstop, since we got to Seattle just yesterday morning.

Is he some sort of magician?

The man himself walks into the bedroom, and his eyes immediately find me. His lips tip up in the cocky smile I love so much.

"Did you have fun today?" he asks me.

"Of course I did. The question is, did *you* have a good day?"

Ry nods, watching me. "Being on the ice with the guys was great, and Aiden's a fucking natural. The fact that you didn't force him to play junior hockey is mind boggling."

"You try to force a teenager to do pretty much anything he doesn't want to do." I shift on my feet and bite my lower lip.

"What's wrong, Trouble?"

"Nothing's wrong. It's been really good to see Aiden relax and laugh. To be comfortable around your friends. Thank you for including him."

For referring to him as your kid. I'm shocked I didn't lose it and crumple into a blubbering mess as soon as Ry said that.

He narrows his eyes on me.

"Aiden belongs wherever we are, sweetheart."

Swoon.

I chuckle and tuck my hair behind my ear. "I always had a crush on you, but if I'd known just how dreamy you can be, I would have embarrassed myself *years* ago."

He slowly walks to me and ghosts his knuckles down my cheek.

"Always?" He tips his head to the side as his eyes roam my face.

"Pretty much."

"Fuck, was I just blind? Or stupid."

I smirk. "I think things worked out the way they were supposed to. Now, I have another question for you."

He kisses my forehead, sending little sizzles of electricity down my body. "Ask, baby."

"How did you do this?" I point to the dress and shoebox on the bed.

"I made some calls," he replies with a shrug, as if it's nothing at all.

"I could have brought something from home if you'd given me a heads-up."

He shakes his head. "I wanted you to have something new. And I wanted it to come from me."

"Thank you."

He brushes my hair back over my shoulder, and there are more sizzles.

"You're so fucking beautiful, you take my breath away."

Hello, butterflies. Welcome to the party.

"I haven't even gotten ready yet." My hands glide up his T-shirt-covered chest and then into the thick dark hair at the nape of his neck.

"Doesn't matter." He presses his lips to my forehead again and then moves them down to my lips for a soft kiss.

"When are we leaving?"

He checks his watch. "In about an hour."

I feel my eyes widen as I gape up at him. "An *hour*? Ryker, I need more than that to get ready."

"No, you don't. Just put the dress on, and you're good to go. I told you, you're fucking gorgeous just like this."

I blink at him. "I need a shower. A full hair-and-makeup situation. I don't know where we're going, but if I'm wearing that LBD, I need to get *ready*."

His eyebrows climb. "LBD?"

"Little black dress." I boost up on my toes so I can kiss his chin. "Now, get out of here so I can get sexified."

"Baby, I'll take you against that wall right now to prove how goddamn *sexified* you already are."

I laugh and bat at him to make him move. "Don't distract me. I'm in a time crunch. It's a good thing I brought all my makeup with me. What are you wearing?"

He smirks at me. "A suit."

"See? I need to get ready. Go away."

"I have to get ready too."

I roll my eyes and start stripping out of the Blizzard sweatshirt and jeans that I wore to the rink earlier. "It takes you twenty minutes to get ready."

He's watching me intently, those dark eyes molten as they journey down my body.

"I don't have time to give you a show, Ry."

He doesn't walk away, and I can't help but roll my eyes as I step out of my jeans and then saunter into the bathroom so I can get the shower started.

"Need help in there?" he asks.

"No. Seriously, I don't have time to waste here."

"Being inside you is never a waste, sweetheart."

Jesus, the things he says should be inside naughty greeting cards.

Exactly fifty-eight minutes later, I finish zipping up the back of the dress and turn to look in the mirror.

I still don't know what kind of sorcery this man had to work, but the dress and shoes fit perfectly.

The dress is off the shoulder and form fitting through the bodice, with a loose skirt that hits me right at the knee. Add in the heels, and the pop of red on my lips, and I'm feeling damn pleased with myself.

With the black clutch that he also got me in my hands, I stride out of the bedroom and find Aiden, Mac, and Ryker standing in the kitchen, talking.

"Whoa," Aiden says when he sees me.

Mac grins.

Ryker turns around, and his jaw fucking drops.

Mission accomplished.

He's so damn handsome in an all-black suit, with a black shirt and tie, with his hair styled. He looks like he belongs on the cover of a freaking magazine.

"I guess we're staying home," he says as he walks toward me.

"Why?"

His hands slide around my waist and down to my ass.

"Because men are going to be checking out what's mine all goddamn night, and I'll get arrested for homicide."

"Easy, killer." I run my hand down his tie and breathe him in. He smells amazing. "You're so handsome, Ry."

"They're gross," I hear Aiden say to Mac, and I chuckle.

"You're still taking me out, because I buffed and polished myself within an inch of my life, within the allotted time frame, and now I'm excited to go."

"It was worth every minute, but there's something missing."

"Did I forget mascara again?"

Ry laughs and shakes his head.

"What is it?"

He kisses my forehead and pulls something out of his pocket, and my breath catches.

It's a blue box. The kind that comes with a white bow and has *Tiffany* written on the top.

"Ry, you don't have to buy me things."

"I like buying you things." He nudges the box toward me. "Open it, Trouble."

I tug on the bow and then open the box and feel my heart pound at the sight of the gorgeous diamond earrings tucked inside.

"Okay, these are too beautiful to pass up. I'm keeping them."

He chuckles and takes one out of the box so he can affix it to my ear. "They're perfect for you."

They're pear-shaped diamonds, easily a couple of carats each, and as he fastens the second earring, I can't help but think that they'd be perfect for *anyone*.

"Thank you."

He kisses me, careful not to smear my lipstick, and then I hear Mac say, "Turn and smile at the camera. You guys got all gussied up—we need a picture."

After posing for a few quick pictures, Ry leads me to the elevator.

"Come on, I have to show my girl off tonight."

"Where are we going, anyway?" I stop short and hold up a finger. "Hold that thought. Aiden?"

I walk back into the common area and see Aiden poke his head up over the couch.

"Yeah?"

"Be good." I smile at him. "It's my job to say that, you know."

"I think I need to say that to *you*," he retorts, making Mac laugh his ass off.

"I raised a smart-ass," I say to Ry as I walk back to the elevator. "Okay, now where are we going?"

"I should probably warn you," Ryker replies as he presses the button for the parking garage. "About six months ago, I bought tickets to this charity dinner thing."

"And that's where we're going?"

He nods.

"What's the charity?"

"I forget the exact organization, but it's for kids."

I narrow my eyes at him. "I don't buy that. What's it for, Ry?"

"It benefits foster kids."

My heart softens even more.

My God, I'm in love with this man.

"Then I'm so glad we're in town for it. Is it one of those silent auction, fancy-dinner situations?"

"No auction." He clears his throat. "It's a mini concert."

The doors open, and he leads me to his sporty little Porsche, opens the door for me, and helps me into it before rounding the hood to the driver's side.

"It's a benefit concert? Why are we all dressed up, Ry? Concerts are casual."

His lips tip up into a smile.

"This one is different. It's held at someone's home."

I blink at him.

"Okay, start talking, James. What in the hell is going on?"

It's a beautiful summer night in Seattle as Ry pulls out of the parking garage and merges onto the freeway.

"So you know who Will Montgomery is?"

I blink at him. "The Super Bowl–winning football player? Of course."

"He's a good guy. Anyway, his family runs this charity. Apparently, it's close to their hearts, and you know that if it's for foster kids, I'll jump on board. Will's nephew is married to Sidney Sterling."

My mouth goes dry. "Sidney Sterling, the megastar who sells out arenas all over the world."

"That's the one." He reaches over and slides his hand up my thigh, under the hem of my dress, caressing my skin. "Christ, you look gorgeous tonight. I'm tempted to pull over and fuck you here in my car."

"Ry, there's no room for sex in this car. Now, focus. Are you telling me that we're going to a Sidney Sterling concert? Not only are her shows sold out, but the resale tickets go for *thousands*."

He smirks over at me. "You're cute."

"Ryker."

"First of all, I could pull you over onto my lap and fuck you just fine, sweetheart. I'll prove it to you before the night is over. Second, we're going to a private residence on the cliffs for dinner and a private Sidney Sterling concert."

My mouth is hanging open, but I don't really care. "How many tickets were sold?"

"One hundred."

"How much were the tickets?"

He flicks his gaze over to me and then back to the road.

"How much were they, Captain?"

His jaw flexes. "A hundred grand."

"*A hundred fucking grand?* Each?"

"Each, Wills."

My heart is going to simply bounce right out of my chest.

"Do I want to know whose house we're going to? If you say Oprah, I will have a heart attack, Ryker. I'm not kidding."

"Not Oprah." He's laughing now, and I want to sock him in the nose. "Leo Nash."

I'm certain I've heard him wrong.

"Leo, Grammy winner, lead singer of the iconic rock band Nash. That one?"

"He's the only one I'm aware of."

"OH MY GOD! I would have had hair-and-makeup people come to me, Ryker!"

"Why? You're fucking stunning. You look amazing. Listen, I know this could get boring—"

"Boring?"

"—and as soon as you're ready to go, you just tell me, and I'll whisk you out of there."

"You think it's going to be boring?"

He smiles that huge, full-on smile that I love so much and eases off the freeway onto an exit ramp. "I love it when you get all worked up, Trouble."

"I'll hand it to you. When you decide to surprise a girl, you go all out."

"I try."

He's still chuckling when he turns onto a driveway and shows his tickets to the security guard at the gate. We're given instructions on where to park, and before I know it, I'm walking around a massive stone house to an area that looks like something out of my wildest dreams.

A rich-people dream.

Puget Sound is in the background, calm and blue as the sun sets behind it. Tables are covered in pretty pink linens and place settings, and people are already seated and talking, or wandering around, mingling.

Servers walk through with trays of champagne, and I can't ignore the little stage set up with instruments and microphones, and *I am so out of my element.*

But there's no time to be shy, because Ryker's recognized immediately, and we're drawn into conversations about his retirement.

I'm surprised by how many people offer condolences about Ray.

And Ryker never leaves my side.

"Ryker." Will Montgomery himself approaches us, his arm wrapped around a pretty redhead—I assume his wife—and shakes Ry's hand. "Congratulations on your retirement. I wasn't expecting that. What are your plans now? Aside from what we're doing, of course."

What are they doing?

"I have a ranch in Montana that needs my attention," Ry replies and glances down at me. "And excuse my manners. This is Willow, my girlfriend."

"Hello." I shake Will's hand.

"My wife, Meg," he says, and I shake her hand too.

"I'm a fan," I tell him unapologetically. "You lead in and continue to hold the record for all-time passing yards, passing touchdowns at *fifty-two* in one season, and, well. I could go on, but you already know your stats."

Will's smile spreads over his face, and Ryker squeezes my hand.

"Great, his head's about to get really big," Meg says, shaking her head with an amused grin.

"I like your girlfriend, Ry."

"I do too," Ryker says with a smile in his voice. "Her mind is a steel trap for stats."

"So what made you start this particular organization?" I ask Will, who smiles at his wife.

"That's on me," she says, pushing her hair over her shoulder. "I was a foster kid. Leo was actually in some of the same homes as me. Anyway, it can really suck, and we're in a position to help. So we help."

"And now, with Ryker joining us, we'll be able to help more," Will says, and my eyes fly up to Ryker, who's frowning down at his untouched glass of champagne.

"It's a big deal," Meg adds, and I'm so damn proud of my man, I let go of his hand and loop my arms around him.

"I'm proud of you."

He kisses the top of my head. "I'll tell you more later."

"I'll hold you to that."

"We have to go welcome everyone," Meg says and smiles at me. "It's really nice to meet you."

"Same here. Thanks for doing this. I love it."

Ry and I stay standing where we are as Will and Meg take the little stage and Will reaches for the microphone.

"Hello, everyone," he says, catching the crowd's attention. "I wanted to take a moment before dinner starts to say thank you for being here, and for supporting our Foundation for Foster Kids. We sold every single ticket for this party, and I know it's not because I'm pretty to look at."

That gets him some laughs.

"I know you're here for Sid, and we'll bring her out in a bit. The ten million dollars that we raised here tonight is going to go a long way toward making some kids' lives better. For that, I am deeply grateful. Now, before we go, I wanted to quickly introduce you to my new cochair of the organization, Ryker James."

Everyone turns to look at Ry, who smiles and gives them a wave. He kisses my temple and then joins Will on the stage.

"Thank you," he says. "I'm proud to be here. I know what it feels like to be a kid without any options, and if I didn't have the adoptive parents who took me in when they did, I likely wouldn't be here, at this fancy party, hanging out with the likes of all of you."

I swallow hard and brush a tear aside.

"So it's an honor to help this organization in any way I can. And yes, we raised ten million dollars tonight, but we're always taking donations."

He winks as everyone laughs, and then steps aside, and Will takes over again.

"Have fun tonight, everyone," Will says, and then Ryker is back at my side.

"We have *so much* to talk about later," I say to him before cupping his cheek and kissing him sweetly. "You're incredible."

He just smiles, and we go back to mingling.

I can't believe it, but as time passes, I actually loosen up. Even though I'm surrounded by movie stars and elite athletes and celebrities that I never thought in a million years I'd ever be in a room with.

Is that Vaughn Barrymore, the actor?

Holy shit.

Dinner is delicious, and then I really need to find a restroom.

"I'll be back," I say to Ry, who frowns down at me.

"Where are you off to, Trouble?"

"Restroom."

"I'll go with you."

I shake my head at him. "I'm fine."

"I'm not." He holds my hand and asks for directions, and then he's tugging me inside the house, and we find the powder room that guests are welcome to use.

"I'll be right out."

I've just washed my hands and am drying them when the door opens. Ry slips in and then shuts and locks it behind him.

"I don't want to watch you pee, Ry."

His lips quirk up, and then he gestures to my clutch. "Do you have lipstick in there?"

"Sure, I—"

But I can't get another word out because his lips are on mine, and my back is against the wall.

"I want my hands in your hair," he murmurs against me, "but I won't mess you up. Everything else is fair game. Got it?"

"Christ, Ry, everyone is *right there.*"

"Then you'd better be quiet. Can you do that for me? Can you be a good fucking girl and stay quiet while I fuck you like I own you in here?"

Holy shit.

"Ry."

He grips my face and makes me look at him. "Answer me."

"Uh, yeah. I can stay quiet."

He brushes his lips over mine. "Good. You're so fucking incredible, Wills. Out there talking with those people like you were born for it, your sexy-as-fuck voice seducing me all damn night as you walk around in this dress, with those shoes."

"You bought them," I remind him, and he grins against my skin as he kisses down my neck.

"And I'm damn proud of myself for it." He reaches under the hem of my dress and works my underwear down my legs, brings them up to his nose and breathes in deep. "These are already wet."

I can't even reply. This might be the sexiest moment of my life.

Ryker unfastens his pants and pulls his already-hard cock out, then picks me up, braces me against the wall, and plunges right inside me.

"I'd love to get on my knees and eat you," he growls against my lips. "To worship you the way you should be right now, but we don't have time, and if I don't feel your sweet little pussy wrapped around me, I might go out of my mind."

I tip my head forward and bite his shoulder, trying to keep my screams inside.

"Good girl. Fuck, you take me so well, Wills."

"Oh my God," I moan against him, already so close to coming.

Suddenly, there are voices outside the door, and my head whips up and my gaze locks on his.

He presses his hand to my mouth and slowly shakes his head as he continues to pound into me on long, hard thrusts.

"Shh," he whispers and then leans in to press his lips to my ear. He grinds the base of his cock against my clit. "Come for me, baby."

I whimper and then quiver around him in a spectacular climax, and he follows me right over, grunting as he grinds into me.

"Shit," I whisper.

"Did I hurt you?"

I chuckle. "No. Holy fuck, Ry."

With a satisfied smirk, he lowers me to my feet, my legs shaky and weak, and then quickly cleans me up the best he can, and I fix my makeup. Aside from flushed cheeks, I don't look any worse for wear.

"I need my panties back."

"Not a chance, sweetheart."

"Ryker."

"Ready?"

I glare at him, but he just smiles, opens the door, and when he sees the coast is clear, leads me back to our table.

"Look, Trouble," he says, "we're just in time for the concert."

"You're a menace, Captain."

"Never claimed otherwise." He kisses my temple as we sit, and then the evening turns completely surreal as Sidney herself takes the stage and starts to sing my favorite song of hers, "Life in the Slow Lane."

The woman plays for almost two hours. Leo Nash joins her for a couple of duets, which feels like a dream.

And when it's all over and we're back in the car, my gaze turns to my man.

I've known him more than half my life.

And yet I forget that there's this side to him. This wealthy, celebrity, elite-athlete side that I so rarely ever got to see. By the time he was über rich and famous, I had a little boy at home to tend to, and Ryker was still just my best friend that I spoke to on the phone all the time.

"Who were you supposed to take to this tonight?"

Ry's gaze whips to mine, and he scowls. "What?"

"You bought two tickets six months ago, Ry. Who did you plan to bring with you? It's okay—I know there were plenty of women before me. Neither of us was a virgin."

But man, I hate thinking that he originally had another date lined up for tonight. I don't want to think about him with anyone else. But did he buy these earrings six months ago too? Were they meant for someone else?

He blows out a breath. "Do I have to fuck you again already, in this car, to remind you just how goddamn obsessed I am with you, Wills?"

"I'm not doubting that. It's just a question."

"I'm not even going to think about any asshole who's had his dick inside you before me because I'll just want to track him down and make him choke on it."

"Ry—"

"But to answer your question, I was hoping Gid would come with me." He shrugs. "He donates to this organization, too, and I thought I'd bribe him into coming out for it. But it worked out well, because I had you with me, and you were amazing tonight."

His praise makes me smile.

So no. The earrings are just for me.

"Gideon wouldn't look as good in these diamonds as I do."

He smirks and kisses the back of my hand.

"But back to what you said about our pasts. I'm not going to write you a list of all the women I fucked," he continues, and my smile fades. "You don't want to know that, Wills."

"No. I don't want to know that. And I don't want you to do that either."

"Good. I don't want to know about your past either. As long as we're both healthy and safe, and on the same page, we're fine."

"Agreed."

"But I will make one thing crystal fucking clear right now, and I want you to listen to every word I'm about to say."

I link my fingers in his and hold on to him. "I'm listening."

"It doesn't fucking matter who was here before. For either of us. Because there will be no one else." I feel my jaw drop for the second time tonight, and he glances my way. "You're mine. You're all I see. You're all I want. That's never going to change."

"Okay."

"Okay." He gives my hand a squeeze. "Now, what was your favorite part tonight?"

"When Sidney and Leo sang together. What about you?"

He huffs out a laugh. "Fucking you in the bathroom, sweetheart."

Chapter Twenty

Ryker

It's three in the morning, and I can't sleep. Willow is warm and naked and dreaming peacefully next to me, and I don't want to wake her, so I ease out of bed, careful not to disturb her.

I'm restless.

And my brain won't stop moving.

So I pull on a pair of sweats and then pad down the hall to my office and step inside. The lights from the city cast a glow, guiding my way to the chair behind my desk. I sit and look around the room. There's no computer on the desk, because I took all my electronics to Montana. So the desktop is empty.

This is the only room that I've designated as a hockey-career memorabilia space. Photos, trophies—anything special from the past fifteen years is displayed on the walls around me, including a photo of me with Mom, Dad, and Gideon after my first Stanley Cup win.

I fucking love that photo. That was the only Cup win that Mom got to see. She passed a month before we won the second.

She's staring up at me in this picture, so tiny next to all of us big men, smiling so bright and proud, it makes me want to puff my chest out, even now.

Christ, I miss her.

That woman is the one who taught me that it's okay to love people. To let them in and show affection without holding back. To trust. Aside from my biological mother, Debbie James is the first person I ever told that I love them. She was the tiniest person in stature, but she loved so big, she might as well have been eight feet tall, and she was not afraid to shower all of us with that love. She left a gaping wound behind when she departed this world.

I understand why Dad never got over it.

Because now I have a woman in my life who's so much the same. She loves big, and the way that I love her would be terrifying if I hadn't had Mom in my life as a young man. Because Willow deserves all of me, and everything I can give her, just the way Dad did with Mom.

And if I ever lost Willow, it would fucking kill me.

I let my gaze roam around the space, pulling out memories of a career that I'm damn proud of. It was everything that I could have ever hoped for. Being here, in the city that's been my home away from home for so many years, has been great this week. I loved being on the ice with my guys, and showing my gratitude to my team, the coaching staff, and the city as a whole was the closure I needed.

Because although I was already considering retirement, I didn't get to go out on my terms. I left the sport because of a tragedy.

And this week, I got to say goodbye.

I'll keep the penthouse for now because I'll need to come here periodically for the foster kids charity that I'm now working with, but I'll likely eventually sell it.

It's not home anymore.

Montana is home.

The Triple Creek Ranch is where I belong.

And wherever Willow is? Well, that's where my heart is. Because that woman owns me, body and soul.

I'm ready to go home, with Wills and Aiden, and get back to work. Sure, this has been great, but waking up with the sun, working my land, breathing that air—that's what I need.

I glance over to the doorway as Willow steps into it.

Speaking of what I need.

She leans her shoulder on the doorjamb, crosses her arms over her chest. She grabbed the shirt I wore to the party tonight and only fastened two of the buttons to close it around her. It's way too big on her.

"You okay?" That sexy voice is soft and makes my cock come to life.

She's so fucking beautiful. Her hair is down, around her shoulders. Her face is clean of makeup, and her lips look so fucking kissable.

"Come here," I say. "Close and lock the door behind you."

She lifts an eyebrow but does as she's told and then pads across the room to me. I push the chair back so she can get between me and the desk, and then she sits on it, and I scoot up between her legs and wrap my arms around her ass. When my forehead lands on her chest, she pushes her fingers into my hair and kisses my head, and *fuck that feels good.*

"Hey," she says softly. "I'm still your best friend, you know."

"Yeah. I know."

She scratches her nails along my scalp, and it makes me groan.

"You can talk to me."

"I'm okay."

She kisses my head again, and I soak her in. "If you're ever *not* okay, you'll talk to me?"

"Yes, baby." I unfasten the two buttons and part my shirt, exposing her soft, creamy skin, and lean in to kiss her breastbone, right between her spectacular tits. "You're fucking incredible. I love your body. Every inch of it."

She hums and kisses my head again, still combing through my hair with her fingers.

I drag my hand up her side, over her breast, and then up until it circles her throat. Seeing my tattooed hand around her neck does things to me.

I run my thumb over her plump bottom lip, and then she gets sassy and pulls it between her lips, grazing it with her teeth, and I can't help the smile that comes as an idea forms.

I stand, but before I can turn her around, her fingertips drag over the tattoo on my ribs.

"Why this tree?" she asks quietly. "It's beautiful, but what's it for?"

With a frown, I skim my knuckles down her cheek. "Are you serious?"

Her blue eyes jerk up to mine, and she frowns. "Yeah. I'm serious."

"It's a willow tree, sweetheart."

"You got it because it's strong?"

This woman.

"No, baby, I got it because it's *you*." I lean over and plant my hands on the desk at her hips and brush my lips over hers.

"Me?"

"I wanted you, right here. At my side and by my heart."

Her breath hitches. "When did you get it?"

I hook her chin on my finger. "About a decade ago." I kiss her nose. "I have Mom and Dad and Gid on my arm, but the tree is you, sweetheart."

Her eyes, almost silver in this ambient light, shine as she stares at me. "Ry."

"No more talking." I shake my head and step back from her so I can push her back onto the desk. "I'm going to fuck you, here in my office."

She bites that lower lip.

"And I'm going to start with your mouth." I gently push on her chest. "Lie back for me."

She does as she's told, and I circle the desk and slide her toward me until her head tips back off the edge.

"If this gets uncomfortable, you tell me."

"Okay."

I bend over to look in her eyes.

"Promise me, Trouble. If you don't like anything that I'm about to do, you'll tap the desk twice, and it stops immediately."

"I trust you."

Those three words are almost my undoing.

I push my fingers into the soft hair that hangs over the side of the desk, and she hums happily in her throat. Bending farther, I drag my tongue down her neck, and then over to her breast, where I suck her nipple into my mouth so hard, her back arches up and her fingers dive into my hair.

"I'd really love to restrain you for this," I murmur as I pull back and watch as her eyes blow wide. "But I won't, not this first time."

That doesn't seem to turn her off at all.

"This is an interesting view," she says, and she reaches over her head to slide her hand up my inner thigh and then cups my balls, her fingertips rubbing against my taint, and it makes my eyes cross, even though her hand is over my sweats.

"Jesus, your hands." I drag my own hand up her belly, between her breasts, and then I hook my thumbs in the elastic of my sweats and tug them down my hips and kick out of them. My cock is already hard as fuck, and my girl licks her lips.

Licks her fucking lips.

Her hands immediately grip onto my hips, urging me closer, and I let her take the lead for a minute. I'm curious where my little vixen is going to take this.

She wraps those fingers around my shaft and pumps up and down twice, opens her perfect mouth, and sticks out her tongue, and that's all I can stand.

"You want this cock, sweetheart?"

She wiggles on the desk and moans in anticipation, and with my hand cupping her chin, I guide the tip inside her mouth, and she licks the precum already gathered in the slit.

With another moan from her sweet throat, my eyes close, and I give her another inch. She's sucking me so perfectly—her hand cups my balls and rubs my taint, and if I thought it felt good over the sweats, that was *nothing* compared to this.

She opens wider, trying to take more of me, but I pull back, checking to make sure she can breathe.

"Are you ready for more, baby?"

"Yes." She opens, and I feed her my dick, and she greedily sucks it in, and when I hit the back of her throat . . . she doesn't gag.

This perfect woman pulls my cock into her throat, and it has my balls lifting and tightening, and I see goddamn stars. I can see my cock moving in and out of her throat, and it's *gorgeous*.

"Jesus fuck, Wills."

"Hmm."

I push my hand down her torso, over her smooth pubis, and into her dripping wet slit, and she moans again.

If I don't stop her, she'll make me come, but when I try to pull out, she sucks harder and holds firm, and the next thing I know, I'm shooting ropes of cum into her throat.

She licks me clean, every single drop, and then smiles up at me triumphantly.

Taking her face in my hands, I bend over and kiss her upside down, tasting myself there, and then I walk back around the desk, sit in the chair, and press the insides of her thighs wide so I can plant my face in her juicy pussy.

"Ry." It's a whisper-shout, because she's afraid of waking Aiden, but there's no way. He's clear on the other side of the penthouse.

But I love it when she struggles to stay quiet.

Her hands tugging my hair, her thighs around my ears, she tastes like fucking heaven.

She tastes like mine.

Pressing two fingers inside her, I feel her walls already quaking, on the precipice of her climax.

"Ry," she whispers again.

"Do you need me to stop?" I ask her.

"Fuck, no."

I grin against her clit and then flick it with the end of my tongue. "Good, because I'm going to keep you busy for a while."

She squirms, clenches her fingers tighter in the strands of my hair, and starts to ride my face.

"There you go. Take what you want, baby."

Fuck me, she's perfect. She's not shy about wanting me, about taking what she needs. She's my sexual match in every way.

"Right there," she says, and I hold steady, sure not to change a goddamn thing. I keep the tempo of my fingers exactly the same, and the next time I brush that tight bundle of nerves with my tongue, her hips buck, and she comes so hard, and so long, it's the most amazing thing I've ever seen.

When her hips have stopped circling, I stand once more. My cock is already hard for her again, and I know she's more than ready for me.

"Look at me."

She doesn't open her eyes, so I reach out and cup her face.

"I said look at me, Willow."

Her eyes meet mine, and I push inside her, not stopping until I'm balls deep. Her mouth is open in a silent O, and with my hand on the back of her neck now, I pull her up to sitting and kiss the fuck out of her as I start to move in long, smooth strokes, in and out.

Her arms wrap around my shoulders, and we cling to each other as I fuck her. Our ragged breaths are the only sound in the room, and when I feel like I can't hold on anymore, when I'm about to explode, she hits me with "You're so fucking *mine*."

There is no holding on after that.

No chance in hell.

I jerk inside her and grind against her, coming harder than ever, and with my chest heaving, I fall forward, holding her firmly in one arm and catching us with my other so I don't crush her.

"Jesus, Wills, you're going to be the death of me."

She huffs out a chuckle and kisses my shoulder. "I'm pretty sure I'm the one who's already sore, Captain."

I grind against her once more, then lift her with me and sit back in the chair, Willow in my lap, and cradle her to me.

"Was I too much?" I ask her.

"Never. I told you, I trust you." She brushes a piece of my hair off my forehead, and then her fingers drift down my face. "You would *never* hurt me."

"No." I kiss her forehead and then her nose. "I wouldn't, baby."

"Do you feel better?"

I frown down at her. "I didn't feel bad before."

"You looked so . . . pensive when I found you. Like you have the weight of the world on your shoulders. But you don't have to carry it by yourself, you know."

Is it any wonder that I'm crazy about her?

"I'm sorry, Wills."

She lifts her head. "For what?"

"That it took me so long to see you like this. To *really* see you, and how good we'd be together. To fight for this."

"Hey, our lives were very different for a long time, Ry."

"I could have brought you and Aiden here, with me. We've lost a lot of time."

She shakes her head and kisses me so softly, so tenderly, it's as if she's kissing my heart itself. "This is how it was supposed to be. We can't change it now, so I don't want you to beat yourself up anymore. Not for one more minute. I haven't been unhappy, you know. We weren't struggling. I've done okay for Aiden and me."

"You've been amazing. I'm so proud of you."

Her whole face lights up at that. "You are?"

"Hell yes. For how well you raised that kid, for your amazing career. I listen to all your audiobooks, you know."

She narrows her eyes. "You do not."

"Every single one. You're so talented, and you have such a sexy voice. It always made me feel close to you to listen to your work." I push her hair over her shoulder. "I love being close to you."

"Same goes." She nestles in against me. "We should go snuggle in the bed before we both fall asleep and Aiden finds us in here in the morning."

Grinning, I kiss her on the head. "Are you ready to go home today?"

"Yeah. I am. I need to get back in the booth, and I want to go back to a routine. But I've loved every minute of this trip, and I know I said it before, but *I'm* proud of *you*, Ry. For a million reasons."

I kiss her again, unable to hold back. Everything about today and tonight has felt so damn intimate with this woman. And now, here in my office, in the quiet, after some pretty intense sex, with both of us sated, I can't keep the words to myself anymore.

"I love you, baby. More than anything."

She blinks slowly, her eyes filling with tears. "I love you too."

Chapter Twenty-One

Willow

"Hey, Shawn, how are you?"

I lean back in my chair and push my fingers through my hair, happy to hear from my friend. I loved being in Seattle for a few days, but the week that we've been home has been *so* productive, and I'm completely obsessed with my new workspace. Ry has to drag me out of here at dinnertime some days because I'm so absorbed in work I lose track of time.

"I'm great, thank you for asking," Shawn replies with that swoony-as-all-get-out British accent that makes all the listeners lose their goddamn minds. "I haven't talked to you in a long while, darling. What's new in your corner of the world?"

"A lot, actually. Oh, let me show you my new booth. I'm putting you on speaker so I can send some photos over."

I quickly tap the screen and then wait for Shawn to react.

"Fucking hell," he says with surprise. "That's brilliant. Did you move, or remodel your adorable house?"

"I sort of moved. For the summer, anyway." I wince at the thought of moving back to Missoula at the end of the summer.

"Why does it sound like there's a story there?"

"Oh, there's a story." I chuckle and swivel back and forth in my desk chair. "A long one."

"Better shared over a beer?"

"For sure."

"Will you be at that conference in Chicago next month?"

"That's the plan, yes. I should be there."

"Excellent, I can't wait to hear this story of yours. Hey, have you started prepping for the project we're working on together?"

"Coincidentally, I finished doing just that a bit ago so I could start recording tomorrow. Wanna talk about it?"

"Yeah, let's compare notes. I'm on page one sixteen."

I bring the document up on my iPad and find the page he's talking about. "Got it. First sex scene. Do you want to run lines, or . . . ?"

"I want to see if we're on the same page with how this reads. Do you think she's scared of him in that first paragraph?"

I skim the page. "Oh, I see what you're saying. I read it as her being apprehensive, but not afraid. Like this: *I don't want you to touch me there.*"

"*Why not, little one?*" Shawn jumps in, reading the lines. His voice has lowered seductively, making me grin.

Holy shit, the listeners are going to love this.

"B-b-because I—"

"You what? Does it make you feel naughty when I kiss you right here, darling?"

"I don't know what it makes me feel."

Shawn chuckles over the speakerphone.

"I think you know. And do you want to see what you're doing to me? Bloody hell, you're so fucking sexy, I can't wait to—"

"He might want to stop there."

Shawn stops reading, and I whip around to find Ryker standing in the doorway of my office, his arms crossed over his chest, his jaw clenched.

I laugh, but he doesn't look amused at all.

"Hold on, Shawn."

But Shawn doesn't hold on. In fact, he initiates a FaceTime call, and I answer.

"Hello, darling," Shawn says to me with that smug grin that all the ladies fawn over on social media.

"Shawn, this is Ryker." I tip the phone so Ry can see him. "Ry, this is Shawn North, a colleague of mine, and we were just going over some notes for a project we're working on together."

"Good to meet you," Shawn says with a nod, and Ry takes the phone from me. "Wait, you're Ryker James. Congratulations on the retirement."

"Are you telling me that Willow's never talked about me?" Ry demands, scowling at me, and I roll my eyes.

"She's mentioned that you're good friends," Shawn confirms.

"More than that now," Ry says, and I reach for the phone.

"Oh my God. Stop it." I yank the device out of his hand and shake my head. "If you've listened to all the books I've done, you know that Shawn and I have worked together a million times. So you can just calm the hell down, Captain."

Shawn's grinning, clearly entertained.

"Don't stop him on my account, darling."

"Call her *darling* one more time," Ry growls.

"Darling—"

Ry taps the screen, hanging up on my friend, and I gape at him.

"Ryker James."

"No." He grips my chin and tilts my face up, and his eyes are fierce as he stares me down.

"Okay." I rub my hands up and down his chest. "Shawn and I are *only* colleagues. You know that."

He closes his eyes and tips his forehead against mine. "I came to see if you were finishing up for the day, and when I got to the door—"

He swallows hard, and I cup his face.

"You heard a bunch of sexy talk."

"*Live* sexy talk. Not in a book."

Ah, I get it.

"I can admit, if I'd heard that puck bunny talking to you like that at the bar that night, I would have ripped her fucking hair out." I show him the iPad. "But this *is* in a book. See? We're starting this project tomorrow, and he wanted to know if I thought this character was afraid in this scene, or if she's apprehensive, and we just started running lines to get a feel for it. Shawn is famous for not liking to text. He calls or sends voice notes almost exclusively. It's just how he works."

"And you're going to Chicago with him."

My eyebrows climb in surprise.

"First of all, I'm not going anywhere *with* Shawn. Second, you knew we were running lines. How long were you standing in my doorway?"

He backs away from me completely and looks . . . *hurt.*

"Whoa. Nope, no shutting down on me, Ry."

"I get it. You were working. Sorry to interrupt."

"No," I say again and reach for his hand, relieved when he doesn't pull away. "Talk to me."

"Anything I say right now will make me sound like a controlling asshole, so I'd probably better *not* talk to you."

"You don't sound like an asshole. Controlling? Maybe a smidge. This is my job. I was not flirting with Shawn. He's a flirt all on his own, but he's harmless. My boyfriend happens to be the hottest man in the universe and does this thing with his tongue—"

He shuts me up by using said tongue, pulling me against him and kissing the hell out of me, as if he's claiming his territory all over again.

"You've never been a jealous man, Ry."

"I've never had so much to lose," he replies, and it makes my heart stutter.

"I'm right here. Completely obsessed with *you*. You don't get to listen to me work anymore if it upsets you like this."

"What's in Chicago?"

I smile. "A book signing, where I've been invited to come and meet readers and sign their books too. Wanna go with me?"

"Absolutely. You're not fucking going without me."

I frown. "You don't trust me? Is that what this is all about?"

"You're the sexiest woman in the universe," he replies, echoing my words. "I trust *you*. I don't trust anyone else."

"Don't scare Shawn."

"I'm not making that promise."

I snort and check the time. "It's not the end of the day yet."

"No, I was going to see if you want to ride into Missoula and check on your place. Aiden wants to go to an electronics store and buy a gaming system so he and Mac can play together in the evenings."

"His money's been burning a hole in his pocket."

"I'm going to teach that kid to be responsible with his paychecks," Ry promises.

"He's fifteen," I remind him.

"It's never too early to start." He kisses my forehead. "Are we good, Trouble?"

"I think I should be asking *you* that question."

He nods and gestures for me to walk ahead of him out of the office. "Let's go. Before I carry you to the bedroom and fuck you so hard, there's no way you'll forget exactly who you belong to."

I pause and squeeze my thighs together. "We could make time for that."

Ry smirks. "Aiden's waiting downstairs."

"Damn."

"I can't believe my fridge died." I'm scowling as we lock up my little house and then walk out to Ryker's SUV. "At least it only had condiments in it. But still. Gross."

"I'll call a crew in to get it out of here."

I don't know how I didn't end up with a ruined floor from any melted ice from the freezer.

"Wait, did you toss the ice and turn off the ice maker last time we were here?" I ask Ry.

"Of course I did."

"You think of everything."

He smirks and has just pulled out of my driveway, headed toward Aiden's favorite electronics store, when his phone rings, showing Andy on the screen.

He accepts the call with an annoyed huff.

"Hello."

"Hey, Ryker," Andy says. From the corner of my eye, I see Aiden take his earbud out of his ear. "Is this a bad time?"

"I have about five minutes," Ry replies. "What's up?"

"I wanted to apologize." His voice *sounds* sincere, but it's that fake kind of sincere, when you know someone is full of shit. "I'm sorry and honestly embarrassed by the way everything went down when you were in Seattle."

My gaze whips over to Ryker, whose knuckles are white as he grips the steering wheel, and he's already clenching his jaw.

"We've worked together for a damn long time," Andy continues, "and you know that I always have your best interests at heart. I don't know how we got so far off course, but I don't think you meant any harm."

"What the fuck?" Aiden mutters under his breath, and I don't even bother to shoot him a dirty look for swearing.

Because *what the fuck*?

Gaslight much, Andy?

"Are you still there, buddy?" Andy asks.

"I'm here. I'm pulling into the parking lot of where I was going, so I'm hanging up. Thanks for the apology."

"You bet. You have a good day, and I'll talk to you soon."

Ryker cuts off the call before Andy even gets the last word out, and I shake my head.

"There's something seriously wrong with that guy."

"Don't worry about him," Ry says as Aiden climbs out of the vehicle.

Ryker takes my hand in his and kisses my knuckles, then threads our fingers together as we walk behind Aiden, who almost has a spring in his step. The whole way into town, my kiddo talked nonstop about which console he wants to snag, and which games he's going to buy, and how he has to get an extra controller so he and Micah can play together in the bunkhouse.

He hasn't been this excited about anything in a *long* time. I offered to pay for it, but he shook his head, insisting that he can buy it himself, and that made me proud.

My boy is growing up.

Ryker and I wander through the store, following Aiden as he zigzags through aisles full of cameras, computers, and even car stereos until he finds what he's looking for.

"Do you need anything while we're here?" Ry asks me.

"No, I upgraded all my work gear last year. I'm good to go. How about you?"

He opens his mouth, but before he can reply, we hear a voice say, "You been hiding from me this summer, pussy? Maybe you're too busy fucking your hot aunt to leave the house."

Ry and I whip around just in time to see Aiden advance on the little bastard from the gas station, and I grab Aiden's arm as Ry gets in the punk's face.

"Who the fuck do you think you're talking to?" Ry demands. He doesn't touch the boy, but he's towering over him, glaring menacingly.

"No one." The boy looks like he's going to pee his pants.

"Which console do you want, Aiden?" I try to redirect his focus, and he glances down at me, his sweet face red with fury, breathing hard. "Don't give him this. Don't let him upset you like this, sweetie."

"No one gets to talk about you like that."

I pat his arm, and suddenly the boy has run off and Ryker turns back to us.

"You didn't have to do that," Aiden says. My happy boy is gone. In his place is the angry, sullen boy I've lived with for the past two years.

"You're mine," Ryker says. "You're *both* mine. No one talks to you that way. Now, we're going to shake that shit off and do some shopping."

Aiden takes a deep breath, clearly reining in his emotions, and then reluctantly nods. "Okay."

He chooses his console, a couple of games, an extra controller, and all the accessories he needs, and when it comes time to check out, Ryker lets him pay for half.

"I'm going to get the other half," he tells my nephew. "And we're going to talk about money management and how to make that money grow."

"I make twenty bucks an hour," Aiden reminds Ryker.

"And you'll make that twenty bucks work for you. Let's go, smart-ass."

Aiden doesn't smirk the way he normally would, and before long, we're back in the vehicle.

"Want to stop for dinner?" Ry asks us.

"I want to go back to the bunkhouse," Aiden replies.

Ryker raises his eyebrow at me, and I nod.

"I'll make dinner at the house," I tell him.

We're quiet in the car for about ten miles. Aiden has his earbuds in, so I assume he's listening to music, but suddenly, he rips them out and shoves them in his pocket.

"Did they run out of battery?" I ask him.

"Why can't we just move out to the ranch full-time?" Aiden's voice cracks, making my heart hurt so much. "What's the point in being in Missoula anyway? I fucking hate it there."

"Let's get out of the car and talk about this." Ryker flips on his blinker and takes the exit for a rest area that happens to be empty right now, and as soon as he parks, we all get out of the vehicle, and Aiden starts to pace. He's so agitated, so upset, and I wish I could pull him to me and hug him.

But he doesn't like to be touched.

"Baby, how long has that boy been harassing you?"

"*Years,*" he says and rubs the back of his hand over his mouth. "I hate him. I wish I could kill him. He's relentless, and his friends are no better."

"I want his full name," Ryker says, crossing his arms over his chest.

"I'm so over it in that stupid fucking town," Aiden continues, as if Ryker hasn't said anything at all. "If I like a girl, that asshole swoops in and makes her hate me. If I so much as smile in class, he finds a way to humiliate me."

"I'm going to kill him." My voice is hard as granite. "And I want to know why you've never talked to me about this."

"Because what are you going to do?" His voice is so loud now, but I allow it because I can plainly see that he's needed to get this out for a long time. "Talk to his *mom*? She doesn't fucking care. She's just like him. I'm sick to *death* of him talking shit about you. About Ryker and hockey and every goddamn thing. I don't even use my phone anymore because he wouldn't stop texting me."

I tilt my head to the side, stunned. "*Aiden.* What in the hell? Baby, you don't have to deal with all this bullshit by yourself, and *yes*, I can do something about it. We can press charges against him. Plus, you don't have to defend me. I'm perfectly capable—"

"Yes I do," he roars back. "Because I love you, and you're the best thing that ever happened to me, and if someone's going to talk shit about you, they're going to get a goddamn broken jaw."

"That's my boy," Ryker mutters, but I don't look at him.

"He's a jealous, miserable kid," I say, keeping my voice calm. "I'm not saying you need to feel bad for him, and I'm not going to tell you to take the high road because he's taken all this way too far, but you do know that he behaves that way because he's jealous, right?"

"I don't care why he does it." Aiden pulls his hands down his face. "I don't give a shit about him. I don't want to ever see him again."

"I fucking hate bullies," I say, shaking my head.

"I want to live at the ranch," he continues. "All the time, not just this summer. I don't want to go to school in Missoula. I can go in Paradise Valley, where Micah goes."

"As far as I'm concerned," Ryker breaks in before I can reply, "you can move in permanently *today*. The ranch is your home. For both of you. I want you with me."

"You do?"

I've gone completely quiet, but for the first time since Aiden saw that little shit in the store, he has hope in his eyes again.

This isn't something that Ryker and I have discussed. The plan was for us to stay on the ranch for the summer and then return to Missoula. I'm a planner. I don't do well with things being shaken up without warning.

Without a conversation.

"Of course I do," Ry continues. "I told you, you guys are mine. I don't want you to move back to Missoula."

"Thank God," Aiden says with a relieved sigh. Then he turns his attention back to me. "That's okay, right, Aunt Wills? We can move to the ranch?"

"We'll talk about it."

"It's perfect. You already have the best recording booth ever, and you like the house. You practically grew up there," Aiden says, trying to sell me on the idea.

"I said we'd discuss it," I repeat. "Now, tell me what you need to make you feel better tonight, buddy."

He shrugs and kicks a rock.

"Can I have a hug?" I ask him, making him roll his eyes.

"I guess."

I walk into his arms and press my head to his chest and give him a squeeze.

"I love you, baby boy."

"I love you too."

I grin up at him as I pull away. "Shall we head out?"

"Yeah, I have to set up my new system."

He climbs into the SUV, but before I can walk around the car, Ryker grabs my hand and makes me turn to him.

"Did I say something wrong?" he asks. I hate the scowl on his face.

"No, of course not."

"Wills—"

"Let's talk about it over dinner. I'm hungry."

His lips flatten into a line, but he finally nods. "Let's go."

Chapter Twenty-Two

Ryker

The majority of this day has been a clusterfuck.

I had to put a cow down this morning. Something attacked her in the night, and she was a fucking mess, suffering in the pasture. I'm glad neither of the younger kids saw her.

That's some shit you don't get out of your head.

Sure, this is a ranch. We have farm animals, and I'll be adding more, but that doesn't mean that I've become completely desensitized when it comes to the suffering of animals.

It fucking sucks.

Then, I decided to cheer myself up with a ride into Missoula with my two favorite people. Aiden was thrilled.

But when I heard that British prick talk sexy to my girl, I would have dragged him through the phone to kick his ass if I could have. I don't want anyone speaking to her like that but me.

Because she's mine.

Just as things were getting better, Aiden's bully came out of the goddamn woodwork and upset all of us, and when I tried to reassure Aiden that he and Wills can both move in with me, Willow iced up.

I don't let my feelings get hurt. I learned that early on in life. But I'll be damned if Willow didn't accomplish it twice in one day.

I need a beer.

I pull up to the house, and Aiden hops out and opens the back of the vehicle so he can retrieve his goods.

"Thanks, guys," he says, his smile back. "I'm going to go set this up."

"Do you want dinner?" Willow asks him.

"I'll eat with the guys at the bunkhouse," he calls over his shoulder as he hurries off.

"You'd think it was Christmas," Willow says with a chuckle as we walk up to the house. I unlock the door and then push it open and wait for her to walk in ahead of me. She rubs her hand over my chest as she walks by, and I want to pull her against me, but I don't. "I was thinking of grilling some chicken with asparagus and salad. Thoughts?"

"That's fine, but I want to talk."

"I know." She strides into the kitchen and starts pulling things out of the fridge. "Can we talk while I work? I really *am* starving."

"Fine." I lean on the island and watch as she seasons the chicken. There are a lot of words rolling through my head right now, so I just start with the obvious. "What the fuck, Trouble?"

She pauses, and her forehead furrows as she looks up at me. "What?"

"What in the actual fuck?" I shake my head and drag my hand down my face.

My girl sets the food back in the fridge—good, I want her full attention—and circles the island to step in front of me.

"I hurt your feelings."

"You got weird on me," I reply. "Are you implying that you *don't* want to live here? Because if that's the case, what in the hell are we doing?"

"Aiden and I moved here for the summer so he could—"

"I know why you moved here. I was here for it." Christ, I'm frustrated. "But things have fucking changed between you and me, and you know it. I'm so in love with you, I can't see straight. When I'm not with you, I get twitchy. You're like a drug, and I constantly need another hit. So explain to me like I'm a fucking four-year-old how I'm supposed to be okay with you and the kid moving back to Missoula at the end of the summer."

Her mouth opens, but no sound comes out, and then she closes it again. Every muscle in her body is tight. Her shoulders are practically wrapped around her ears.

I take a breath and step to her, cradle her face in my hands, and kiss her forehead.

"I need you to talk to me, Wills. Because I'm not letting you move out of this house. Not at the end of the summer, not ever. Unless we're going somewhere together."

Finally, she exhales and braces her hands on my sides.

"It's not that I don't want to stay with you. Not at all."

Thank God.

"Of course I do. It's just . . . you know how I am with surprises."

She's shit with surprises. "You never did like having plans fucked with."

"I like structure. I *need* it, because after what my mom pulled, I just—"

"I know." I tug her to me and hug her close. Shit, it's like I fell in love with her and forgot who she is.

This is *Willow.*

"I should have talked to you privately before I told Aiden he didn't have to go back to Missoula. It was the heat of the moment, and I wanted to reassure him."

"Yeah. We should have discussed it first. I don't like being handled."

I pull back and frown down at her. "Do you seriously think that's what I was doing?"

"Yeah. I do. Aiden was upset, and you handled it. My refrigerator died, and you're gonna handle it. You simply take over."

I'm staring down at her when my phone rings. I pull it out of my pocket and see that it's Gideon and let it go to voicemail. I'll call him back later.

I'm having my first fight with the love of my life.

"I'm not *handling* shit. I'm helping."

"Without asking if I *need* help."

My phone rings again, and this time I answer the call.

"Hey, this isn't a great ti—"

"Put me on speaker. I'm only saying this once."

My eyes fly to Willow's as I put Gideon on speaker.

"We can both hear you, Gid."

He clears his throat, and now I notice that he's breathing kind of hard. "I need you both to know that I'm okay."

Willow's eyes immediately fill with tears, and she reaches for me. I pull her against me.

"What's going on?" I ask him before I plant my lips on the top of Willow's head.

"I was shot today, but *I'm okay.*"

"Oh, God," Willow cries, covering her mouth with her hand. "Where? How? Gideon, if you die, I will kill you."

"I'm fine," he repeats, softer now. "Hey, Wills, don't cry."

Shit, even *I'm* tearing up.

"What happened?" I ask him.

"It's classified."

"Fuck that," Willow interrupts. "We're your family, and I demand to know what in the fucking hell is going on. Did that little brat cause this? Gideon—"

"Stop." His voice is harder now. "I'm in the hospital, and I've had surgery."

Christ.

"I'll be in the air in less than an hour," I tell him. "I'll charter a plane, and I'll be there late tonight."

"No. For fuck's sake, will you two stop panicking and listen to me? What part of 'I'm okay' did you not understand?"

"It was overshadowed by the whole 'I was shot' thing," Willow informs him before she buries her face in my chest.

"If you think I'm not coming there, you don't know me at all."

"You won't be able to get in here," he says with a sigh. "It was two shots in the leg. They missed the important stuff. I can't tell you where we were or who did the shooting. I've already had surgery on the leg, and now it's just recovery time and physical therapy so I can get back to work."

"You should come home to recover. I'll come get you."

Gideon sighs. "Listen, I'm about to pass out from some really good drugs that I tried to refuse but Nurse Ratched insisted on giving me. I'll stay here to recover. I have the best doctors and physical therapists in the world here. I'll be back to work in less than a month."

"And you'll check in with us every day?" Willow asks.

"Of course."

"I love you," Willow says into my phone. "I love you so much, Gid. Don't ever do this to me again."

"I love you, too, baby girl." His voice is getting sloppy. "Don't let Ry get on a plane. I'm gonna be okay."

"I love you, too, you know," I tell him. "Even when I want to strangle you."

"Same." He takes a deep breath. "Gonna sleep now. Night."

He hangs up, and I throw my phone across the room into the couch and then pace away from Willow. My brother is in a goddamn hospital bed, and he doesn't want me to come to him.

He could have died today.

He could die every day. That's the truth of his job, and it's something that I always have in the back of my mind, but Jesus, I hate what he does for a living.

"Ry."

I hold up a hand and continue to pace.

"Why." I swallow hard and then try again. "Why won't the people I love let me help them?"

I stop and face her and watch as a tear falls down her perfect cheek.

"Even my birth mother." I keep pacing, pushing my fingers through my hair. "I *begged* her to move away, to stop bringing the men home, to be happy with just the two of us."

I'll never forget her face, broken and bloody. She was still convinced that the man who did that shit loved her and she couldn't live without him.

"But she didn't listen, and she stayed until it killed her."

Willow shakes her head. I don't know if I've ever told her that story before.

"My dad. Ray. I asked him a hundred times if he needed me to come home to help him after Mom died, and he always said no, which we know now was a huge fucking lie. I could have hired people for him. I could have come here myself and taken care of him."

I am so goddamn *pissed.*

"Gideon is lying in a hospital bed somewhere, and he won't let me come help him. Do you know how absolutely hopeless it feels to know that someone you love is hurting and they won't let you do anything to fucking help? And then there's *you.*"

"Me?" She blinks rapidly as she brushes away her tears.

"Your fridge died, your kid feels safe here, *you* thrive here. Don't think I haven't noticed."

I should probably stop yelling and take a deep breath, but goddamn it, I'm so fucking pissed off.

"I have an amazing house with everything we could need or want. I want you with me, always. I want Aiden. And you're fighting me on it, as if you planned to just fuck around with me this summer and then—what? Get me out of your system? Once upon a time, I might have been down for that with someone, but not with you, and not now."

"That's not—"

I pace over to her. "Maybe my feelings aren't reciprocated like I thought they were. Apparently, you don't feel the same."

I turn to pace away, but she catches my wrist in her hand, keeping me close.

"It's my turn to talk," she says. "You had your say, and now I'll have mine. I *know* you're upset, and I agree with you. Gid should let you go out there, even if it's just for a few days."

I pull out of her reach. I can't let her touch me right now.

I feel too raw, too vulnerable.

"Please let me touch you."

"Not yet."

"You're a fixer, Ryker. That's who you are as a human. It's who you've always been, and it's one of the things that I love the most about you. If I got hurt on this ranch when I was a kid, you were the first one there to help me get cleaned up. When my bike had a flat tire, you fixed it. When I dropped my journal in the creek because I thought it would be magical to sit on a rock and write down all my feelings, you swam in to get it for me and then painstakingly used my blow-dryer to get every page dry, and you swore you didn't read it."

"I might have read a page or two," I mutter.

"When Aiden was dropped off at my apartment, and I called you from the ER because he was *so sick*, you dropped everything and flew out to be with us." She swallows hard. "You sent me money during the leanest months when I was getting my feet under me and had to hire an attorney to get legal custody of him, even though Sabrina had abandoned him to me, and the state of Montana was being a royal pain in my ass. *You have always helped me.*"

I shake my head.

"I'm not done." She steps closer but doesn't touch me, because I haven't told her she can and she's always respected boundaries. "I love you so much it hurts. I always have, from the moment that angry, hurt, skinny boy stepped out of that car in front of this house. You are my person. My best friend. And now you're so much more than that, and I don't ever want you to think that I would want to move Aiden and myself in here because you want to fix something for me. I only want you to love me."

"I do, baby." I reach for her now and take both of her hands in mine, threading our fingers together. "And I don't want you here just because I think you need me to rescue you. You don't. You're fucking badass. You would replace the stupid fridge and get on with your life, but—"

"There is no getting on with my life unless you're in it," she says and loops her arms around my neck. "And as far as the rest? Well, your mom, your birth mom—you couldn't have saved her, Ry. You were just a little boy."

My chest is cracking open. That's the only explanation for the pain just behind my sternum.

"I hated her for letting them do that to her," I whisper. "And then I hated her for dying while I sat in that hospital room and watched."

"God." She pulls me down in a hug, and I bury my face in her neck. "I'm so sorry. That's not okay."

"No, it's not okay." I breathe her in and feel myself start to settle.

"You also couldn't save Ray. He didn't want to be saved. He just wanted Debbie."

I nod, feeling the tears come. "I know. I get it. Because if anything ever happened to you—"

"Shh." She pulls back so she can see my face. "Look me in the face. I'm *right here*. And I'm not going anywhere for a long, long time. I have too much to do. Of course Aiden and I will move in here. He can go to school in Paradise Valley."

"He's going to be really happy to hear that."

"Only him?"

My lips twitch, and I feel better after my . . . tantrum? Outburst? Fucking panic attack? I don't know what that was. But I feel better.

"I'm happy too. Debbie and Ray would love it, you know. You and me here with Aiden."

"Carrying on their tradition," she says with a nod. "Yeah, they'd be happy about it."

"So you're going to let me handle things?"

She lifts an eyebrow. "No. I'm going to love you, and we're going to work together to keep things running smoothly."

"I'm going to handle you," I reply, my voice getting deeper as I slide my hands down her back to her perfect ass.

"Oh, will you?"

"Yes. After you make dinner, because I'm fucking starving."

"You can help me, and it'll go faster."

"Deal."

The mood has lightened considerably as I help make the salad and get the grill going. Dinner is delicious, and I've just finished loading the dishwasher when my phone rings, and I see that it's Dusty.

"Hey, what's up?"

"I found the cow murderer," he says with a heavy sigh.

"What is it?"

"Coyotes. If you step outside, you can hear them."

I open the back door and step out on the porch, listening.

Sure enough, they start to call.

"They're fucking hunting again tonight."

"We're going to have to kill them, Ry. Or they'll make their way through our whole herd."

"I know. It fucking sucks. We need to get a donkey."

"I've already put out the word that we're in the market for one," Dusty replies. "In the meantime, those coyotes won't stop on their own."

"I'll be ready to go out to the pasture in about twenty minutes. I'll meet you out there."

I hang up and go back inside and find Wills in the kitchen. She already took a shower and changed into her sleep shorts and my jersey, which never fails to wake my dick up.

"Hey," she says with a grin. "Wanna watch a movie and make out until we ignore said movie and fuck on the couch?"

God, she's perfect for me.

"Hell yes, I want to do that, but I have to go out to check on the herd. Coyotes are killing our cows."

"Oh no." She scowls. "We need a donkey."

I let out a loud laugh and pull her in for a kiss.

"Why was that funny?"

"I just said the same thing to Dusty."

"Great minds think alike."

Chapter Twenty-Three

Willow

"Just so you're aware, the house won't come with a fridge," I say to Susan, my real estate agent. I can't believe that not only am I moving Aiden and myself to the ranch, but I'm also selling my house. I won't need it anymore, and I don't want to be a landlord, so it makes sense to sell while the weather is good and people want to move. "The existing one broke, and I'm not replacing it."

"That's fair," Susan says. I can tell she's writing that down. "What about the other appliances?"

"Everything else stays, including the washer and dryer."

Ryker just replaced everything in the farmhouse. We'd have no need for my older appliances out here.

"That's a good selling point," she says. "Have you done any upgrades since you bought it six years ago?"

I lean back in my desk chair and swivel side to side. "Not really. I did have a walk-in closet soundproofed so I could use it as a studio. I'll be leaving that as is, but a buyer could easily remove it."

Susan asks me a few more questions, and I give her permission to go to the house without me to take photos so we can put it on the market.

I know that it surprised me when Ryker first mentioned us moving here permanently, and that made me pause, but now that I've had time to think about it and soak in the idea, I'm excited. There will be no more driving back and forth. Aiden will be away from the kids who mercilessly bullied him.

And we'll be here, with Ryker.

"Okay, I'll get over there and take some pictures, and we'll get an appraisal. It should be on the market by next week."

"Thanks, Susan. Let me know if you need anything from me."

"You bet."

She hangs up, and I stand up to stretch before I walk downstairs to find some lunch. I have a few hours of recording time left today, but I need a pick-me-up. Maybe I'll even take a short walk and get some fresh air.

I can hear my guys in the kitchen, and it makes me smile. Ryker brings Aiden here almost every day for lunch. They've been doing this all summer, and I love that Ryker takes time to hang out with my boy.

"Why do you think that idiot says what he does about Willow?" Ryker asks, and I pause outside the kitchen, out of sight. I shouldn't eavesdrop, but, well, I'm human. Sue me.

"Because he's an asshole," Aiden replies. I can hear the scowl on his face.

"It's weird that it started out of the blue," Ry counters. "Did something happen?"

Aiden's quiet. I can hear him chewing from over here. "A couple years ago, I was doing summer league baseball, and we had a game. Miles—that's his stupid name—was on the team, and his dad coached."

I remember this.

"His dad's single, and he asked me if Wills was single."

He's quiet again, obviously chewing his lunch.

I hated that guy. He always gave me the creeps.

"I told him I didn't know about stuff like that with her. I was, like, twelve. How would I know? She never brought anyone home, but hell, I don't know what she did when I was with friends, or whatever."

"Sure, makes sense," Ryker says.

"At first he let it go, but as the season went on, he'd ask me more. Finally, I told him to ask her himself."

"What did he do?" Ryker asks.

"Don't know. He didn't ask me again, but he was also an ass to me after that. Liked to embarrass me in front of the other guys at practice."

"So his kid comes by being an asshole naturally."

Aiden snorts. "Totally. I don't know what he said to Miles, but after that, Miles had it out for me. He's relentless. I'd block him, and he'd figure out a way to change his number on an app or something to still get through. It was actually really creepy. Can I change my phone number?"

"We'll make it happen," Ry says, and those four words make me fall in love with him even more. I didn't think that was possible. "Now, tell me about the girl you were with the night before you first came out here. The night school got out."

Aiden's quiet for a heartbeat. "She's not important."

"Important enough for you to have your hands on her."

I cringe. I do *not* want to think about that.

"I liked her. Her name is Hilary. She's cool, but she moved to Texas after we got out of school for the summer, so I probably won't ever see her again."

My kid has had so much going on, and I knew *nothing*.

That breaks my heart.

I walk into the kitchen and force a smile onto my lips before I stop by and kiss Aiden's cheek, making him cringe.

"How's it going out there today?"

"It's hot," Aiden says.

I saunter up to Ryker, who's sweating like crazy, and carefully kiss his cheek as well.

"And how are you?" he asks me.

"I'm great. I called the real estate agent, so Operation Sell My House is underway."

"Thank God," Aiden mutters. "You can just toss my stuff. I have everything I need here."

"That's not how it works, buddy. We'll be going back to pack up, and you'll be going with us. I need your strong muscles to move all my heavy stuff."

He scrunches up his nose and then shrugs. "I guess it's worth it."

Ryker's phone rings, and he scowls at the display. "It's fucking Andy. Again."

"You should answer it."

The man has been calling Ry every day for the past couple of days since we took our afternoon trip to Missoula, and Ryker always sends him to voicemail.

"This is Ryker," Ry says as he puts the phone on speaker and sets it on the counter.

"Hey, man, how are you doing up there in the boonies?"

I feel my brows pull together. Why is Andy calling like he and Ryker are besties?

Aiden opens a bag of Cheetos and starts crunching away.

"What's up, Andy?" Ryker asks.

"I've been trying to get ahold of you," Andy says, and there's an edge to his voice now that I don't like.

"You didn't leave any messages," Ry replies.

"No, I'd rather just talk to you. I might have some appearances lined up for you, if you're interested."

Ryker shakes his head. "I made it clear that you're no longer my agent. I'll have my attorney send a cease and desist if I have to. Stop trying to line shit up for me."

"Fine. I didn't know how convinced you were of that decision."

Aiden and I share a look.

"Listen, Ry, I could use some help. Just a loan, only a hundred eighty thousand, that I'll pay back as soon as I'm able to. There are some guys who said they'd, well, hurt me—"

"You have lost your motherfucking mind," Ryker replies. His voice is cold and hard, and it's full of fury.

Andy is a stupid, stupid man.

"If you'd take the jobs I have lined up for you, I wouldn't need the loan—"

"Stop talking," Ryker barks. "I'm going to make myself perfectly fucking clear. I don't owe you shit. I will not loan you money today or any other day. You no longer work for me. I want nothing to do with you ever again. Lose my goddamn number, Andy. If you keep calling me, I'll sue you for harassment."

"*Sue* me?"

"That's right. Go. The fuck. Away."

He hangs up on the man, and Aiden shakes his head. "You need to block his number."

"Good idea," Ryker says, tapping the screen. "There. Done."

"We got a donkey," Aiden says, cool as a cucumber, as if Ryker didn't just threaten his former agent.

"Yeah? Is it here already?" I ask, raising an eyebrow.

"Out with the herd now," Ryker confirms, blowing out an agitated breath. "We named her Molly."

"She's gonna kick some coyote ass," Aiden informs me before popping more Cheetos in his mouth.

"Let's hope she just scares them off," I reply. "I'm going to take a quick walk before I go back to work. I need some air."

"It's damn hot out," Ry reminds me and reaches out to drag his fingertip down my bare arm. "Don't get sunburned."

"I won't go far." I boost up on my toes, and he leans down to kiss me.

"Here, take this sandwich with you." Ryker passes me a turkey sandwich.

"Were you making that for me?"

"No, I was making it for me, but I can make another. Eat while you walk, Trouble."

"Why do you call her Trouble?" Aiden wants to know.

"Because from the moment I met her, I knew that she'd get us all in a whole lot of it," Ryker answers him with a smirk. His dark eyes find mine, and they're full of humor and memories. "And I was right."

"Hey, most of the trouble we got in was *not* my fault." I take a bite of my sandwich and saunter out of the kitchen. "See you later!"

"Wait," Aiden calls out, and I poke my head back into the kitchen. "I'm not coming for dinner tonight. Mac and I are gonna kill some zombies, so I'll eat at the bunkhouse."

"Does Dusty know?"

"Yeah, he's cool with it," Aiden says.

"Okay then. Have fun. Call me if you need me."

"She's such a mother hen," I hear Aiden say as I walk through to the front door.

Of course I'm a mother hen.

He's my boy.

Ryker and I have just settled back on the sofa, ready to watch a movie, when my phone rings with an incoming video call from Gideon.

He hasn't called every day like he promised last week, but it's been close.

"Hey, handsome," I say as I answer and smile at him. Then I notice that he's not sitting on a hospital bed. I recognize that couch. "Wow, are you home?"

"Yeah, I'm home. I'm doing outpatient PT now."

"How are you feeling?" Ryker asks him, and I point the phone so we're both in the picture.

"Like I got shot," Gid replies. "I don't want to talk about that. What's happening there?"

So, for half an hour, we fill him in on Molly the donkey, Andy losing his ever-loving mind, and the fact that Aiden and I are moving here permanently.

"It's never boring with you two," Gid says with a sigh.

"You'd hate it if we were boring," I tell him. "Will you ever tell us what happened?"

"When you get the security clearance you'd need to know the details, I'll tell you."

I roll my eyes. "Lame."

"I think you just like to say 'security clearance,'" Ryker says, pulling a laugh out of Gideon. "You like to sound cool."

"I *am* cool," Gid replies. "And I have the highest security clearance you can get, which makes me *extra* cool."

I snort out a laugh.

"Have you ever won a Stanley Cup?" Ryker tosses back, and I roll my eyes.

"Have you ever protected a president?" Gideon volleys.

"I've got *two* of them," Ry continues.

"You're both giving me a headache. And if you pull your dicks out to compare the size, I'm out of here."

Now we're all laughing, and it feels so damn good.

We're the Three Amigos.

These guys are my besties.

"Now that you're out of the hospital, are you sure you won't come home to rehab your leg?" I ask Gideon. "I know I'm annoying you because I'm asking you this all the time, but there are physical therapists here."

A text from an unknown number flashes across the top of my screen, but I flick it away.

"I'll stay here and work with the team I've started with," he replies.

"I think you just don't want to see me." I pretend to start crying and wipe an imaginary tear from the corner of my eye. Gideon lets out a gusty sigh and rolls his eyes. "Don't mind me and *my* feelings. I'm fine. Everything's fine."

"You're a pain in my ass," Gideon informs me.

"But you love me." With no tears in sight, I wink at him and grin. "Seriously, take it easy. Don't work that leg too hard. This is a marathon, not a sprint."

"Ry?" Gideon says.

"Yeah, man."

"Rein in your girl."

My jaw drops, and then I glare at Gideon. "You did *not* just say that."

He's laughing again, and that makes me happy.

"I will cut off your balls and feed them to you."

"You've always had a mean streak," he says as he wipes the tears from his eyes from laughing so hard. "Okay, I'm headed to bed. Thought I'd check in and make sure you two are staying out of trouble."

"We are."

"We're not."

We say that at the same time, and Gid grins at us.

"Call me soon," I tell him.

"Yes, boss." He winks. "Love you guys."

He hangs up, and I start to set the phone aside and then remember the text.

Expecting it to be something about my car's warranty, I open it up and then freeze.

"Uh, Ry?"

"Yeah, babe."

"What the fuck is this?"

Chapter Twenty-Four

Ryker

Willow turns her screen my way, and I frown, sure that I'm not seeing what my brain tells me I'm seeing.

"What is this?" she asks again, her voice full of hurt. Not anger. Hurt.

And that sets me on edge, because someone has hurt my girl.

"May I?" I hold my hand out for her phone, and she gives it to me. I don't hide what I'm doing from her. I zoom in on the image.

It's a photo of me with a girl named Darcy, the same one from that night in Seattle when Wills and Aiden were at my retirement party. The one that Willow said had been eyeing me all night. But this photo was taken a different night, months ago.

We're in the same place, Darcy is in my lap, and my lips are on her neck.

"Who sent you this?"

"It's an unknown number," she says. I can hear the hurt growing in her voice, and it both pisses me off and makes my heart ache because I *never* want my girl to feel insecure. The fact that my past was thrown in her face like this makes me fucking feral. "Talk to me, Ry."

"Obviously, it's what it looks like. This was probably close to a year ago, or more, and I was partying with the guys."

"And you hooked up with her."

I tap her screen, send the photo to myself, and then delete it off her phone. She doesn't try to stop me.

"First of all, I sent that to myself so I can have Gideon look into it, not so I can save it. And I probably did hook up with her, yeah. We already said that we aren't going to bring up who we fucked in the past."

"If someone sent you a picture of me all over one of the men I'd had sex with before you, you'd be cool about it and not get your feelings hurt?"

"Fuck no, I'd want to find him, cut off his hands, and bring them to you in a box."

She blinks and then blows out a breath. "This is fucked up."

"I have *not* touched another woman since you and I—"

"I know." She shakes her head and stands to pace. "I know that. So what was the point of that text? Someone just wanted to piss me off?"

"Probably." I stand with her and pull her to me, wrap my arms around her and rock her back and forth. "I didn't delete the number from your phone. I'll see if Gid can find out where it came from."

Suddenly, her phone blows up again, and she reaches for it, and her eyes widen as she scrolls on her screen. I have a bad feeling about this.

"Jesus."

She closes her baby blues and swallows hard and simply passes the phone to me.

When I look down, the fire of a thousand suns streams through my veins.

So many photos.

Of me, with plenty of different women. Some in bars, some at the arena after games. But some are inside my motherfucking penthouse.

Naked.

I'm fucking them in my bed.

Willow lets out a shaky breath and brushes a tear off her cheek, and I immediately call Gideon.

"Miss me already?"

"I'm sending through some photos that you'll want to bleach from your brain. They were sent to Willow just now. All of me, from an unknown number. I need to know where these came from."

He's all work now, his voice hard and cold.

"Send me everything you've got. I might need her phone to trace the caller, but I'll reach out to the cell provider first."

"Whatever you need. Find this asshole. They hurt my girl, and now we hurt them."

"Understood. I'll be in touch."

I forward everything to Gideon, who replies with one word.

Gideon: Fuck.

Yeah, fuck.

Gideon: Are we going to find out that there are photos of you fucking Willow that get leaked to the goddamn media?

Fuck.

Me: There better not be, but I don't know anything right now. Jesus fucking Christ, Gid.

Willow's standing by the windows, looking out into the darkness. Her arms are wrapped around her, and she's rocking back and forth, as if she's trying to soothe herself.

"Sweetheart."

She shakes her head. "Don't apologize. You didn't do anything wrong. I just can't unsee that, and I *never* wanted to know—"

"Hey, I know." I want someone to bleed for this. Anger is a living thing inside me, but I need to reassure her, to remind her that she's all that matters.

"They were in your house. Do you film the women you fuck? Christ, did you film us—"

"Absolutely fucking not."

I turn her to face me and hold her neck and jaw between my hands, gently rubbing her lips with my thumb.

"Look at me right now. In my eyes, Trouble." Her stormy gaze finds mine. She looks *scared*, and that fuels my rage. "I did *not* take those photos. Someone planted that camera in my place, and I'm going to find out who, and when I do, they're going to regret it. I would *never* violate someone that way. What happens between you and me is just that: between you and me."

She swallows hard and closes her eyes again before she nods and another tear escapes, spiraling down her cheek.

"I know you wouldn't do that."

"That's right, you *know me*. Christ, baby, just the thought of it makes me sick. Those women might not have meant more to me than that one night, but they absolutely did not deserve that, and I will make sure those images are destroyed. He violated me *and* them, and he'll pay for it."

"Oh, God, you're right. Those poor women. I'm so selfish."

"Stop it." I kiss her forehead, and then her nose. "Come here."

She walks right into my arms, and the relief is immediate. She's not running away from me, even after my past was literally thrown in her face in glaring detail. She's right. She can't unsee that.

But I can do my best to wipe it from her memory.

I lift her bridal-style and walk up the stairs and to our bedroom. It's no longer mine. It's been ours for weeks now, and that's what it will always be.

She's clinging to me, her face buried in my neck, her hands in my hair.

When I get to the foot of the bed, I set her on her feet, and then I peel my shirt over my head and toss it aside.

Her hands immediately fall to my chest.

"The tree." I drag her hand over to my side, and she gently traces the dark lines of the willow tree, and every brush of her fingertip sends heat through me. "Look carefully."

She frowns up at me, but then she turns her attention to the ink. Then she blinks, and her eyes widen.

"Ryker."

"What do you see, baby?"

Her eyes fill with tears, and she leans her forehead against my chest. "Ry."

"Hey." I cup her chin and make her look at me, wiping at her tears with my thumb. "What do you see, Wills?"

"I see me." She swallows hard. "In the branches—it's my face."

I kiss her then, so tenderly, breathing in her breath, consuming every bit of her sweetness.

"It's you," I whisper against her lips. "Always you, baby. And it will only ever be you for as long as I'm breathing. You're it for me. You're in the marrow of my bones, seeped into every broken crack of my being. You smooth out my rough edges. You always have, since the first day I met you. You're all I want, and all I need, and I'll spend the rest of my life proving it to you."

"Get naked, Captain." She brushes the last of her tears away, and she's watching me with hungry eyes that I'll never say no to.

I kiss her once more before I push my jeans down, along with my boxer briefs, and then I reach for her. I ease her little white tank over her head and toss it aside, then push my fingers into the waistband of her denim shorts and tug her close, drag my lips down the side of her neck and grin when goose bumps break out over her soft skin.

"You're so fucking beautiful it almost pisses me off," I murmur and feel her chuckle.

"Why would that make you mad?"

I kiss the ball of her shoulder as I unfasten her shorts, and they fall around her ankles, leaving her in pink-and-green-striped panties that have my already-hard cock weeping. I cup her and feel that the fabric is soaked, and groan against her neck.

"Because every man will look at what's mine and want you. But they can't have you, can they?"

"No."

"Why is that, Willow?"

"Because I'm yours."

Fuck me sideways.

"That's right, baby. Because you're mine." I push my fingers farther down her slit, over the soaked panties, and bite the fleshy part of her shoulder. "You're so wet for me."

"Always." Her hands coast down my sides and around to my ass, and then I simply lift her around the waist and set her down in the middle of the bed. Sliding my fingers into the elastic of her panties, I pull them down her legs and bury my nose in them, breathing deep.

"You smell fucking fantastic."

She bites her lip, and I set the underwear aside.

I'll be keeping those.

With her legs spread wide, I can see her cunt glistening, just begging for my mouth, for my cock, and this sexy-as-fuck woman cups her breast and pinches her own nipple.

"Christ, you're beautiful."

She grins. "Yeah? You like what you see, Captain?"

I cover her body, my pelvis cradled between her legs, and rest on my elbows so I can kiss her sweet mouth.

"I don't like it. I *love* it. Every gorgeous inch. Now, I need to ask you something, and I want you to be honest."

She brushes her lips back and forth against my own. "Okay. I'll be honest. As long as you keep hitting my clit like that with your cock, I'll tell you anything."

"Anything?" I feel a sly smile slip over my face, and I move my hips back, then forward, and graze over that hard bundle of nerves. "Do you really think that I'd take photos like that without someone's consent?"

She pulls back and scowls up at me. "No, of course not. *No.*"

"Do you not see that you're it for me?" I slip my dick through her sopping wet slit. "That you're all I see in this world?"

"I know." She cups my face and kisses me tenderly, slides her tongue over mine.

"Do you know how much I love you?" I push inside her, making us both groan when I bottom out, and push my hands into her hair. I'm covering her, I'm inside her, I'm *everywhere*. And yet it's not enough.

It'll never be enough.

"I love you too."

"There is no one before you or after. It's only you, Willow. And I'm going to make you forget what you saw. I'm going to wipe it from your mind, because you're all I want, all I need, and the only thing that matters."

"Fuck, Ry."

My hips are moving faster, and my anger from earlier is starting to come back to the surface. That *anyone* would try to fuck with what I have with this woman makes me lose my mind.

I pull up onto my knees and look down to where we're joined together, and then I pull out and flip Wills onto her stomach.

"Head down, pussy up, sweetheart."

She eagerly sticks that perfect ass in the air, and I push a pillow under her hips to keep her up before I smack her ass and push inside her once more.

"Oh, God, that angle is *incredible*." She's hugging a pillow and buries her face in it, but I want her moans.

"Don't muffle your sounds, beautiful. Give them to me. I'm fucking greedy for every noise you make."

"Ry," she groans, pushing back against me with every thrust. "God, yes."

I slide my hand up her spine, around her neck, and then stick my thumb in her mouth.

"Suck it."

She does, without hesitation, and when it's good and wet, I pull it out of her mouth and cover her puckered hole with it, just teasing her there. She stiffens up on me but doesn't pull away.

"I won't do anything you don't want me to do," I assure her as I rub the pad of my thumb back and forth over that tight opening.

She doesn't tell me to stop, and she doesn't pull away, and with my next slam into her, I push just the tip of the digit inside her, and she *growls*.

"Why is that so *good*?"

I grin and lean forward so I can kiss her, right between her shoulder blades. "Do you like that, Trouble?"

"Yeah. God, I like that."

With each thrust, I ease into her a little more, until I'm in as far as my knuckle and Willow is writhing and moaning, and I know that I'm not going to last.

With my free hand, I reach around and rub her clit, and she immediately shivers around my cock.

"That's it, baby. I want you to come on this cock. Come all over me, sweetheart."

"Oh my God," she yells out before she comes apart, squeezing me so hard that I have no choice but to succumb to my own climax. I fall forward and cover her, kissing her neck, her shoulder, and then I finally move to her side, and she pops an eye open and smiles at me. "Hi."

"Hey." I can't stop touching her. My hand glides down her back to her ass and then back up again. "You okay?"

"I can't feel my body right now, but I'm sure I'll be fine in about two years, when I've recovered."

With a chuckle, I bite her arm, and she yelps. "You felt that."

"I guess I can feel my arm."

"Hmm." I reach out for her and drag her to me so she's lying on top of my chest. "Come here. I can't get close enough to you tonight."

"We're okay, Ry. What happened earlier made us a little needy for each other, but we're okay."

"Promise?"

She smiles up at me so sweetly, it steals my breath. "Promise. Gideon will find the asshole. He might kill them, even with an injured leg."

"Not if I get to them first." I kiss the top of her head. "I don't ever want you to feel insecure about us. Because I'm not going anywhere, and I don't give a rat's ass about anyone but you and that boy in the bunkhouse. And probably Gideon."

She smirks and nuzzles into me. "I don't feel insecure. Mostly, I was just jealous."

"I don't want that either." I shake my head. "You have no reason to be jealous, Trouble."

"But it's normal, Ry." She nudges back so she can look at me better. "It's one thing to know you've been with other people. For fuck's sake, you're thirty-five. Of course you're not a virgin. But it's another thing altogether to see images of it. So yeah, I was jealous. And let's not forget, it wasn't that long ago that you were irrationally jealous over a phone conversation that you overheard between me and a colleague. So I won't apologize for being jealous of literally *seeing* you fuck other women. Because I overthink literally everything."

"Okay, let's talk about that." I brush my finger down her cheek. "What are you overthinking?"

Her blue eyes go stormy, and I nudge her chin up. "Nope, just tell me. Don't get all up in your head."

"I believe that's the very definition of overthinking."

I narrow my eyes, and she sighs. "I was so enjoying the afterglow. I guess my mind wanders to silly things like, was she better at something than me? Did he like it when she did this or that? Does he think about the time he had *her* on her knees and she—"

"Okay, whoa." I roll her under me and kiss her senseless until I feel her relax into the mattress. "I'm not like that. I can't speak for all men, but *I* don't think that way. It may sound callous, but I don't give a fuck, because we're in our safe place and I can speak freely."

She nods, watching me with wide eyes.

"I don't remember much about most of those girls. Maybe bits and pieces, here and there. I was probably a little drunk with some of them. Or they were just a quick fuck, and then I moved on with my life. What you and I have is completely and utterly different. The sex is the best of my life."

"You don't have to say that for my ego."

"Good. Because I'm not. It's the truth." I raise an eyebrow, and she rolls her eyes.

"Yeah, it's the best of my life too."

"You sound so convincing, baby." I chuckle and nibble on her lips. "But it's more than the sex. It's this. Talking with you, laughing with you. It's the whole package, and that's something that I've never had with anyone else. So whatever you saw in those motherfucking pictures is *not* applicable to us. We're so much more than that."

She sighs and kisses my chin. "Okay."

"That's it? *Okay*?"

"I mean, what else do I say to that? I do wish I could sterilize my mind's eye."

I lift an eyebrow and nuzzle her cheek as I press inside her. "I guess I'd better get to work making you forget. I'll fuck you until this is all you remember, Trouble."

She sighs and wraps her arms and legs around me, pulling me into her. "I won't argue with that."

Chapter Twenty-Five

Ryker

The sun is already up. Usually, I'd be out at the barn by now, checking in with my guys and getting to work. But I texted Dusty and told him I'd see them after lunch.

Last night was about reassuring Willow. Loving her, and making her feel safe after some piece of shit sent her those photos and upset her. We both needed the time together, to be intimate.

But today, as soon as I leave this bed, I'll start finding out who did that and figuring out how to make them pay dearly.

Wills is still sleeping soundly next to me. She should be. It was a rigorous night of sex. I wasn't lying when I told her that making love to her is the best of my life. None of the women I was with before her can even hold a candle to her.

I think, by round four, I finally convinced her. But if she needs a reminder, I'll be happy to give it.

I kiss the back of her head, breathe her in, and then gently roll away, careful not to wake her as I slide out of bed, pad into the closet for some clothes, and then go downstairs for coffee and to do my business.

Less than ten minutes later, I sit at my desk, open the laptop, and then stare out the window to the mountains and wonder . . . *Where do I start?*

I've never had something like this happen before. Sure, there were women who claimed they were pregnant with my child, though I'd never laid a finger on them, or people who found out where I lived and hung out on the sidewalk, waiting for me. But I always had the team to call to take care of it. The PR department, or attorneys.

I'm no longer on the team.

I frown and then remember that Will Montgomery told me to call him if I ever needed anything. I never thought I'd have a reason to take him up on that offer.

I'd say this is a damn good reason.

It's still early, especially on the West Coast, so I send him a text.

Me: Good morning. This is Ryker James. Do you mind calling me at your earliest convenience? I have some questions.

Will's been retired from professional football for a few years, and he was one of the best quarterbacks of all time. I'm sure he'll have wisdom, and maybe some contacts, to share with me.

Before I can even set the phone down, he calls through.

"Hey, Will, I hope I didn't wake you."

"No, I was just finishing up in the gym. What's going on, Ryker?"

I swallow hard and push my hand through my hair. "Someone has decided to dick with my girl."

"Go on." His voice is hard now, and for some reason, that makes me feel better.

I tell him about the photos that Wills received last night.

"A few things here. First of all, *they're in your home*?"

"Some of them were, yeah. And based on the women in them, I'd say it was from more than a year ago."

"Nothing recent?"

"There hasn't been anything recent to document."

Aside from Wills, but we never had sex in the bedroom. Thank Christ.

"That's the first thing to look at. You're in Montana now?"

"I am, yeah."

"My brother is a cop," Will says, thoughtfully. "With your permission, he can meet someone there and sweep the place."

"My buddy Mac would meet him there, no problem."

"Good, we'll make that happen today. Now, the next thing. There was no threat sent with the photos?"

"No, no message of any kind. Just the images."

Just then, my phone pings with a text.

From an unknown fucking number.

"Wait, I'm getting something now. Hold on, I'm putting you on speaker so I can read it."

I tap the screen, put Will on speaker, and then open the text.

Unknown Contact: I'm sure I have your girlfriend's attention. To keep all these images out of the press, you'll need to pay me $180,000. I'll be in touch with more instructions.

I read it aloud to Will, but my ears have started to ring.

"What a stupid motherfucker," I growl.

"I take it you know who it is."

"For fuck's sake he's *stupid*. My former agent. He called me just yesterday and asked me to *loan* him that exact amount of money."

Will huffs out a laugh. "It's amazing you did as well in your career as you did."

"He's desperate. He owes the wrong people."

"Not your problem."

"No, not my problem. But now I have to prove it. I have my brother, who's with the Secret Service, looking into the phone records."

"Wow, that's a cool connection to have," Will says.

"I know. I'll call Mac and get things going on that end."

"I'll call my brother, too, and be in touch. And Ryker, I know you think you know this man, but if he's desperate enough to do this, don't let your guard down."

"Yeah, I thought of that too. Thanks, Will."

I hang up, drag my hands down my face, and take a moment to feel . . . *sad.*

Andy was my agent since I started in the league. He always went to bat for me, got me good contracts, and was good to me. Hell, I recommended him to other players. It was only in the past year, when he could sense that I was nearing the end of my career, and he got desperate, that things got bad.

He was never my friend, but I respected him.

I trusted him.

And now he's nothing.

I hear movement from the bedroom, so I leave the office and walk to the kitchen to make my girl some coffee, and when I return upstairs, I find her just coming out of the bedroom, ready for the day, yawning.

"Is that for me?" she asks.

"Of course." I pass her the mug and lean down to kiss her pouty lips. "Good morning, sweetheart."

"Morning." She sips her coffee and hums. "That's good. It always tastes better when you make it."

I can't help but grin at that. Christ, she's cute. "It does?"

"Mm-hmm." She steps into my arms and snuggles against my chest. "I thought you'd be out with the guys."

"No, I have to figure some stuff out first."

She frowns up at me. "What's happening wi—"

I cup her face and kiss her softly. "Don't worry about it. I don't want you to think about it. I'm handling everything, and when there's news to share, I'll fill you in."

"Promise?"

"Yes. I promise." I kiss her again. "You need breakfast. What do you want me to make for you?"

Her eyes soften again. "You're always feeding me."

"I've been hungry before. The people I love will never go through that. We have eggs and potatoes. Or oatmeal. Or bagels and smoked salmon."

She rubs her hand up and down my chest. "I'll go make myself something. My voice isn't quite awake enough to jump into work yet anyway. Do you want to join me?"

I start to say yes, but my phone rings, and it's Mac.

"I have to take this. Rain check?"

"Of course."

"Oh, and how about if you and I go swimming this afternoon? Just you and me. It's going to be hot again."

"You, mostly naked and wet and all to myself? It's a date." She winks and then heads downstairs toward the kitchen, and I take the call and walk back into my office.

"Dude, what the fuck is going on?" Mac begins before I can even start talking.

"What do you mean?"

"What do you mean, what do I mean? The retirement was a publicity stunt, and you're coming back to the team? That's kind of fucked up. I mean, I'm one of your best friends, and I had to find this out from the team?"

I pace my office as more anger pulses through me.

"Mac."

"Yeah?"

"I'm not coming out of retirement. Jesus, no."

"But Andy told Barry—"

"Andy has lost his motherfucking mind." I shove my hand in my pocket and stand at the window. "He's trying to extort money out of me, man. And I need your help."

Mac is silent for a moment, and then the fun-loving persona is gone and his deep voice rumbles through the phone.

"What do you need?"

I lay it out for him, and by the time we hang up, we have a plan in place.

Then, I make a call to Barry, the owner of the Blizzard. After the press conference, he told me to call anytime, so I'm taking him up on that.

"This is a surprise," he says into my ear.

"Hello, sir. It sounds like we have a situation."

"If you're talking about your idiot of an agent, no. There's no situation."

I feel my shoulders drop with relief. "He no longer speaks for me, sir."

"I know that. But I can plainly see that he's hell bent on fucking with you, son. What are you going to do about that?"

How is it that literally every single other person in my life is so damn supportive? How did I luck out this way?

"There are several moving pieces right now, but I have a feeling that Andy's going to end up in jail. That's between the two of us, of course."

He's quiet for a moment. "The team's legal and PR teams are yours to use as you need," he says. "You may no longer be on my starting lineup, but you're still one of ours, and we'll take care of you, Ryker."

"He threatened my girl."

"Then we'll take care of her too. Like I said, whatever you need. Just give me the word."

"I can't thank you enough."

"You don't need to. You lived and breathed for this team for fifteen years. We haven't forgotten that. Just let me know how to help."

"Thank you, sir."

"We'll speak soon."

I hang up and let out a deep breath. As long as Andy doesn't send those photos to anyone else, everything is going to be fine.

Chapter Twenty-Six

Willow

All my voice work is done for the day, since I wrapped up a project, and then I took a couple of hours to prep the next. I haven't turned my phone on today. I was worried that I'd get more photos, and I don't think my mental health can stand any more.

Don't get me wrong. Ryker did a damn good job of making me forget all about it through the night, and I love that he wanted to do that. That he needed to be as close to me as I needed to be to him.

But it doesn't change the fact that it happened, and I don't know if I'll ever get all the photos out of my head. Seeing him in intimate situations with beautiful women honestly makes me sick to my stomach. I don't know, and I don't *want* to know, how many women he's been with. He's been a professional athlete at the top of his game his entire adult life. Of course women threw themselves at him. I watched it happen.

It was disgusting.

But I'm no virgin. Sure, I've only been with four men in my life because I've raised Aiden for the past decade, and dating when you're a single parent isn't easy.

But there were men.

Four of them.

I bet I saw Ryker with fifteen different women, easy, in those photos. And I know that's only scratching the surface.

Ugh, stop thinking about it.

I power on my phone, because as much as I'd like to leave it off, I use it for work, and I need to know if anyone has tried to reach me.

I pace behind my desk, trying to work off some nervous energy, and my phone pings with a few messages.

No missed calls.

"Thank God," I mutter to myself when I see that the messages are just work related, and one from Gideon.

Gid: How you doing, baby girl?

Since he's injured, I know he's not working, so I simply call him. I know that I can always talk to Ryker, but right now, I need a best friend who *isn't* my boyfriend.

"Hey, you," he says.

"Hi, handsome. Wanna FaceTime, or is this okay?"

Suddenly, the phone rings with an incoming FaceTime call, and I accept it and set the phone up on my desk so I'm hands-free.

"I guess that answers my question."

"I want to see your face," Gid says, eyeing me. "You didn't answer my text this morning."

"I just turned the phone on. I left it off all day because I didn't want to get any more pornographic photos of my man with random women."

Gideon blows out a breath and cringes. "I'm sorry, Wills."

"Unless it was you that sent them, you have nothing to feel sorry for."

He shakes his head. "No one should have to see that. I'm tracking down the sender. I have calls out to your phone carrier."

"The things you can find are kind of scary."

He laughs and then just smiles at me. Gideon doesn't often smile. He never has, so when I get one, I tuck it away in my heart.

"Is it always going to be like this?" I ask him.

"What do you mean?"

I blow out a breath and lay my forehead on the desk, close my eyes.

"Wills, talk to me."

"I don't want to anymore."

He chuckles, and I squint one eye open and stare at him.

"He has baggage, Wills."

"We all do," I counter. "We all had tough childhoods—"

"I'm not even talking about that. He's always going to be *Ryker James*, the phenom, the GOAT of professional hockey. Two-time Stanley Cup winner, MVP, and all the other things that make his ego big."

I smirk at that. "I'm proud of him."

"Fuck, I am too. He worked damn hard for all of it. He deserves it."

I nod slowly.

"But it comes with the fame, and even if he's moved to the ranch and isn't in the sport anymore, the fame won't ever really go away. What happened last night isn't part of that. This was malicious and, honestly, illegal. This isn't something you'll have to deal with often, if ever again. It's mostly people asking for autographs and photos when you're in public."

"I don't mind that."

"Are you telling me that last night gave you second thoughts about your relationship?"

"No." I sit up and push my hands through my hair. "No, I'm in love with him, Gid. There's no going back for me. He's it—he's the one—and I'll fight with everything in me for him. I'm not pulling away."

"Then why do you look so fucking sad?"

I smile at him. "I love you. You know that, right?"

"I love you, too, baby girl. What do you need? Need me to come home and fix it?"

I raise my eyebrows. "*That's* what it takes for you to come home? Not getting shot in the leg?"

"Getting shot in the leg is part of my job. You're my family. Those are two different things."

"You're kind of badass. You know that, right? You got *shot*, Gid. With bullets."

"Yes. I was there."

I snort.

"You changed the subject on me, Trouble."

With a sigh, I shrug a shoulder. "I'm not . . . *sad*. I don't know what I am. You saw them. I wouldn't want to see that if it were *you*. And you're my brother. How do you think it feels when I'm in love with him?"

"I imagine it sucks."

"Understatement."

"And it's not your fault. It's not his fault. It's not those women's fault."

"Exactly. So who am I supposed to be mad at?"

"The asshole who took them, without consent, and sent them to you."

"Who is it?"

He shakes his head. "I have a pretty good idea but can't prove it yet. As soon as I know, you guys will know. Now, what do you need to feel better?"

"To know, I guess. So they can be dealt with and we can just move on."

"Take them off your phone, Wills."

"Ry already did. I don't ever want to see them again. I think Ry and I are going to head out to the lake and swim this afternoon. It's been hot as fuck here, and a swim sounds good. That might help."

"Go scare the fish," he says. "Everything else is being dealt with."

"I know. Ry was in his office all morning on calls. Maybe it doesn't help that there's nothing I can *do*."

"If I had a job for you, I'd give it to you. But I don't."

"You would not give me a job."

Gid laughs again. Wow, two in one day. He must be feeling better. "No, I wouldn't. Go enjoy the sunshine."

"Okay. Did you have therapy today?"

"Yep."

"How did it go?"

"Hurt like a bitch."

"I've never understood that phrase, but I'm sorry you're hurting. Anything I can do for *you*?"

"Go have fun, kiddo."

"Okay. Love you."

"Love you back."

He hangs up, and I walk to the bedroom to change into a bikini. I only own two bathing suits, because summers in Montana are short and I don't spend a ton of time on the water. Maybe now that I live out here, I'll do more swimming, since the lake and the creeks are so close.

I've just pulled on a loose cover-up when Ryker walks into the room and wiggles his eyebrows.

"Well, hello, gorgeous."

"Hi. Are we going swimming now?"

"Hell yes. I just have to change." He disappears into the closet for five minutes and then comes out wearing only a pair of swimming trunks.

Good God, his body still does things to me. All the muscles. All the ink.

That knowing grin.

"Don't you dare touch me." I point a finger at him and skirt my way to the door. "If you get started, we won't leave this room."

"Would that be a terrible thing? I saw the way you were checking me out. You can have all of me, sweetheart."

I snort and start down the stairs. "Easy, big guy. Inflate your ego much more, and you won't fit through the door."

We're both laughing when he takes my hand and kisses my knuckles, and then we walk the quarter of a mile to the nearby lake.

"Why didn't Ray build the house on the lake?" I ask Ryker as we follow the path. "It's a nice size, and the views are just as good there."

"I asked him once, and he said it was because Debbie was worried there would be snakes and a bunch of extra bugs from the water, so he built it a little ways away for her."

I rub a hand over my chest. "God, he loved her."

"I'd never seen anything like it," Ryker says, shaking his head. "I think my biological mom cared about me. But I'd never witnessed someone truly loving the hell out of someone the way those two did each other. And then the three of us too. I had one hell of a shitty attitude when we were brought here, and I had every intention of being good enough to stay, but I wasn't going to win any awards for being a good kid."

"You and Gideon were both so angry. You'd beat the hell out of each other before you got here."

"That was only the latest time out of dozens before that." He chuckles. "I liked that Ray was up front and honest, right from the get-go. The one rule was 'We don't hurt the girls.' I'd never respected anything more in my life."

I squeeze his hand. "You wouldn't have hurt us anyway."

"Who could ever even think about being ugly to Debbie? Christ, she was a tiny thing, but she was pure sunshine. She just spewed happiness and love onto everyone."

"She was irresistible," I agree as we walk over a small hill and see the lake come into view. "Now, I have a serious question for you."

He looks down at me and quirks up the side of his mouth. "Okay. Shoot."

"Are you going to get my hair wet?"

His eyes flick to my topknot, and then he smirks. "Fuck yeah, I'm gonna get *all of you* wet, Trouble."

"Damn it." I wiggle out of my cover-up, toss it aside, and then run toward the water. There's a beachy area that Ray built when we were teens so it would be easier to swim, and I dive right in, hair and all, and swim just under the surface.

It's so hot today, and the water is nice and cool, and suddenly, Ryker's with me and holding on to me.

I wrap my arms and legs around him and fuse my lips to his as he keeps us afloat in the water.

"You're so fucking sexy," he says against my lips.

"Is that a fish in the water, or are you happy to see me?"

He chuckles and grinds against me. "That's all me, baby."

"We're not having sex in this lake, Ryker."

"Says who?"

"Says me. Anyone could come out here at any time."

His brows lower over his eyes. "No way. All the guys are working. There's no one around."

Suddenly, we hear horse hooves, and Ryker's eyes widen.

"You've got to be shitting me."

I rub my nose over his. "Told you."

"Hey, we want to swim," Aiden calls out as he and Micah dismount their horses. I haven't spent much time with Micah. He's a quiet boy, but I can see that he's eager to get in the water.

They both strip down to their underwear and then run and cannonball in, splashing us.

"So much for lake sex," Ry mutters in my ear.

"Don't worry. I'll make it up to you later."

He leans in and bites my neck and then whispers, "I can't fucking wait."

Chapter Twenty-Seven

Aiden

I've gotten used to getting up at the ass crack of dawn. Actually, it's before the ass crack of dawn because the sun isn't even up yet. But Dusty's already in the kitchen, making us all breakfast. He makes us breakfast every day. We offer to take turns, but he still does it.

I don't know what I would make if it was my turn. I'm just a kid. I don't cook so good. I guess I could toast bagels or something.

It's probably for the best that Dusty cooks.

Micah and I share a room in the bunkhouse. He's cool. Since I bought the gaming system, he bought the TV in our room, and we spend a lot of time in here in the evenings, playing around.

"I smell bacon," Micah says as he climbs out of bed and scratches his chest. Without saying anything else, he leaves the room, and I yawn.

Neither of us is a big talker. That's probably why we get along so well.

I get up and pull on my jeans and a T-shirt, grab my hat and boots, and walk out to the kitchen, where sure enough, Dusty's finishing up breakfast and the other guys are already having coffee at the table.

Even Ryker's here this morning, which isn't typical for him. He usually meets us later on.

"Is Aunt Wills okay?" I ask him with a frown.

"She's still sleeping," he replies and then sips his coffee, and I immediately feel better.

Good.

I call her Aunt Wills, but she's really my mom in every way that matters. She's the only mom I remember. I don't know much about my real mom. I just remember being hungry. And sick.

I was really sick.

"I hear you all had fun yesterday," Dusty says as he piles the bacon on a plate. "Went for a swim."

"Yeah, it was fun," Micah says as he joins us. "I didn't know that lake was there."

Ry grins. "As long as you finish your work each day, you can swim as much as you want. We lived in that lake when we were kids. It's the best way to cool off."

"Just no swimming alone," Micah's dad says, giving us both a stern look. "Be safe about it."

We nod and dig into the food. I'm hungry here, but never because I haven't been fed. It's because we work so fucking hard. And I kind of love it. I like the horses and the cows, and we got chickens last week, and that's pretty cool. I don't know dick about chickens, but I guess I'll learn. I mean, won't they freeze in the winter? It's weird.

"Hey, Aiden," Ry says as we finish eating, "there's something that came for you yesterday. You'll be with me in the barn this morning."

"For *me*?" I raise an eyebrow. "It's not my birthday or anything."

Ry just laughs, and then we get our stuff and set off for the barn.

"How's everything going?" he asks me.

"Great."

"Do you still like living out here?"

I frown. Is he going to tell me that we have to move back to the city after all? *I won't go back. I'd rather run away.*

"I love it here," I tell him honestly. "Will I really have to move into your house when the summer's over?"

"Yep, you'll live with us during the school year," he replies.

"So I don't have to go back to Missoula?"

He stops walking and turns to me, takes me by the shoulders the way he does when he's telling me something serious.

"Aiden, you are staying here. You and Willow live here now. Wills even put her house on the market. You're not going back to Missoula, okay?"

"Okay. Good."

"Have you had any weird messages come through on your phone from a number you don't know, or an unknown number?"

Now he's making me nervous again.

"I haven't looked at my phone since last night," I reply. "I got a text from Mac to hop on and play *Call of Duty* with him. But there's nothing weird."

"That's what I want to hear. If that changes, you tell me right away."

"I will. I mostly ignore my phone. I'm too busy to pay any attention to it."

"That's not a bad thing." Ry opens the barn door, and we walk inside.

"Hey, girl," I say to Sunflower, the horse I ride the most. She can be skittish, but she loves me. I rub her head and then follow Ry to the other side of the building, where a big box sits in the corner. "What's that?"

"The punching bag I promised you."

One thing I've learned this summer is that if Ryker promises something, he comes through. Always.

"I know you're not quite as angry as when you first came here, but we can all use a round or two with a punching bag once in a while," he says with a shrug. "I need your help hanging it."

"Sure, I can do that." I like it when he needs my help. I like feeling useful.

"What's your favorite part of the ranch?" he asks me as he cuts open the box.

"What do you mean?"

He shrugs and gestures for me to hold on to the closed end so he can shimmy the bag out of the cardboard.

"When I first moved here, when I was about your age, my favorite part was the quiet. I liked that there isn't a lot of noise out here. And the stars are cool too."

I nod, thinking it over. "I guess I just like that I feel safe here."

He stops what he's doing and turns to me. "You didn't feel safe with Willow in the city?"

"I always feel safe with Aunt Wills, because she's a mama bear and she will cut a bitch."

Ry smirks and nods. "Yeah, she is that."

"But I didn't feel safe at school. I never knew what to expect, you know?"

"Yeah." He sighs and pulls a hook out of his pocket, then stands on a stool to screw the hook into the beam above us. "I know that feeling, and it fucking sucks."

"I know what to expect here. I'm kind of nervous about starting a new school, but it'll be a million times better than the last one, so it's no big deal."

"If there is ever even *one minute* that you don't feel safe, you come to me or Willow and tell us. No more keeping that to yourself. Got it?"

"I didn't want to worry her. She already has so much going on—"

"She's your mama bear, kiddo. It's her whole job to worry. And, news flash, she'll worry whether you give her a reason to or not. Might as well keep her in the loop so she's worrying about the right things."

I never thought about it like that.

"Yeah, you're probably right."

"Of course I am. Here, I need you to lift this thing so I can slip the loop onto the hook."

I bend my knees and get under it, then lift, and Ry guides it onto the hook, and then it's all done.

"One punching bag." Ry pats it and then ruffles my hair. "Now, let's saddle up and ride some fence line today."

I nod and turn toward Sunflower. I'm good at saddling her up, keeping her tack clean and taken care of.

She's my best girl.

First, I brush her down and give her some carrots, and then I lay a blanket on her before lifting the heavy saddle onto her back. Once it's secured, I turn to see that Ry's done the same for his horse, and we ride out of the barn.

"It's already hot out," I say to Ryker as we head out into the sunshine.

"Yeah, we might all end up in the lake again this evening," he says. "It's handy. I could put in a pool, but what's the point?"

"Aunt Wills would probably prefer a pool."

His gaze whips to mine. "Why?"

"She doesn't love swimming with fish and bacteria and all the other creatures in the water. Those are her words, not mine."

"She didn't say anything yesterday."

I smirk. "Of course not. It's not like she can *choose* a pool out here."

He starts to say something, but his phone rings. "I have to take this, buddy. Ride ahead, and I'll catch up."

I nod and turn Sunflower toward the fence line closest to the house. But as I get closer, I frown.

Why are there people here?

They aren't anyone that works here. Half of them are women.

Girls.

As I approach the fence, they start to wave, and I feel Sunflower hesitate.

"Whoa, girl, it's okay. We're just going to say hi."

"You're not Cap," someone says with disappointment in her voice.

"You all need to leave," I announce, keeping my voice strong. The girls are pretty. They're not wearing much of anything. Bikini tops and jean shorts, their hair up, and their eyes hidden behind sunglasses. There are four of them, along with two guys.

They all look older than me. Maybe in college.

"We don't have to go anywhere," one of the guys says. "Where's Ryker James?"

"This is private property," I reply, keeping my eyes hard. "And you need to get the fuck off our property."

"We were invited," one of the girls says. "And you're kind of cute. I'd do a lot of fun things to you if you introduced us to him."

What the hell?

"Oh my God, I think that's him!"

The girls start to squeal, and Sunflower spooks. She rears up on her hind legs and then bucks, and I can't stay on her. The next thing I know, I'm airborne, and then I'm in the dirt, and everything hurts.

Chapter Twenty-Eight

Ryker

"Good morning," I say, answering the call from Gideon as Aiden points his horse toward the fence. I love seeing my kid on his horse. He's a fucking natural.

"You're not going to like this," Gid says in my ear, and I let out a gusty breath.

"It's Andy, isn't it?"

"Right the first time."

"That motherfucker." I filled my brother in yesterday on the cops going to my condo with Mac. "They found six cameras in my house, Gid."

"I know. I talked with a Lieutenant Matt Montgomery. How did you get a high-ranking murder cop to help with this?"

"He's Will Montgomery's brother."

"Ah. Makes sense."

"There were two cameras in my bedroom, two in the living room, one in the kitchen, and one out by the rooftop pool."

Thank Christ there wasn't one in my office.

"They ran fingerprints," Gid informs me. "All Andy's. He wasn't even smart enough to wear gloves."

"He wasn't even smart enough to demand a different amount of money from what he'd asked me for not a day before he sent those photos."

Gideon scoffs. "I never liked that guy."

"Yeah, yeah, so you and Wills have said many times."

"There's a warrant out for his arrest, and he'll likely be picked up today. I can prove that he's the one who sent the photos, so in addition to stalking and a host of other charges from the cameras, extortion . . . hell. A ton of things—he'll be arrested and is likely going to prison for a while."

I think of Willow and how upset she's been, and I can't help but be okay with that.

"Hopefully he's arrested before he sends those photos to the press."

"I believe it's happening as we speak," Gid replies. "I'll keep you posted on that."

I notice some commotion at the fence, and that Aiden is talking to . . . a group of people?

"Why are there people on my property?"

"What do you mean?"

I head that way. "There are six of them. Four female, two male, and they're harassing Aiden."

"I'm calling the sheriff," Gid says. "Christ, can't you live without drama for one day?"

"Yeah, yeah."

I hang up and urge my horse to move faster. As I approach, one of the girls squeals.

"Oh my God, I think that's him!"

They start jumping up and down and high-fiving, but I don't give a rat's ass about that, because Sunflower rears up and then bucks Aiden off, and he's in the air, falling from the saddle.

When he lands in the dirt, I know it's not good. He moans as I dismount my horse, run over to him, and fall to my knees beside him.

"Hey, sorry," someone calls over. "We just got excited."

"Why the fuck are you *here*?" I demand, still not looking their way.

"Hey, if you didn't want people at your new guest ranch, why did you post the address on Insta?"

I spare them a glare. "I didn't."

"Sure you did. We all follow you, and you don't post very much, but you announced the new guest ranch today, and we came right over."

Aiden groans.

The front door of the house flies open, and Willow comes running at top speed.

"What the hell happened to my boy?"

"Don't touch him," I order as I pull my phone out of my pocket and call emergency services. "The horse threw him because these idiots scared Sunflower."

"Don't hurt Sunflower," Aiden murmurs.

"Shh," Willow says, brushing his hair off his forehead. "No one will hurt her. What hurts, baby?"

"Everything."

"This is Ryker James at the Triple Creek Ranch," I say when the phone is answered. "I believe you have deputies on the way, but I also need an ambulance."

"That's right, we have two men on the way out there. I'll dispatch an ambulance now. What is the injury?"

"Thrown from a horse. His shoulder is either broken or dislocated. I don't know what else is hurt."

"ETA is ten minutes," she says in my ear.

"Longest ten minutes of my fucking life," I reply as I hang up and then call Dusty. Jesus, I've been on my phone more in the past forty-eight hours than I have been in the last year combined.

"Hey, boss."

"I need you by the house to collect our horses. Aiden's been hurt. We have unwanted visitors."

"Two minutes" is his clipped reply before he hangs up.

"I want to cradle him," Willow says, tears running down her cheeks.

"Until the ambulance gets here, I don't want to move him," I reply softly and reach out to rub my hand up and down her back. "Buddy, what hurts now?"

"Shoulder," he says. "Doesn't feel right. Head hurts. Foot got twisted."

"Did it get caught in the stirrup?" I ask him.

"Think so." He huffs a breath in and out, and I can see tears gathering in his eyes. "Scared me."

"I know." I pat his good shoulder as Willow brushes her fingers through his hair. "I know, kiddo. It's scary as hell."

"Listen, we didn't mean to hurt anyone," one of the guys says. "We really thought it was okay for us to be here."

"I told them to go," Aiden says.

Two sheriff cars roll up the driveway, and the men hurry over to us just as Dusty comes riding up to take care of the horses.

It's chaos for several minutes, and all I can think about is getting my boy to the fucking hospital.

"I want them gone," I say, pointing to the unwanted visitors. "They're trespassing. An ambulance is on the way for my boy."

"Can you give us a rundown on what happened?" deputy number one asks, and I stand to give him the information. His face is grim as he turns to the strangers. "Let's go, folks. And for future reference, if someone tells you to leave, you *leave*."

As they file away, an ambulance *finally* pulls in, and the EMTs rush toward us with a stretcher.

"I go with him," Willow says, not leaving Aiden's side. "He's mine. I go with him."

"That's fine, ma'am," one of the EMTs says and then turns to me. "We'll be at Paradise General. You can follow us in."

I turn to Dusty, who gestures with his chin. "Go. I have everything here handled."

I jump into my truck and immediately call Gideon, and then the PR department for the Blizzard, and they assure me they'll get my social media handled.

Fucking Andy.

I'd bet a year's salary it was that asshole who put my address on social media.

He's going to pay for all this.

Chapter Twenty-Nine

Willow

My heart is going to burst out of my body. Jesus, I can't calm down. My boy is on a gurney, moaning in pain, and there's nothing they can do for him until we get to the hospital.

"His blood pressure is good," the EMT named Sandy says. "Good heart rate too. And I don't think he has a concussion, because his pupils are the same and not dilated."

I know she's trying to calm me down, but until a doctor tells me that I can take him home, nothing is going to calm me down. My kid is in pain, and there's absolutely nothing I can do about it.

Talk to him, Sandy mouths to me.

"Hey, kiddo, remember that time that we went to Disney World when you were ten?"

"You got sick after Space Mountain," he says with a smirk.

"Are you seriously making fun of me for getting motion sick?"

"Duh." He winces when we hit a bump. "It was cool that Gideon and Ryker met us there."

They surprised us both the day after we got there, and the four of us had a whole week of rides, time at the pool, and all the park food in the world, and I'm pretty sure Ryker spent a mint on all the souvenirs that

Aiden wanted. It was one of the few times over the past decade that I got to spend significant time with Ryker, and I soaked in every minute of it.

"Where are your Mickey ears?" I ask him.

"In my room at the ranch," he says. "In the big house, not in the bunkhouse."

I smile softly. "Aw, you still have them?"

He purses his lips. "Don't tell anyone."

"Hey, I still have my Little Mermaid ears," I inform him. "They're cool."

Finally, I see the hospital come into view, and when we park, the back doors fling open, and the paramedics carefully pull Aiden out, trying not to jostle his shoulder.

"I'm here," I hear Ryker call out as he runs from where he parked just about ten yards away, and then his hand is in mine as we walk right behind the gurney and EMTs.

"Take him to bay six," someone calls out, and then suddenly we're in a cramped room with curtains rather than walls in this small ER, and the medics, along with two nurses, gingerly move Aiden onto the bed.

Ryker pulls me against his chest, my back to his front, and wraps his arms around my shoulders. I soak in his strength, his warmth, as my emotions flutter all over the damn place. I want to scream at them to hurry up, but I don't want them to hurt my kid, and I need to stay out of their way.

"He's going to be okay," Ryker murmurs into my ear. "See? He's alert, and he's answering questions."

I nod, but there's a huge lump in my throat, and I can't answer him.

"Trust me, sweetheart, I've had my fair share of knocks on the head and injuries, and I'm telling you, he's going to be fine."

"Okay," I whisper and squeeze his forearms against my chest.

We're ushered out when they wheel in an x-ray machine, and then after we've waited about twenty minutes, a doctor roughly our age walks in. He's in a white coat, and it reads "Dr. Ashby."

"Well, I have good news," the doctor says with a smile for Aiden. I'm clasping his good hand in mine. "The shoulder isn't broken, but it *is* dislocated, and that means we have to reset it."

"And that's going to hurt like a bitch," Aiden guesses.

Dr. Ashby's lips twitch with humor. "Not gonna lie. It's going to hurt. But we can give you meds—"

"Just do it," Aiden says, shaking his head. "It feels weird, and I'd rather get it over with."

"You don't want to be here for this," Ryker tells me and tries to pull me away, but I adamantly shake my head.

"I'm not leaving."

"It's okay, Aunt Wills," Aiden says and squeezes my hand. "You should step out. I'm okay."

"No."

"I can also report," the doctor continues, "that there is no concussion, and the ankle is just twisted. You have some scrapes that we'll clean up for you, but you'll be able to go home in about an hour."

"Good," Aiden says. "I have work to do."

"No work for quite a while," the doctor says. "You'll need to keep that shoulder immobile for about six weeks while it heals."

"No way."

"Yes way," Ryker says. "You'll move into the ranch house with us."

"Sonofa—" Aiden pouts, and I squeeze his hand.

"Hey, you're fine, and that's all that matters. If Sunflower had stomped on you—" My voice cracks, and I can't complete the thought.

"Whoa, baby," Ryker says and kisses my temple. "No going there. She didn't, he's going to be fine, and you can baby him for the rest of the summer."

"Hey, Ry," Aiden says, "we were talking about that time we all went to Disney World in the ambulance. Remember when Aunt Wills got sick after—OH MY GOD!"

The doctor took that opportunity to reset the shoulder, and I'm pretty sure Aiden just crushed my hand.

Ryker hisses behind me.

"That hurts so bad," he whispers.

"You've had a dislocated shoulder?"

"Twice," he confirms.

"You didn't tell me!"

"No need to worry you, Trouble."

"We are having a conversation when we get home, Captain."

"Captain," Dr. Ashby says with a nod. "I thought you looked familiar. You're Ryker James."

"Guilty."

I feel Ry tense up. Normally he doesn't mind talking with fans, but this isn't a good time. Luckily, the doctor just nods and then goes about his business. At least he didn't ask for an autograph.

Aiden wipes a tear from his cheek.

"It's just a reaction to the pain," he says, trying to talk all of us into believing that he wouldn't cry.

"Of course it is." I lean down and kiss his head. "I love you, buddy. I'm so sorry it hurts. We'll take you home and get some good drugs in you, and you can rest."

"Lame," Aiden says, but he leans into my touch. There are moments when he's still my little boy.

Finally, an hour later, after they've given him a full bag of fluids, cleaned his cuts and scrapes, wrapped the ankle, and put his arm in a sling, we can head home, armed with a few days' worth of pain medicine so we don't have to rush to the pharmacy. Ryker is careful to avoid bumps as he drives the truck, and it takes both of us to help Aiden inside and up the stairs, thanks to his twisted ankle.

"This sucks ass," Aiden says as I help him lie down on his bed. "I have to go out to the bunkhouse and pack up my stuff."

"That'll be done for you," Ry replies. "Just rest for today, buddy. Take a nap."

"I think the medicine is making me sleepy," he says. "But it's hard to get comfortable."

"I'll adjust your pillows when needed," I assure him and then kiss his head again, breathing him in. His hair is always so soft against my lips. "Nap for a while, and then I'll bring up some food."

"Okay."

He's asleep before we leave the room.

"Jesus, I'm tired," I say as Ry and I walk down to the living room and curl up on the couch.

"If we never relive that, it'll be too soon." His lips are in my hair, brushing back and forth. "I have news about the other stuff, but if you're too tired to talk about it, we can do it later."

"No, I want to know. It's killing me." I lean back so I can see his face. "What's going on?"

"It was all Andy," he says and brushes a lock of my hair behind my ear. "He's been arrested this morning on a bunch of charges."

"And he didn't send those pictures to anyone else?"

"As far as we know, no. He just wanted to get money out of me."

I sigh and lean against him again. "I'm so sorry, Ry. You trusted him."

"Yeah, well, I'm just glad it's over. But I'm thinking about going to Seattle to check on the penthouse and talk with the attorneys and PR people in person."

Panic shoots through me.

Jesus, I don't want him to leave. I know I can do this alone. I've taken care of Aiden during illnesses and injuries by myself since he was little, and if I had to, I could do it now too. And I *hate* to ask for help.

I hate feeling like a burden to anyone. It was drilled into me as a kid, by the one woman who was supposed to love and protect me, that I was just that: a burden.

But I have Ryker now. And I really don't want him to go to Seattle.

"No. Please don't go, Ry."

He scowls down at me in concern. "Hey, I won't be gone long. Just a day or two, so I can check in with the authorities, my penthouse—"

"We need you here." I don't even care that I'm being needy as fuck and that I sound a little unhinged. I straddle his lap and wrap my arms around his neck, almost clinging to him. "I *never* ask you for anything, Ry, but I'm asking for this. You have the police, the team, and even Gid helping with the mess in Seattle, but Aiden and I need you here at the ranch. I know I'm asking a lot. I *know*. But if you leave right now, I'll fall apart, and that's your fault."

God, I'm so close to tears. The adrenaline from dealing with Aiden has worn off, and now my emotions are all over the place, and *I do not want him to leave me*.

He lifts an eyebrow and runs his hand up and down my back. "Why is it my fault?"

"Because you made me love you and depend on you, and he's hurt, Ry. Under literally any other circumstances, I would tell you to have a good trip. I would even offer to go with you, but Aiden—"

I feel a tear slip down my cheek, and he smooths it away with his thumb.

"I have done it by myself for all these years, and I *can't* anymore. Not now that I know how fucking good it feels to do it with you, and if you go away for a few days, I might lose my mind."

"Okay, take a breath. Deep breath for me, sweetheart."

I do as he asks, and he breathes with me. I'm on the verge of a panic attack. His hands ghost up and down my back, and he's soothing me with that deep, calm voice.

"That's it. You're doing great, baby. It's been a shitty day, but Aiden is safe upstairs, and he's *fine*."

The tears keep coming. I held it together until Ryker said he wants to go to Seattle. And it would make sense for him to go. If I were in his shoes, I'd want to as well.

But I can't deal with it right now.

"I hate sounding weak like this."

"No. You don't sound weak at all. I'm glad you're asking for what you need." He wraps his arms around me and hugs me to him, and I bury my face in his neck, clinging. "Always tell me what you need, baby. And if this is what you need, I'll stay home. You're right, everyone's handling everything for me, and I can ask Mac to get eyes on the penthouse."

"I'm sorry."

"I don't want you to be sorry." He's peppering my shoulder with kisses. "I like that you need me, and I'm happy to be here with both of you."

"Today scared me."

"I know. It scared me too. I'm usually the one getting injured, and I can take it. I don't like it when it's my family."

His family.

Just when I think my heart can't melt any more, he goes and says something like that.

"It's been a rough week," he adds, still hugging me close.

"I'm ready for boring now, please."

He huffs out a laugh and tugs my face up so he can see me. "Me too. There will be press surrounding the Andy shit. There's nothing I can do about it, but the team will help keep it to a minimum."

I nod and kiss his chin. "It'll die down after a while, and something else will be interesting."

"That's how it works," he agrees as his dark eyes skim over my face. "Everything's going to be okay, sweetheart. I promise."

"I know. But please, stay here, okay? Even if it's just for the next week or so, and then we can reevaluate."

"That works." His hand cups my cheek. "Whatever you need, Trouble. You're the priority."

I close my eyes and rest my forehead against his. "Thank you."

"Always. I love you so much."

"I love you too."

Chapter Thirty

Ryker

One Month Later . . .

"You may be out of the sling, but you still have to take it easy," Willow informs Aiden, who just rolls his eyes. "Don't you sass me, young man."

"With my *face*?"

"Yes, with your face." She grabs said face and kisses his cheek, making him scrunch up his nose. "You've done a really good job of healing and taking it easy. Let's keep that trend going, okay?"

"Yeah, okay." He pats her back. "But I'm swimming today."

She frowns, but I jump in.

"The swimming will be good exercise for him," I say. "Just not for too long, and don't overdo it."

"You're a bunch of nags," Aiden decides.

"You're just *now* figuring that out?" Wills demands with a laugh. "Go swim and have fun with Micah. School starts Monday, so we need to run into Missoula tomorrow for some school clothes and supplies."

"I have clothes."

"Yeah, and you've grown three inches this summer," she says, propping her hands on her curvy hips. Jesus, my girl is beautiful. "Plus, most of your clothes have gotten so dirty, it's impossible to get all the stains out."

"I don't care."

"I do." Willow shakes her head. "Go swim before I kick you in the butt."

Aiden smirks. "Yeah right." But he hurries out the door and meets Micah at the path that leads to the lake.

"Alone at last." I waggle my eyebrows at her, and she grins.

"I have work to do, you know."

"Do you?" I advance toward her and cup her face, brush my thumb over her lower lip. "I can be quick."

"You're *never* quick."

I smirk. "That's because I like to savor you, baby. Every inch of you. Once I get started, I lose myself."

"I think you just upped the swoon factor to get into my shorts."

I lick my lips. "Is it working?"

"Possibly."

I bend and lift Willow onto my shoulder and carry her upstairs.

"Hey, I can walk, you know."

"You're not getting away from me. I'm getting you naked, and by the time I slide inside you, you'll be begging me for it."

"I don't beg for anything."

I smirk. "Challenge accepted, sweetheart."

After dumping her on the bed, I don't bother to take her shorts off. They're loose and short, and I can push them to the side to slip inside her.

But I do want to see her gorgeous-as-fuck tits. So I push her shirt up and off, then unfasten her bra and pull one tight nub into my mouth, making her back arch and her hands plunge into my hair.

"God, Ry. It always feels so good."

It's only been one summer with her like this, and yet it feels like she's been mine forever. I nibble my way up her chest, over her collarbone, and to her ear, where I press my lips against her smooth skin.

Reaching between us, I shimmy my sweats down, pull her shorts to the side, and push two fingers into her wet heat.

"Shit," she moans.

"Mine," I growl before replacing my fingers with my cock, and then I pause when I'm balls deep. "I used to think that it was this ranch that was my safe haven, but I was wrong."

I nudge a lock of her hair off her cheek and sweep my thumb under her eye.

"It's you, baby. You're my safe place."

"You're all I need," she says, tightening her walls around me. "Always."

I pull back, then push inside her all the way and grin against her when she gasps.

"Always, Trouble."

Epilogue

Ryker

One Year Later

"I'm not sleeping without you tonight."

Willow is sitting at the kitchen island, marking things off her long-as-fuck to-do list. She glances up at me and raises an eyebrow.

"It's tradition."

"Fuck tradition. We've been living together for over a year."

She pops that lower lip out because she knows that I can't resist it, the little minx. "But, Ry, it's bad luck for us to sleep together the night before the wedding and then see each other before the ceremony tomorrow."

"Wait, let me get this straight." I hold up a hand. "You expect me to not only sleep without the love of my life tonight, but also not even see you until the ceremony tomorrow afternoon?"

"That's how it works."

"Fuck that."

"Ryker."

I shake my head, not even a little embarrassed to discover that a tiny bit of panic has set up in my stomach. Call me codependent, but unless there's no other way around it, I have no plans to stay in the bunkhouse tonight, away from her.

"It's one night, babe. Besides, we have so much going on, the time will fly by. The tents are being set up as we speak. There are so many people coming to town—it's crazy. You invited your *whole* hockey team. Everyone you've ever played with. That's a *lot* of people."

"I couldn't leave anyone out," I reply reasonably.

"Even the owner is coming."

"Barry expected an invitation."

"And yet you threw a fit when I told you that I was inviting Shawn North. He's a colleague and a friend."

I shake my head. That guy wants my girl. I went to that book event with her. Hell, we've been to several, and this Shawn guy is constantly trying to charm her pants off with that British accent.

"He does *not* have a crush on me," she continues.

"Agree to disagree, sweetheart."

"Well, he's coming, with his *girlfriend*."

I smirk and cross my arms over my chest. "Whatever."

Great, he can watch her come permanently off the market.

"My point is, there will be so many people around, and so much going on, that one night won't matter."

"Let me make myself clear." I cross to her and hook her chin on my finger, tipping her face up. "I will not today, or any other day, sleep without you in my arms when you're literally yards away from me. No. This is one tradition we're breaking, Willow, and I won't compromise on it."

"Well, you don't get to see me in my dress until I walk down the aisle."

"I can live with that." I smile and lean down to kiss her soft lips. "We're so good at this marriage thing already."

"Stop kissing in front of the rest of us."

Our heads whirl to the doorway at the sound of Gideon's voice, and Willow hops off her stool so she can run over and hug him.

"Hey, handsome."

"Hi, baby girl." He kisses the top of her head. "I'm sorry I couldn't get here sooner."

"Always did avoid the heavy lifting."

Gid flips me off, making me laugh.

"You're here now," Wills replies and pats his cheek. "You okay? You don't look quite like yourself."

"I'm great. Don't you have enough to worry about without adding me to the mix?"

"I always have room for you," she assures him. "Did you try on your tux?"

"Yes. Why am I wearing a tux in a field?"

"Because that's what Willow wants, so that's what she's getting," I reply.

"Fine." He heaves out a breath, but then he grins. "Where's the kid?"

"He's helping with the tents," Willow says.

"That's code for 'He's bossing everyone around out there,'" I add.

"He was a born leader," Gideon replies. "He'll be an NHL captain before we know it."

Gideon isn't wrong. Aiden played hockey last year, and he *slaughtered* it. He's naturally talented, and if he wants it, I know he could make it to the NHL.

But he has two years left of high school, so we'll see what he decides to do. I won't push him into hockey.

"Okay, boss," Gid says to Willow. "Give me my marching orders."

Willow

Ryker was true to his word. There was no keeping him out of our bedroom last night, but I have successfully avoided him all day today.

I purposefully planned an afternoon wedding because I knew that I wouldn't be able to stay away from him until a sunset ceremony.

And I wasn't wrong.

I'm in my pretty lace gown with short sleeves and a V neckline. It hugs my curves in all the right places. Ryker insisted that I go to Seattle to shop for my dress, and we made a week out of it, all three of us. Ry sold his penthouse, and I found my dress.

I would live in this dress if I could. I love it.

There's a knock on the door, and I turn to find Gideon poking his head in.

"Are you ready, baby girl?"

"As I'll ever be." Gid's walking me down the aisle, and he's standing up with me. I cried like a baby when Ry asked Aiden to be his best man. Aiden asked if he could also change his last name to James so we're all the same, and then I cried some more.

"He's going to swallow his tongue when he sees you," Gid says as he holds his elbow out for me to take.

"That was the goal." We walk through the house and out the front door, toward the field that has the best views of the mountains. There are tents set up, ready for the reception with a ton of food and cake and drinks. Enough for all three hundred people.

"Do we have you here for a couple of weeks?" I ask him, to keep my nerves down.

"I'm here forever," he says in that deep, rumbly voice. "I'm not going back, Wills."

I stop and stare up at him. *"What?"*

"I talked with Ry about it last night. I'll build a house over by the lake."

"Gid, you love your job."

"Yeah, well, the job doesn't love me anymore. The leg will never be the same. Not good enough to protect the president or her family, and if I can't do that, I might as well retire."

I squeeze his arm. "I'll selfishly be happy you're home."

"I know."

We turn a corner, and there's the aisle, leading me to my man.

He's standing by the judge in his tux, my boy standing next to him. And when Ry's gaze lifts and finds me, his lips press into a hard line, and I see tears in his gorgeous brown eyes.

"That's what I wanted to see," I whisper as Gideon guides me down the aisle.

"You're happy?" Gid asks.

"More than I probably deserve."

Out of the corner of my eye, I see him shake his head. "No, baby girl. You deserve every minute of this happiness. You both do."

We reach the men, and Ryker joins us. Gideon passes my hand over to Ryker's, then kisses my cheek and moves to the other side of me to stand as my witness.

"You're so fucking beautiful," Ry says after swallowing hard.

"Hey, let me kiss her," Aiden says, making everyone laugh as he leans in to kiss my cheek. "Love you, mama bear."

Oh, God, my makeup.

"I love you too, baby boy."

"We are gathered here today—"

The words are beautiful. We repeat solemn vows to each other, slide rings on our fingers.

Debbie's and Ray's rings.

Gideon had given us his blessing to use them, and the three of us finally went into the master bedroom, which had been closed up for the past year and a half, to find them. It was a bittersweet day.

"I'm honored to pronounce you husband and wife. You may kiss the bride."

Ryker's smile is wide as he bends me backward and plants one on me that has the entire crowd applauding and whooping.

"Come on, wife." He kisses the back of my hand. "Let's go live this amazing life."

ACKNOWLEDGMENTS

Dear Reader,

I would be remiss if I didn't take a moment to thank a few people for making this book happen. First and foremost, to my agent, Georgana Grinstead. Thank you so much for believing in me and fighting for me so fiercely. I don't know what I would do without you!

To Megan Sakoi, my editor at Montlake, you have been a dream to work with! Thank you for your calm and steadfast support and for your love of this story. You are wonderful.

To Lindsey and everyone else at Montlake who helped this story shine. You're the real heroes, and I appreciate you more than I can say!

As always, I have to express my love and gratitude to my assistant, Crystal, who goes above and beyond every single day so I can focus on the writing. You hold it together. You're the best there is.

What I'm saying is, behind every single book there is a village of incredible people who support me every single day.

Thank you so much for being my village.

Love,
Kristen

A Teaser From

Book 2 in the Triple Creek Ranch series
Available April 2026

Lena

"Holy lobster, Batman, look at this."

My best friend, Chelsea, snickers into her glass of champagne and points to the enormous painting in front of her.

It's a lobster.

Dancing with a squid.

This painting is the size of the windows that span behind my mother's desk in the Oval Office. I should know. I was just in there this morning.

Sipping my one and only glass of champagne, I tilt my head to the side, still staring at the painting. There's a *lot* going on. "Is that a—"

"Starfish fucking a clam? Yeah, I think so."

I blink over at Chelsea, and she grins at me.

"What did you bring me to?"

Chelsea laughs and pats my shoulder. "An art exhibit opening in New York City. Come on, it's fun. We're dressed up, drinking bomb champagne, surrounded by your hot security guys."

I glance over to my Secret Service men. There they are, like always. Dressed in suits, with things in their ears, just like in the movies. Only difference is, we're not outside, so they're not wearing sunglasses. Richie has been with me since I was a teenager. But the other one is new. I don't remember his name.

I frown at my best friend of twenty years, since our first day of kindergarten.

"They're not *hot*." Only one has ever been hot, and he hasn't worked for me for years. "They're annoying."

"If you have to have annoying security, they might as well be hot. They can be both." She winks at me, and we move along to another piece that features a sink full of dirty dishes and a golden retriever humping a poodle.

"My eyes may never recover from this," I mutter, making her cackle with delight. Chelsea's laugh always makes me smile.

We couldn't be more different. She's the wild one. The risk-taker, the loud person with no filter.

She's also stunning, with long blond hair, bright-cerulean eyes, and an hourglass figure that fills out her blue dress perfectly.

She's a showstopper.

I can never tell her no about anything, including this last-minute trip into New York City for this exhibit. Chels loves the city, and I would rather be anywhere else.

Somewhere quiet, where I can think, where there aren't many people. Or any people at all.

"You should have an exhibit of your own, Lena," Chelsea says, sobering. "You're way better than this."

"You can't compare my art to this. It's not the same."

Chelsea rolls her eyes as she loops her arm through mine, and we click on our stilettos to another room, another gallery. And of course security follows.

"You know what I mean," she says. "Your art is fucking beautiful, and it should be displayed for others to enjoy. To buy. You could make a *killing*."

Shaking my head, I give her arm a squeeze. "Thanks for the vote of confidence, but I'm okay."

I've told her before, I don't want to draw more attention to myself. My mother is the president of the United States. I get plenty of attention already, and I hate it with a passion.

"Maybe once your mom's term is over, and things settle down a bit," she says and tips her head against my shoulder.

Probably not.

But in my usual fashion, because I can't tell her no, I simply say, "Maybe."

"Oh! I could totally be your manager. You could just do the art side, and I could run the business side."

Not in this lifetime.

I love her, but Chelsea can't manage her own allowance from her parents. She's twenty-four and has already spent her entire trust fund, and her parents *still* give her ten grand a month for living expenses.

And yet by the middle of the month, she's broke and asking me for a *loan*.

Which I always give her.

And I hate myself for it. I know I'm enabling the shit out of her, but damn it, she's like a sister to me. I don't have siblings. Just Chelsea. She battled a cocaine addiction for years, and she's finally clean. She has so much potential—she just doesn't have any self-esteem.

Because her parents, while filthy fucking rich, are assholes.

"Oh, look!" She points to the side of the room. "A dessert buffet. Let's be naughty and eat some calories rather than just drink them."

I blink over at her. "Chels."

With a huff of her breath, she shakes her head. "Come on, *Mom*, I want some of that cake."

I nod at people that I know as we walk through. This is definitely a who's who of New York's elite, and I know the only reason I was invited is who my mom is.

"Well, you look delicious."

I know that voice.

Pasting on a plastic smile, I take a steadying breath and turn to find Howard Tobias Matthews III ogling my tits as he lifts his glass to his lips.

Not champagne.

Bourbon.

His diamond-studded Rolex flashes beneath the cuff of his white dress shirt. He's in a custom black suit, which molds over his body perfectly.

On paper, Howey is the perfect man.

A Harvard Law grad, attorney with a prestigious New York City firm, tall, dark, and handsome, with a muscled body and an impressive financial portfolio, and he comes from the kind of family that would have hosted grand balls during the Gilded Age.

He's also a selfish, narcissistic asshole, and I only learned that after I dated him for a year.

"Hello, Howey."

"Goodbye, Howey," Chelsea says and flips the man the bird, and I have to press my lips together so I don't laugh.

Chels always hated this guy.

"Still have your yappy friend by your side, I see." Howey's voice is like honey.

If he wasn't such a monumental asshole, he really would be a catch.

Seeing him makes me feel *nothing*. I never thought I was in love with him, but I enjoyed dating him. Especially in the beginning, when he was attentive and kind. Sexy. He really was good in bed. He didn't cause trouble with my detail, and he was respectful to my mother.

And then, it all went to shit so fast, my head spun. So no, I don't feel anything at all when I look at him. No remorse. No longing or sadness.

"Are you enjoying the exhibit?" I ask him, ignoring the dig at Chelsea.

"It's interesting." He glances around the room, and then his brown eyes fall on me once more, flicking down to my cleavage. "It just got better."

"Yeah, well, I think we were getting ready to head out. I need to get back to DC tonight."

That's a bald-faced lie. We're staying in the city for the weekend to shop and eat at our favorite restaurants.

But Howey isn't invited to tag along.

"Come out on the veranda with me," Howey says, and I shake my head.

"I need the restroom." I turn to Chelsea, who's suddenly chatting with a woman I don't recognize. "I'll be back."

"Okay, I'll grab you some cake," she says with a smile, and I turn to walk away.

"Lena," Howey says, stopping me. His eyes have softened, and he reaches out to tuck my hair behind my ear. "I'd really just like to talk to you."

I sigh and back out of his reach, which makes his eyes narrow.

"You lost that right the day you smacked me across the face. Goodbye, Howey."

I walk across the room, toward the hallway where I noticed the sign for the public restroom. My detail is right behind me, and I glance back at them, directing my comment to Richie.

"I don't want him near me again."

"Yes, ma'am."

My detail makes me wait to enter the restroom until it's empty, and then they stand outside the door, making sure no one can get in with me.

It's over the top and ridiculous. It's always driven me *nuts*. I wonder if they can hear me pee out there. When I was a teenager, I rebelled against the security. Chelsea would talk me into ditching them all the time, which we'd do, and then go get ice cream, or go shopping. We never did anything too crazy—we just loved the adrenaline rush of losing the security guys.

And then I always got into a heap of trouble afterward.

When the *incident* happened five years ago, I put my foot down and told Chelsea we'd never do it again. Because people got hurt that day, all because of me.

And it still haunts my dreams.

Once I've washed my hands, I open the door and step out of the restroom, but then frown when I don't see Richie. The new guy glances my way, and I look down the hallway.

"Where's Richie?"

"He had to handle something."

No, that's wrong.

My guys *never* leave my side. Not for anything.

The hair on the nape of my neck stands on end as I hold this guy's stare.

"What did he have to handle?"

"Don't worry about it. He'll be right back. Your friend's waiting for you in the car out back."

He points with his thumb toward the opposite end of the hallway, where there's an exit sign.

I can hear Gideon's voice in my head. He was with me from the minute my mom took office until the night of the incident.

"Trust your gut. If something feels off, it likely is."

My heart beats faster, but I manage to keep my face calm.

"Chelsea wasn't ready to go yet."

"She is now. She's out back with Richie."

I tilt my head to the side. "You said he was taking care of something."

"He's taking care of Chelsea." His jaw tightens, that muscle twitching with his frustration. "Come on, we need to go."

Slowly shaking my head, I start to move to the other end of the hallway where the party is still happening, but his hand catches my upper arm, and he starts to drag me away.

I have an emergency button on my watch, which I immediately press, and within seconds, more Secret Service rush in.

Cold metal is pressed against my neck.

"I'm taking her," this asshole says. His voice shakes a bit, and my eyes find Richie's. *Where was he?*

Without hesitation, Richie raises his gun and fires, and my would-be kidnapper falls to the ground, dead.

Oh, God.

I stare down in horror at the blood as it spreads over the floor, and then I'm flanked by three men and taken out to the SUV. They're talking into phones and communicators, but the blood is rushing so loudly in my head, I can't hear a word they're saying.

He was going to take me.

"How?" Is that *my* voice? So small and breathy.

Richie turns to me, but I don't understand the words coming out of his lips. His face is set in concerned lines.

Was he in on it?

He wasn't there.

He was supposed to be there.

"Blackbird is secure. ETA two hours," I hear someone say as we zoom through Manhattan, just as I start to shake, and I'm hurled back in time five years.

"Get her out of here!" Gideon pushes me toward Richie, but I don't want to leave him. No one makes me feel as safe as Gideon. No one can protect me like him.

I shake my head, clinging to him.

"No. I'll go with you."

"Go with Richie. That's an order."

I shake my head again, but then shots ring out, and Gideon grunts, then collapses to the ground.

"Oh my God!"

"Go," Gideon says. His face is white, his voice strained. "Get the fuck out of here, Lena."

Strong arms pull me back, but I'm yelling for Gideon. I won't leave him.

"Lena." Richie shakes my shoulder, pulling me out of the past. "Shit, she's going into shock."

"Of course she is. She just saw a man die."

"I've told you exactly what happened five times," I tell my mother, who's sitting with me and my detail in the living room of the White House, in sweats. Her eyes are cold and hard. She's in scary executive president mode right now.

Which is better than the terrified-mama mode she was in about an hour ago. I don't know what to do with that. My mother is not emotional. And she's *never* gone into mama-bear mode with me.

My dad's pacing behind the couch, pushing his hand through his salt-and-pepper hair over and over again.

"He passed *everything*," Richie says for the fifth time. "There were no red flags to make us think that he was a threat."

"Well, he clearly was," Mom says. Her voice is like ice, and it makes Richie shift on his feet. "The mess has been dealt with?"

"Yes, Madam President," Bishop, the head of the Secret Service, says. "It's been dealt with, and it won't make the press. The other people in the gallery have been debriefed. There won't be any mention of it anywhere."

The press only knows what those in charge want them to know. Politics is like the Mafia on steroids.

"You'll stay here for the immediate future," Dad says to me.

"I have a life—"

"And you'll be here, where we can protect you better," Mom adds, her voice leaving no room for disagreement.

I love my apartment. I don't want to live in the White House.

I hate this haunted house.

Resigned, I let out a sigh. "Do you need me for anything else, or can I go to bed?"

"Go on up," Mom replies, and catches my hand as I walk by. "Try to get some sleep."

"I'm sure that won't happen." I kiss her cheek, then give Dad a side hug before climbing the stairs to my old bedroom. But suddenly, a thought occurs to me, and I turn back. "Wait. What about Chelsea?"

"She's fine," Richie says. "She's at the hotel, and she'll be back in DC on Monday."

"She's staying in New York after everything that happened tonight?" I frown and reach for my phone, but there aren't any missed calls or texts from her.

"She doesn't know what happened," Bishop replies, with no emotion on his face. "She thinks you were pulled back here on official business."

"And you won't tell her otherwise," Mom adds. "Good night, Lena."

Fuck my life.

ABOUT THE AUTHOR

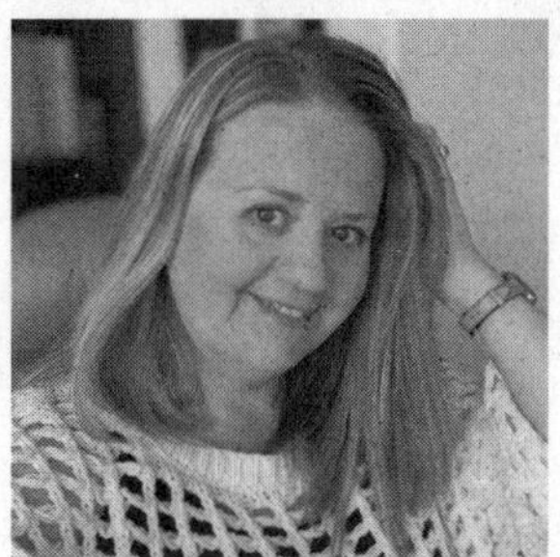

Photo © 2025 Kristen Proby

Kristen Proby is the *New York Times*, *USA Today*, and *Wall Street Journal* bestselling author of more than seventy titles. Making her publishing debut in 2012, she continues to captivate fans with spicy contemporary romances about families and friends, packed with plenty of swoony love. She also writes paranormal romances and recommends leaving the lights on while reading them. When not under deadline, Kristen enjoys spending time with her husband and their fur babies, riding her bike, relaxing with embroidery, trying her hand at painting, and of course, enjoying her beautiful home in the mountains of Montana.